THE DESERTER

Scene in Plymouth Sound in August 1815, by John James Chalon. The HMS *Bellerophon* is at the centre of the picture, surrounded by crowds of people in small boats who have come to see Napoleon.

THE
DESERTER

BOOK ONE of the ALFORD SAGA

PAUL ALMOND

McArthur & Company
Toronto

First published in 2010 by
McArthur & Company
322 King Street West, Suite 402
Toronto, Ontario
M5V 1J2
www.mcarthur-co.com

Library and Archives Canada Cataloguing in Publication

Almond, Paul, 1931-
        The deserter : book one of the Alford saga / Paul Almond.

(The Alford saga bk. 1)
ISBN 978-1-55278-901-8

        I. Title. II. Series: Almond, Paul, 1931- . The Alford saga.

PS8551.L585D47 2010   C813'.54   C2010-903982-3

The publisher would like to acknowledge the financial support of the Government of Canada through the Canada Book Fund and the Canada Council for our publishing activities. The publisher further wishes to acknowledge the financial support of the Ontario Arts Council and the OMDC for our publishing program.

Design and composition by Szol Design
Map design by Szol Design
Printed in Canada by Webcom

10 9 8 7 6 5 4 3 2 1

For Joan

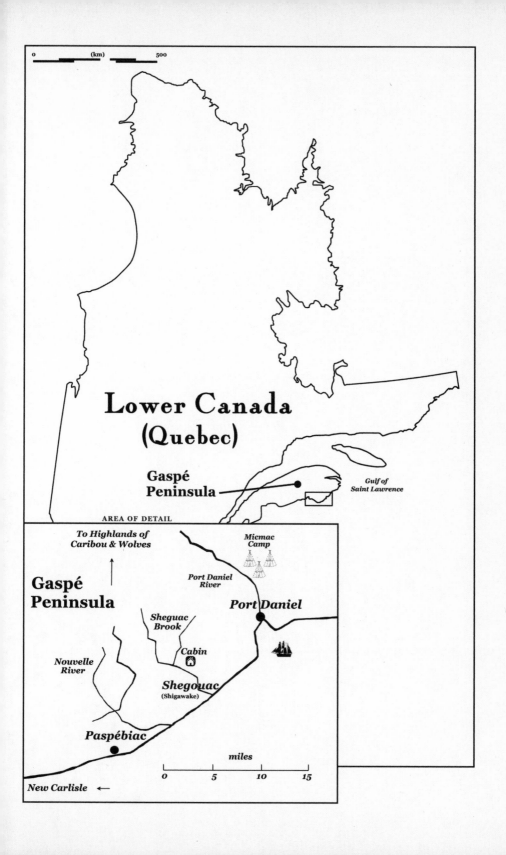

0   (km)   500

Lower Canada
(Quebec)

Gaspé
Peninsula

*Gulf of
Saint Lawrence*

AREA OF DETAIL

*To Highlands of
Caribou & Wolves*

*Micmac
Camp*

Gaspé
Peninsula

*Port Daniel
River*

Port Daniel

*Sheguac
Brook*

Cabin

*Nouvelle
River*

Shegouac
(Shigawake)

Paspébiac

miles

0   5   10   15

New Carlisle ←

Chapter One

On his wildly swaying hammock in the Midshipman's quarters below deck, Thomas Manning tossed and turned. He faced a huge dilemma: would he take his regular watch in the morning at eight bells? Or would he jump ship and set off for a perilous adventure in the New World?

All hands on the *Bellerophon*, a seventy-four-gun vessel in His Majesty's Navy, were exhausted from a two-day chase of a privateer up and down Chaleur Bay. They had been given leave to go to their quarters and sleep while their man o'war waited out the spring storm in this sheltered bay. But Thomas could not stop fears crowding into his consciousness.

Just jump overboard and swim ashore — yes, but in waters so close to freezing, the human body could not last more than a few short minutes. And if he did reach the shore, a good hundred yards away, what then? Chilled senseless, would he not make the perfect prey for wild animals that abounded hereabouts? Whatever would possess him to try?

Apart from two settlements the *Bellerophon* had visited, nothing covered this coastline but trees, wild animals, and Indians. Tales of terrifying tortures by savages were traded below decks in the evenings, one more horrific than another: they'd cut a man's entrails out and drape them round his neck as he hung in front of a fire, or eat his heart out in front of him as he died. No, put that right out of your mind, Thomas reprimanded himself. Aren't you afraid enough?

Afraid of swimming through the spring storm that rocked and pummelled this heavy ship? Certainly. Afraid of starving to death on those snow-covered rocks? Of course. Afraid of being attacked among the barren trees by hibernating bears as starving as you are? Well, yes. And to boot, chased by the whole British Navy as a deserter? No, you must stop this, Thomas ordered, do not let yourself conjure up too much, no more thoughts of the waiting tortures. Think only of what you can achieve.

Think of a farm on the cliffs, built from the very trees among which it stands. Think of a wife, broad skirt blowing in the wind, holding a child — your own son. Think of trudging behind sturdy oxen, ploughing deep red furrows in rich Gaspé soil. Think of the companionship of settlers, hear their pounding hammers erecting your barn, just as you would help with theirs. Think of the warmth on a frosty night by your very own fireplace, built from stones picked on these beaches, while your wife roasts one of the chickens you've raised.

But cramped in the orlop deck with its five feet of headroom, bounced in his swaying hammock with the other Midshipmen, Thomas Manning was afraid. Because he knew he was being foolish. That was the key. Foolish and inviting disaster. To take on all those bold challenges of the New World, the empty forest, the wild animals, with no experience of a pioneer life, no tools, no food, only a long-held and overpowering dream. No wonder no one else had tried to escape along this shore.

Rough as His Majesty's Navy might be, hard though these disciplined quarters were, if you toed the line you were safe. Until you struck another battle. Yes, or until Wickett, the scourge of the vessel, got hold of you.

He saw his grim face again, black eyes smouldering under thick eyebrows, seeking out young Thomas, following, awaiting some slip-up. The Chief Petty Officer (nicknamed Wicked Wickett) was all the British Navy personified: a harsh disciplinarian and a bold fighter. Unafraid to sentence a man for a lashing at the slightest infringement, he had proved himself so courageous in battle that Thomas at first had admired him. He had witnessed the man's consummate bravery after his left forearm had been blown off. Tourniqueted by the surgeon, Wickett had insisted on returning to the main deck, exhorting the sailors with a rare valour, calling out encouragement in his heavy Cornish accent. Small, dark, and swarthy as befits a true Pict from the depths of Cornwall, he represented at the same time everything that Thomas hated about the rigid structures on the ship, that same rigidity he had left behind in the Old Country. Never had he fathomed, when he joined the Navy years before, that he would be placed on a ship with such a merciless disciplinarian. He had even gone so far as to find himself slitting Wickett's throat in nightmares.

One of three who had played a practical joke on the man, Thomas would rue the day he ever joined the Navy, Wickett promised. The other two had been caught for some minor infraction, tied to the grating and lashed senseless. What Wickett threatened, he carried out. The only one left unpunished was Thomas.

But if he were to continue as a Midshipman, and if he

were to evade Wickett's threats, he would be in line for the rank of Fourth Lieutenant. With that rank he'd be safe from Wickett. So should he really give it all up? Throw it all away for the life of a deserter?

Why not? Thomas hated being forced to line up and watch some poor wretch flogged for a minor offence. British "justice" was more than he could stomach or understand. Discipline did not sit well with him, even at the Raby Castle, where his hours had been planned, jobs laid down, and all for so little reward and often few pleasures.

All this month patrolling the coast for privateers plundering merchant shipping, Thomas had waited for his chance. But a barrier of high cliffs protected the dark forbidding forests that covered the land. And there were damn few settlements along the two hundred miles of coast, certainly: one they had visited, New Carlisle, where loyal British families had fled north from the Thirteen Colonies after the Revolutionary War in 1776. But ever watchful, Wickett had made sure to cover the gunports with mesh, and had sent redcoated marines (the soldiers carried on every naval ship) to circle in their longboat to prevent would-be deserters escaping, even to the point of having them patrol the broad beach and muddy alleyways inland. The villagers were well aware of what would happen to anyone harbouring a deserter. So no hope there. Paspébiac, another remote settlement, was entirely French and Thomas did not speak the language; again, the marines were, as ever, watchful.

Why did the British Navy go to such lengths to stop escapees? So few men were volunteers, as Thomas well knew: most poor devils had been caught in their country villages and press-ganged into the service. Some were criminals who preferred the unknown of a shipboard life to the filthy prisons, even though every couple of weeks, the ship's crew lost a member to accident or disease. On his one trip down from the north of England to join up in Portsmouth, Thomas had become acquainted with the perils of London life. A thief could be imprisoned for stealing food for his starving family, and sometimes, even hanged.

Vividly he recalled a lashing Wickett had arranged in the waters off Finland. A deserter had been caught in the woods after jumping ship, just as Thomas himself was foolish enough to contemplate doing now. The seaman, a country lad press-ganged in a Devon village, hated shipboard life, the food, fleas, rats, scurvy, weekly lashings, and many deaths from accident or disease. The lad had swum ashore one night, and then, without the means to survive, had finally given himself up. One thousand lashes was the punishment for desertion, standard throughout the British Navy: a hundred on each of ten ships of the line. Brought back to the *Bellerophon* for his third dose, he was barely alive. Wickett had him strung up by the wrists, and kept sloshing icy water over him to keep him awake. Not long after they had begun with the cat o'nine tails on his back, His Merciful Lord had taken him. But they kept on lashing the body, and then passed on the lifeless meat for further floggings on other ships, to set a well-remembered example. That sight had stiffened Thomas's resolve to leave. But not until they got to the New World.

And now, his last chance. After chasing the privateer, the *Billy Ruffian* (as the *Bellerophon* was called by the crew), would sail out of Chaleur Bay into the Gulf of Saint Lawrence, littered with icebergs, through Cabot Strait and on past Newfoundland to cross the Atlantic, where they'd rejoin the war with Napoleon. Would he survive those future naval battles? Midshipmen got wounded or killed just as the officers and crew did. He had been lucky to survive so far. And if he were to be so lucky again, would the ship return to the New World? The war between Britain and America would soon be over. No need for the British Navy to patrol the shores then.

He thought of his mother, the undercook at Raby Castle, of Goodman the butler, and the chambermaids who had tossed precious pennies into the passed hat as he left. They all expected him to do well in this New World, and would be awaiting word, due when he landed. They'd been waiting a long time. Each time the ship called in at Portsmouth, he had sent messages, divulging of course only the brighter aspect of life on board. But with no hint of the New World. In the comparative safety of the castle (always drafty but at least never dangerous), did they have any idea of the ultimate horrors of battle on board ship? Or of the almost unimaginable challenges awaiting him on this perilous coast?

Aboard his man o'war, he had fought grisly battles, faced demise and dismemberment, without a qualm. But this was different. This was the moment of a lifetime.

Such an appalling risk! But then again, why else had he joined the service? To wage war against Napoleon? Hardly. He had joined, through the good offices of the Marquis, his mentor, precisely to find a new life abroad.

He thought of his canvas bag, filled with items he had

carefully collected over the last month. Firearm, tinder-box, small axe, precious ball of marline, razor, and so on. Would it all be held up by the watertight bladder he'd made and tested one night in the icy waters? He hoped to tow it behind him when he swam for shore.

But was life here in this apparently unmanageable wilderness all he had so often imagined? The Robin's workers he'd seen in Paspébiac, did they look any happier for their so-called freedom than the staff at Raby Castle? Well, he had found the settlers in New Carlisle prosperous, indeed flourishing. A settler's life, that is what he wanted.

So take your chance of surviving those icy waters. Have a go at your life's ambition, he told himself. At least you'll die in attempting a new life. Was this not a laudable aim?

In an hour, the first light of dawn would give him the visibility to try. One tortured hour of rumination left. But then, all rumination would cease — to be replaced by either action or inaction.

In his bones, Thomas knew which it would be.

Chapter Two

Thomas Manning eased himself through the gunport of the pitching man o'war and held onto the cannon's icy barrel as he peered down. Waves leapt and crashed against the *Bellerophon*'s wooden hull. He lifted his eyes to the outline of the rocky and wooded shore, dimly visible in the dawn. Too far to swim? He hesitated. Then swallowing hard, he grabbed his canvas bag with its inflated bladder, tied its line round his waist and threw it into the angry waters below. Then he thrust himself through the gunport, and fell.

The glacial Atlantic shocked his system as down he went under the violent waves. Before he could surface, a surge threw him against the hull, knocking the wind from his lungs. Air, his brain screamed. His legs thrashed him upwards through the foaming water to burst forth, gasping for oxygen. He ingested more saltwater and was thrown against the hull a second time. His feet found the timbers and he rammed himself away. After another struggle, he surfaced again. This time a wave hoisted him, he gulped air and water, got a quick sighting of the shore, and struck out.

Had anyone heard him jump? Those battering seas, tearing wind, flapping yards of canvas, creaking two-hundred-foot-high masts, they would have covered the noise. But to make sure, he swivelled to check the watch lantern by the forecastle. No, it had not been whisked off by some watchman giving the alarm. Thomas Manning had gotten away.

Chilling fast in the paralyzing waters of the bay, he drove for the shore. Waves choked him with spray, lifted and dropped him, but he kept his arms churning, tugging his survival bag behind. Ten minutes in this subarctic water would finish any man; sailing through the Gulf of Saint Lawrence earlier this month, they'd passed a plethora of icebergs. So concentrate, he ordered, pump your legs, ram through the waves, you'll make it, God is surely with you.

On the man o'war now dropping farther behind him, he had endured the great naval Battle of Trafalgar in 1805, which claimed his Admiral Nelson and his Captain Cooke, and he had survived. For years he had dreamed of this New World where there were no more lashings, no summary British Justice, just the land itself and what you could make of it.

For the last month patrolling Chaleur Bay, he'd watched and waited. He could not allow himself to fail.

Rocks, head for those red rocks piled on the beach, not the sand bar, don't leave traces of a landing: they'll be after you, all right. Wickett would see to that. Forget all that, he commanded himself, gasping and choking, and forced himself on through the bucking sea. Thoroughly chilled, he began to tire. His sodden canvas bag tugged at him — would it stay afloat? He had tested the bladder in the sea late one night, but not in a storm. And surely the bag must have struck the hull as he had done.

Dragging every ounce of effort out of his frozen limbs, he could feel the twine of the precious bag riding lower.

The choppy waves kept thrusting him under, as an arctic cold gripped him, froze his joints, choked his breathing. His exhausted body began to rebel. And behind him, he felt his bag begin to sink.

The bladder had failed.

He grabbed at the twine, doing his best to keep it up. But now his frozen hands refused to work. He wound the line around a wrist, but he was so cold, so tired. Lashing out with the other arm, he pressed himself on, but every stroke needed a huge effort. His legs were refusing to obey. He found his senses slipping and he grew disoriented, the chill numbing his mind, choking his heart. The will to survive slipped away.

Hoist up the bag, he exhorted, you can still stay afloat, but no, it dragged him under. Let the line go? These frigid waters were dulling his ability to think, his muscles to respond. Just let the sea take him? So good for it all to be over...

But then he felt the line give a different tug. Had the bag hit bottom? Three fathoms of line, yes, that made sense, so now, so very exhausted, at least he wasn't doomed by the weight of the bag. Drag it along the bottom. Thomas gulped air as another wavecrest lifted him. He saw rocks about thirty feet away. He threw every ounce of effort into his swim, and began to gain on the shore.

Then, the bag caught.

He tried to pull on it while treading water, but his limbs would not respond. Stiffer by the second, he tried grabbing with both hands, only to be pulled under. He let it go and resurfaced, spluttering. The shore seemed so close, so very tantalizing. But that bag was stuck; that line around his waist tethered him. Get rid of it, and come back later? No, never, he'd have to get away from the shore fast, even run for his life. But he needed that bag, those necessities.

He threw himself backwards, kicking toward the ship again, still buffeted by waves. He tried looping the line round an arm, but the hands didn't respond. Dragged under, but holding his breath as he went down, he kicked himself upwards and in a miracle unsnagged the bag. Now, thrust forward! But these last few yards seemed endless. At last a huge wave gathered him and threw him with tremendous force against the boulders on the beach.

His hands and feet thrust forward so that when he struck, smashing his knees and scraping his hands, he protected his head. The wavecrest sucked him back for another throw. But he swivelled and let it throw him sideways and forward, twisting to avoid sharp edges. It drove him into a crevice and, as the water receded, he managed to stay, stranded.

He braced himself for the next wave, wedging his feet and knees against jutting rocks. It struck him and tore at him, but stubbornly he held fast and then, as the water receded, managed to pull himself up higher. The next icy wave washed over him, to no effect. Gathering himself, he heaved his nearly naked body up above the water line. Worn out, he rolled onto his stomach, arched over a boulder, head down, and let the water drain from his spluttering, heaving lungs. His body shuddered mercilessly from the paralyzing cold.

He pictured the other Midshipmen asleep in their hammocks on the cramped orlop deck, with less than five feet of headroom. He had stuffed his Midshipman's uniform into in his own hammock to simulate a sleeping form. The others might not notice when they got up for the watch at four this morning, but at eight bells, which began the forenoon watch at eight, he'd surely be found out. Not much time left.

He couldn't stop shaking. The spray from the crashing waves had chilled him so much, almost wiping him out. This May weather was snapping cold. Get up and out of the spray. Unsteadily and still shaking, he tried to rise. How close he'd been to surrendering! But nothing could stop him now.

Except the bag.

His hands could not get a grip on the hempen line. He flexed his icy fingers, moved his arms, swung his shoulders to get the feelings back. Already the darkness was lifting and he saw the outline of the bucking man o'war across the estuary. With wary eye on it, he struggled onto a rock and tugged at the line. Still snagged. Shaking, he bent forward and managed to wind the twine round his frozen hands, and lifted again. No luck.

Now what? Dive out again? Never. But what else? Shaking like a fluttering pennant, he was not at all ready for more of the same. So leave the bag — head off into an unknown woods, with no clothes, no weapons, no knife, no tinderbox, nothing?

You need that bag and those clothes, he ordered, stand up straight, breathe deeply, stretch, swing your arms, get warm, get some strength back, and quick, in you go!

He plunged again into the raging waters. The first wave struck him and threw him flat. But he hit bottom — shallow! He leapt up, swimming, and in two strokes found himself above the snagged bag. As the wave withdrew, his feet hit bottom again, and he leapt, tugging on the bag, and tore it free. A surge knocked him down again, this time pulling him under and out from the beach. Choking great gulps of saltwater, he somehow righted himself and, as the next wave gathered, he aimed for a space between boulders and was thrown up onto the shore again.

Winded, gasping, but now clutching his bag, he clambered up the slippery rocks. Off balance, lurching this way and that, he headed for the cover of spruce trees twenty feet back. Then he let himself fall exhausted on a mound of dead needles. He had arrived in the New World.

Chapter Three

Thomas lay, trying to collect his thoughts, a few feet back from the breaking sea. Not much time, he knew.

The rain was stopping and the storm abating: more worry. Would the Captain take off after the privateer they had been chasing? He hoped so. Or would he listen to Wickett and stay here to put the marines ashore? Thomas knew the drill. Wickett would send out three boats: one around the mountain to his left to cut off any escape westward towards Paspébiac, the nearest settlement, some days' walk away. Another would surely row straight in to the trading post in the centre of the curved shore. A third contingent of marines would row around the eastern cape to cut off any escape towards Pabos, again some three or four days' walk eastward.

Should he head for the trading post? If the owner traded with the Indians, he'd be French, and so not friendly to the English, having been conquered by them within living memory. But suppose the trader were English? Worse still. He would support the penalty for sheltering deserters.

So should Thomas make a beeline westward over the mountain, and count on beating the search party? No chance. They were fast rowers and he knew the tactics: string marines out at distances of one hundred feet perpendicular to the shore to form an impenetrable barrier among these bare and wide-spaced trees not yet in bud. Then why not stay hidden here until the danger passed? No, he'd heard dogs in the night at the trading post — the marines would enlist their help. They'd cover this area in no time.

All right, strike back, avoiding the trading post, and head for the river. Its fresh water would sustain him and if he hiked up it, he'd leave no scent for the dogs. But wouldn't the search party chase him far into the interior? To the north lay one hundred miles of mountain wilderness. No one could reach the distant shores of the great Saint Lawrence River over those snow-covered hills, they'd know that. So no, they probably would counsel against that. Now, he decided, he would just have to head back the river up into the northern hills.

What about Indians? For certain they'd be all over the place no matter where he went. This river — maps showed it large enough to sustain an Indian band. Bloodthirsty savages — the thought froze his already beating heart. They hated Englishmen, he knew. When the French had been chased out of Louisbourg down Cape Breton way, the tribes had harassed the British hard. But wasn't that a long while ago? He wished he'd paid more attention.

Well at last, he'd arrived; the New World was his. If he could avoid capture.

His breathing had slowed, his lungs felt clearer, and strength was seeping back. With it, his inflamed imaginings began to cool. Everywhere lay danger. So plan slowly, take time, make good decisions. But first, put on those wet clothes. In the light wind they should dry on his body. And then go. Go fast.

Shaking hard, he reached over and wrestled open the knot that closed his bag. Feeling around, he pulled out the trousers he had bartered when the ship had stopped last week for supplies in Paspébiac, several miles to the west. Sheltered by the pines, Thomas rose and tugged them on over his freezing legs. He was so tall that they stopped halfway down his calves, and so large they fell off his waist, but he found the drawstring and tightened it. He reached down and pulled from his bag the special shirt his mother had given him, which he'd carefully kept for this moment. He tugged its dun linen over his nearly dry torso, and then put on his rough North Country jacket, now so sodden. Finally, he sat down to lace up his black boots. The transformation was complete, from Midshipman to man of the soil.

Now he was ready for anything.

***

Thomas carried his bag up from the beach into the heavier woods on the low mountain. Well hidden, he could soon make out, on the stormy waters of Port Daniel cove, his anchored British man o'war with sails furled. No abnormal activity as yet. Good. He turned and hurried through patches of snowy underbrush until he caught sight of the river estuary behind the causeway, where the trading post centred on a few nondescript dwellings. Avoid that, he decided. Panting and chilled, he hiked on vigorously through the dim dawn light, stumbling, and twice falling. But the exertion kept him warm and he felt his clothes drying.

Making sure to keep on the hillside until he had passed the trading post, he found the land sloping downwards. He headed down towards the estuary where the river widened, and where a few ducks and lots of dark geese rode the choppy waters. Glancing northward, he saw the river curving into woods that stretched northwards for a good hundred miles.

He came upon a path that ran along this side of the river. A route used by traders from the Post? Or a path worn by animals? In any case, fearing to leave a scent, he leapt across, then plunged through low bushes to the edge of the water. Without hesitation, he stepped in.

Freezing. Of course, because the river flowed from those dark northern hills patched with snow. Lifting his knees high, he half walked, half ran along in the water. His ankles began to pain from the cold.

The choppy surface would conceal any rings spreading from his strides, but he edged out from the shore bushes to check the trading post. A second-floor gallery had been built out behind, but he saw no sign of life. Feet aching, he made himself splash forward as fast as he could, carrying his precious bag.

But what about Wickett? Would the ship be putting out to sea again? Or would Wickett prevail and get the Captain to send in landing parties? Better climb a tree. Ahead, he saw a half-dead spruce.

Bag around his neck, he struggled up the scratchy trunk until he could see, over the sandbank and through the bare trees, the masts of his ship. Sails still furled — that meant search parties. Quickly, he clambered down and forced himself ever faster through the water.

The sun had not yet risen. Early bird calls from

unfamiliar warblers and the gossiping of crows bespoke the beauties that surrounded him in this dawn, now breaking into hard light.

Hope surged strong. Keep wading, keep going, he told himself, but his ankles ached horribly. Without any feeling in his feet, he tended to trip. His freezing wet clothes were almost dry so he made sure not to fall and drench them all over again. Here, on the banks of the Port Daniel river, all he had to do was evade capture.

Ahead, a low cedar bent out over the water. He hurried forward, sat, and with both hands massaged his numb ankles and feet. How they hurt! But the vision of the landing party and their baying dogs spiked his brain. No time. Put your boots back on. Push on quickly. But for a few moments he stayed, rubbing and praying.

Perhaps now he should take to the bank and race along the trail; he'd make much better time. But the words of his mentor at Raby Castle came back: caution must prevail. The dogs would be coming, avoid leaving them any scent. If they did not find him quickly, surely the Captain would override Wickett and give his previous Admiralty orders priority, rather than staying too long to search for some deserter. Privateers from the American Colonies plied the coast, striking at local ships and other British commerce. The *Billy Ruffian* was here solely to provide safe passage for the schooners bound for Europe, or indeed South America and Africa with their cargoes of fish and lumber. He must remain out of sight and scent for at least two full days. So get going fast. With circulation vaguely restored, he splashed handfuls of water over the trunk of the tree to get rid of his scent and jumped down. When he did, he glanced up and through cedars forty feet away, he saw a face.

Bronzed, broad features, dark eyes. An Indian.

Shivers shook his spine. In an instant, the face had disappeared. Nothing. He listened. No sound. Was it a mirage? Should he go search the ground, the dead leaves and moss, for a footprint?

Fear swarmed over him. He grabbed his bag, forgetting caution, and set off at once through the underbrush up the sloping hill due west. Run, run fast. Oddly enough, he was far more afraid of that one face than a boatload of Wicketts. He leapt over the trail, fearful of the dogs, but had he not travelled far enough upstream? He pushed through the evergreens and reached a maple forest of wide trunks, but plenty of smaller growth springing up. Using the rising sun behind him as a guide, he made for the destination he had picked out while on the ship. Westward up the bay towards Paspébiac, he had seen an opening in the cliffs that indicated a stream. Fresh water — only a day or two's hike from here. Once there, he'd make camp and, being far from habitation, should find himself safe for the time being.

Would the Indians have dogs? Fool, he thought, Indians need no help in following a trail. So what could he do to hide his progress? Avoid patches of mud and melting snow? But even on this carpet of old leaves and moss, just one disturbance of leaf or twig would betray him. If they wanted to track him, they'd find him.

Panting hard, he tried to force them out of his mind and just keep going. But terror had a way of gripping him. He'd heard so many sailors' tales. How they would strip the flesh off you while you were alive, and eat it in front of you. Or tie you to a stake over a fire, and then cut your heart out. His imagination leapt with more and more gruesome yarns, until he found himself actually shaking. Forget that, he ordered. Be positive: look, you're in this beautiful country, a free man! Everything you asked of your Maker, He has given you: the survival through many naval engagements, the crossing of the Atlantic, and now this territory — all yours for the taking. No, the Good Lord would support him.

Head down, leaping fallen trees, racing across open patches, concentrating on moving swiftly, Thomas did not bother to look up. When he did, he stopped short.

Four Indians stood waiting.

Chapter Four

Thomas Manning stared at the Indians in the maple wood. The moment he feared most had come — capture by savages. Their jackets reached down to their knees, a curiously European cut. Under them, he could see shirting, mostly soft leather like chamois, and all wore leather leggings fixed below the knee by a garter, and held up by strips attached to their broad belts. Knives hung in pouches round their necks. Three carried bows and arrows. No point in him trying to get his firearm out and load it with the powder and shot from his waterproof sack. He lifted his hand in greeting.

No answering wave.

Thomas thought fast. No weapons were raised, but the four looked menacing, no doubt. So what next? He'd learned, when in difficult situations with the crew, always contrive a smile. He nodded pleasantly and walked forward, putting on a brave face. "Hello..."

No reaction.

He kept moving. Stay calm, he told himself firmly, look friendly, hope for the best. Ten feet away, he paused and smiled.

Perhaps he ought to divert them with presents? He lifted his bag to open it. One of the natives barked a command and another came quickly forward to grab it.

Without that, he was finished — but what could he

do? He handed it over.

The Indian with long black hair cut square across the forehead pulled out a strip of leather. Another grabbed his wrists and tied them behind his back.

An impulse to strike out seized Thomas, but he quashed it. Don't provoke them now.

Once the hands were tied, they gathered about solemnly, looking Thomas up and down. They spoke little.

His brain churned with alternatives. Run? No hope of that. Reason with them? Obviously, they spoke no English. What about the landing party from the ship? They might be within earshot, though he doubted it, and anyway, if he were rescued, it would only be for another, though just as cruel, death.

The natives reached a consensus. They placed their prisoner firmly in between, two ahead and two following, and motioning, headed swiftly off through the forest.

Thomas noted how effortlessly they travelled, placing each foot down deliberately but with speed, avoiding thickets, ducking under dead trees. Soon they came upon a trail and broke into a trot. With arms tied behind and no way of balancing, he found it hard going. But he did his best; at least this speed was taking him away from that other certain punishment. But was he not heading into another, possibly worse?

No words were spoken. He wracked his brain for ideas that might save him. Would they skin him alive? Roast him? Torture him? Bizarre thoughts from shipboard romances, sailors' tales he wished he'd never heard, jostled his sanity. Stop, he told himself sternly, who trusted sailors' yarns? All right, what books had he read? Unusual though it was for a serving lad to study, he had always been an eager student. Back at the castle, he had made a point of getting on the good side of the noble childrens' tutor, doing small favours. As a result, the tutor had helped him learn to read. In fact, together, they had delved into the history of the New World, firing Thomas's imagination even more. But the tutor had steered away from Iroquois and their unusually cruel tortures.

All signs pointed to him being led to his execution, but Thomas tried to make believe that, in their village, the Chief might be willing to listen. He would explain his circumstances. In fact, why not offer to barter his belongings? Barter? They had them already. So then, lend his services? But to do what? Well, a young man, healthy like himself, perhaps he could live among them, help them trap or whatever on earth they did; he was able-bodied. But could he get them to see that? To see that his body could be of use? Or would they rather *eat* it? Ridiculous to speculate.

Panting hard after three or four exhausting miles, Thomas felt himself ready to give up and beg for rest — a cardinal sin he knew. But he heard the barking of dogs ahead. Was he approaching their village?

Then he saw through the trees a grouping of strange structures randomly scattered around. Each wigwam, for that is what Thomas figured them to be, was covered in birchbark sheets laid like shingles over poles, starting from the bottom and overlapping as they worked upwards. The bark had been stitched together with spruce roots and the doorways all seemed to face east. Slender poles on the outside held the birchbark down, with the top left open for smoke to escape. On some he saw a separate collar to cover the open top in bad weather. Some coverings had been painted with figures of birds and animals. He noticed hides in preparation everywhere: skins of what he took to be squirrel stretched on Y-shaped twigs, other pelts drying on larger frames. Among the wigwams, he saw smaller structures with straight sides from which smoke issued, perhaps smoking meat. One of his four captors had run on ahead, and now an assortment of villagers was gathering to watch the arrival of this tall, thin, white man with brown tousled hair, beardless, in his borrowed trousers and North Country jacket.

Were they hostile? He searched the faces, but found them hard to read. Curiosity, rather than hostility, seemed to dominate. Two or three dogs, small and half starved, ran up to sniff at him but then retreated hastily. Many of the women and surely the children seemed never to have seen a white man. But the Iroquois spent their lives fighting the white man. Perhaps these were not Iroquois? No, think hard, yes, from somewhere he came up with the name Micmac; yes, the officers had mentioned them while patrolling this coast. They had been apparently the first to meet Jacques Cartier in this very bay in 1534. One of the Basque crewman told him that Basques spoke of Micmacs who had fished here for centuries, but the other officers had just laughed.

At the sight of Thomas, two smaller children burst into tears and were hushed by concerned mothers. Another little boy grabbed a small bow and arrow and began gesturing arrogantly. Women pointed, seeming to discuss his clothing and his every feature. Two began laughing. Modestly dressed, all wore long skirts, dark blue, or brown, with geometric designs, and soft leather shirts tucked inside their skirts. Some had short vests; many wore tall, strange hats that curved up and forward to a point, embroidered with ribbons and glass beads.

At one side of the central wigwam, two large logs had been felled and placed opposite each other to form a kind of meeting place. From it arose a tall, sturdy man set off from the others by his clothing: a jacket obviously bartered from Europeans, and leggings of finest leather held up by a wide belt, from which hung various pouches. His handsome face was fixed by a great broad nose, and his well-defined features suggested courage and wisdom. The Chief.

The four men who had captured him hurried across to tell him the circumstances of their capture, while others, whom Thomas took to be tribal Elders, joined the Chief in deep discussion. Thomas stood apart, guarded by a young man and another youth who eyed him curiously.

One little girl came forward cautiously, and on impulse, Thomas made a funny face.

She squealed, whirled, and raced back to her mother, hiding behind the cloth skirt. The mother turned to the woman next to her and they both hid smiles behind their hands.

One brave little boy, who had pretended to attack with a child's bow and arrow, tried the same trick and this time Thomas made an even uglier face. He too screamed and raced off. Others joined in the game, much to the amusement of the women. Thomas kept it up, if nothing else but to take his mind from the horrors he might face. Well, they'd have a real treat when that show began. They liked amusement, he decided. But he did wish that someone else would be the butt of their barbarous devices.

The Chief held up his hand and called out a rebuke to the children, who then hurried back to their watchful families. He turned and spoke a few short sentences. The women gathered their children and retired to wig-wams, while Thomas found himself led to a prominent tree. Another youth brought a length of stripping, and Thomas was securely tied.

Was a process of torture about to start? He had an im-pulse to lash out, to die fighting, but here he was, held by two strong youths in the centre of their encampment. What good would it do? They bound him to the tree by his elbows, which Thomas found painful, adding a strip around his waist, another round his ankles. The rising sun was warming the air and the scent of cedar now began to soothe his nostrils.

The Chief walked across to his two logs, and began what seemed a formal meeting with the Elders. Time to panic? Well, time to pray. And pray hard he did.

Chapter Five

Thomas was jerked from his reverie by a strange native grabbing his hair and yanking it back to bare his neck. He found himself staring into a demented face with the man's knife poised at his throat. Done for, he thought.

A short stubby native came quickly up, calling out in Micmac. He spoke strange words at his fierce friend and then took his place in front of Thomas. Loudly and firmly, he asked, "You, trading post?"

English! A flash of hope. "No." Thomas shook his head.

"You live trading post!" the translator repeated loudly.

"No, not live."

"How long live trading post?"

"Not live trading post. No! Not live there."

"Yes. You live trading post!" The angry bark prompted Thomas to keep quiet. No point in arguing, they wouldn't listen.

After a pause, the translator frowned. And spread his hands in a questioning gesture. "Not trading post?"

"Ship," Thomas enunciated. "Navy. British Navy." He paused. "I am from ship."

The translator frowned, then made his hands into a prow and undulated them.

"Yes." Thomas nodded vigorously. "Yes, ship. I am a seaman. Midshipman. Almost an officer."

Behind the translator, the fierce Indian grabbed his knife tighter, staring into the captive's eyes, but the translator restrained him, muttering in Micmac. The Chief called out and the translator turned and walked back to the gathering on the tree-trunk benches. After a look of hatred, the angry Indian followed.

Thomas watched as the translator explained what had been said. The Elders fell to discussing this with their Chief.

Thomas found his body begin to wilt. Exhausted and chilled, he willed himself to keep awake, and alert. Watch them, he told himself, stay focussed. Think. Plan. Not often did one's whole existence lie in the hands of so few supposedly uneducated brutes. Though probably not much worse than those gossiping dolts he had attended as an occasional footman in the castle dining room. He'd been noticing that on the logs, each Elder got his chance to speak. The words came methodically, slowly, sometimes halting. Sometimes a long silence followed to allow reflection. Clearly they were giving each speaker their whole attention. And in an orderly fashion.

All at once, some of the Elders rose from their logs and approached their captive, followed by the others.

Oh-oh, Thomas thought, this is it.

They stood around while the Chief directed some questions at his translator. The translator came close and eyed Thomas keenly. "British ship?" he said.

"Yes," Thomas replied, "British."

"Fight with French?"

"No," said Thomas, "not here. Fight with French in Europe. England and France still at war. With Napoleon."

The translator nodded, seeming to understand, and then turned and explained that to the others. He turned back. "Napoleon win?"

"No sir," Thomas replied smartly. "Well, yes, he's already conquered the half of Europe. But not winning, no. Goes on forever, this bloody war."

The translator passed this on to the others and Thomas watched while a good deal of discussion went back and forth, as some seemed to grasp the concept, others not. The translator turned for further amplification.

Thomas shook his head, wearily. "Now we've got Austria against him, and looks like Russia and Sweden and some German states are with us British, too." Thomas warmed to the subject: after all, wasn't that what most of the officers talked about on board? "But the bastard went and captured Moscow, then they finally beat him back last winter, and now he's in Paris, just got there before our ship came over. Seems like he's set to go off again, he just never gives up." Thomas realized he was getting too carried away, as he saw the translator's eyes glaze over. To save face, he was probably having to make things up, so Thomas stopped short, letting go one final remark, "Wellington, our General in Spain, he's certainly knocking him about…"

After more discussion, the translator turned to him and pointed the finger at him. Oh-oh, thought Thomas, what now?

"You," the translator barked, "you here? Why?"

"My ship? The Admiralty sent us here to protect our shipping from privateers."

The translator turned. No one seemed to grasp that concept. He turned back to Thomas. "Privateer? Navy?"

Thomas shook his head and spoke slowly. "Privateer means ship. Merchants in a company that sells things, they put guns on their ships. Special 'articles of war.'" Thomas stopped himself: don't get too complicated; they'll be angry again. "When they catch a local ship, they keep all the cargo, everything. But they do not hurt the sailors. The send the crew back. Very bad for our merchants, like James Robin in Paspébiac. We British do not like American privateers."

"Your ship?" The translator gestured with his hands. "Big how."

"Man o'war." Damn, thought Thomas, that will get me nowhere. "Biggest ship on sea. Very strong. Many big cannons. Seventy-four, in fact."

The translator nodded and passed it on. The others seemed to understand.

"Privateers very afraid of my ship," Thomas repeated, pleased. "My ship can beat every other ship. Best ship in Navy, I say." Thomas smiled. He would almost be enjoying himself, if his life were not somehow hanging in the balance. "But now she sails back to Europe, to fight Napoleon again. He is trying to blockade England. We are going to stop him."

The translator let all that go by. "This country," the translator said, "you say this country, English?"

"Yes, of course. The British general Wolfe, he beat French Montcalm outside Quebec, on the Plains of Abraham, fifty years ago. Then the Treaty of Paris, 1763, France gave Canada to the British." Damn, there I go again. "France gave Britain all this country." He gestured with his head, his arms being still tied securely behind him, causing him to be conscious of the pain once again.

By now, some of the women had come out of their wig-wams and, with the younger men, stood at a respectful distance, watching and listening. He watched the Elders discussing his view of events, as there seemed to be some disagreement among them.

"French live here," the translator barked. Then he spread his hands in a questioning gesture. "How?"

"Good old King George III," Thomas replied, searching for simple words, "he said he'd permit the French to live just the way they want. Keep religion. Keep customs, keep habits, he gave the French all freedom to live just as they wish."

This seemed to shed a good deal of light, and they fell to discussing it among themselves. One of the older men, who stood leaning on a staff, asked a question of the translator, who turned to Thomas. "This general in Spain, good general?"

Thomas nodded. "Wellington? Very good general."

"Now, English fight French here?" another Elder asked, to be translated by the short stocky Indian.

Thomas shook his head again "No. No French war here, only fighting now in Upper Canada. Faraway. President Madison, he declared war on Britain," Thomas added, then kicked himself again, because what would they know of the fourth American President? "We were interfering with their shipping, so Americans start war again with British. But here, in Chaleur Bay, all fine, I think." Keep it simple, he told himself, and easy to understand. That is the only way he might get off, if indeed he were eventually to escape with his life.

They all stood around, discussing what they had heard, and Thomas began to realize that their quest, that this trial, might not be so much the discovery of his guilt or innocence, but rather a hunger for more knowledge. Smarter than one thought: these Indians probably had not been treated with courtesy by the traders so as to allow for much exchange of information. And perhaps, he went on to think, they had heard some of this from the French in Paspébiac, when they went there to trade, and now they were seeking an opposing viewpoint from a British citizen. Most of this would very much concern them, even though they had little contact with civilization. Might the Micmac find themselves in action once more? They had harassed the British in Nova Scotia after they took Louisbourg, the last French garrison on Cape Breton Island, not five days' sail from Chaleur Bay. But he remembered the word in his Navy that the natives were nowadays more or less at peace, accepting the status quo.

Now what bearing might this all have on his release, or his imprisonment, or torture, or eventual death?

He studied their attitudes as they stood talking, and for the life of him, he could not discern the hostility that characterized the savages in his overheard yarns of brutal torture. On the other hand, he reasoned, better be vigilant. No use trying to divine what is in the mind of a creature so alien as one of these warriors.

They turned and headed back to their conference logs, continuing to speak to one another without the formality of a meeting. It was almost as if they had enjoyed this session that gave them, Thomas presumed, food for discussion around their fires this evening.

He felt himself sag against the bindings. So tired, so very tired. His head dropped forward. After all, he had not slept last night. And the previous two days spent chasing the privateer through a rising, buffeting spring storm had taken all his efforts. Then his chilling swim through icy waters, the bushwhacking, freezing river — it had all been very hard on him, physically and psychologically.

A set of new sounds brought him back to consciousness. The men were heading for their wigwams, from which smoke issued. Time to eat? He repressed the fierce hunger that took hold of him. Would they bring him something? Of course not, why feed a dying man? So they were not going to save him, after all. His heart sagged along with his body, and his eyelids flickered shut. But his mind raced. Maybe they'd take him to civilization for a ransom? But would the Navy pay? No, because all they'd do was flog him to death. Cheaper to let him die here.

Why not ask the band to conscript him? After all, he was strong and healthy. After the harsh winter, most of them seemed so lean, just skin and bones. He'd talk to the translator, whom he sensed to be a man of intelligence. Later, he'd find a way to escape. On the other hand, even now they might be discussing the manner of his death.

Then he looked down and caught sight of the canvas bag at his feet. Some hidden honour had not allowed anyone to touch it. So might there be hope for him, too?

Three Indian children, playing games with miniature bows and arrows, kept their eyes on him. Two women made their way down a path toward the river with vessels for water. They studied him as they passed, and then discussed him in low tones. Crows and jays traded taunts in the trees above, until a merciful darkness came down into his brain.

Soon afterwards, he awakened to hear the men still on their tree trunks in earnest discussion. The angry native was haranguing them, and pointing at him. Oh-oh, more trouble. He watched out of the corner of his eye, but the man seemed at the end of his torturous oration, and soon sat down. After an appropriate pause, another Elder took his place. Would this one put forward an opposing view? Again, impossible to tell. Before long, it appeared as though a decision had been reached, and the meeting broke up.

Curious how his life hung on such a whim. Almost better to know, he reflected: the uncertainty had been terrible. He only hoped that if an end were coming, it would be fast. Not like those Jesuit priests, tortured for days on end, or other settlers who had been scalped and gutted and then tied in the sun to die in horrible pain. Having said many prayers, he felt ready for whatever might come.

Chapter Six

The meeting of the Micmac Elders having taken place, their Chief arose and gestured. The encampment fell silent. He called out to the two who had tied him up and were now working at repairing a canoe. Then he turned and retired to his wigwam.

The two young men came forward. Thomas tensed.

They proceeded to untie him. From their demeanour, he could guess nothing. He stood, submissive, while they released him. Then feeling so horribly cramped, he stretched his arms overhead and twisted his body around. How stiff he felt! Stiff, cold, and hungry.

He was tempted to grab a knife from one teenager beside him as the other knelt to unbind his feet. But no chance. The young man stood up and they both led him to the Chief's tent. They stood back and indicated he should enter.

Thomas paused, looked at them both, and they repeated their gesture. What lay inside? Taking a deep breath, he dropped to all fours and made his way in.

His eyes slowly widened and he made out the form of the Chief sitting on the right of his fire. Behind him, he felt another enter. He turned to see the stubby shape of the translator come to sit at one side.

Thomas was ushered to the back of the wigwam. He noticed on the left side, a woman's cooking tools, provisions of wood and food, and her bags and blankets. Smoke rose into an opening where the poles joined. He waited.

Then he realized he'd better forget being a prisoner — he should behave as a guest. With manners. The Chief was dignified enough; why not he himself? He turned to the translator. "My bag?" He gestured as to its size and the manner of carrying it.

The translator spoke to the Chief, who nodded, and out he went. He soon returned with the bag, and the Chief watched impassively as Thomas worked at undoing the sodden canvas. He rummaged inside with one hand, but stopped as he noticed the Chief stiffen.

He wanted to dump it all out, to show it contained nothing dangerous. Then more slowly, smiling at the Chief, he took his time, feeling out his waterproof pouches. One he knew held tobacco. How carefully he had oiled and re-oiled with linseed oil its several cloths to make a good waterproof covering. An arduous process, but now that stood him in good stead.

Finally he found and drew out his stash of navy tobacco. As the Chief watched, he peeled off its coverings and handed it over.

The Chief looked at the sticky black mess, shaped like a large sausage. He smelled it. Then he held it up and examined it again. Thomas motioned for the Chief to hand it back, and gestured for a knife. The Chief frowned, looked at the translator, who shrugged and handed his knife to Thomas.

Thomas carefully shaved some flakes, and then rolled them in his hand as he'd seen the officers do on the man o'war. He handed that to the Chief.

Thomas watched him put a little in his mouth, tasting it.

Then he stuffed a portion solemnly into the stone bowl of the pipe, which had been set on the ground before them. Packing the bowl with his forefinger, he drew a brand from the fire with cedar tongs and lit the pipe. From the stem hung an arrangement of beads and feathers. The Chief inhaled and breathed out a cloud of smoke. Were his eyes glowing? Had Thomas somehow hit on the appropriate gesture? He handed over the pipe.

But Thomas didn't smoke: what should he do? Better not refuse. He took the pipe, undecided. Then he drew in a small puff. He held the smoke in his mouth and blew it out. The Chief looked stern.

"Not smoke?" asked the translator.

Thomas took another puff, and then made himself inhale.

He coughed furiously.

The Chief began to laugh, and so did the translator. The more Thomas coughed, the more they laughed. Finally clearing his throat, Thomas was able to stop his coughing and began to laugh too, wiping away his tears.

Well, he thought, at least they're not going to skin me alive.

***

He awakened to morning sounds of the New World: songbirds, crows squawking, dogs barking, children playing. He lay on comfortable skins covering a moss underlay. Disoriented, he tried to remember where he was. Oh yes, the laughter and the exchange of views with the Chief, after which he'd been brought to this wigwam.

The translator had said "cousin," pointing at the Chief. So for the moment he was safe; and knowing that, though starving, he had fallen quickly asleep.

He rolled over and saw a woman studying him with dark eyes, black hair parted in the middle and held back in braids. She was seated, legs bent to one side, lit by her fire, glowing in its circle of round stones smoothed by the river. He became conscious of his enormous hunger.

They looked at each other. Then she reached over and picked up a wooden bowl. Holding it, she gestured. Her large, round eyes set in a moonlike face appeared to glisten; youthful, in spite of her worn features.

"Food? Yes please, oh yes!" He nodded as vigorously as he could in this sleep-glazed state. But then he remembered his precious bag, towed behind him in the swim. Where was it now? Had they stolen it? No, he saw it at one side of his sleeping blanket.

He watched as she scooped out a porridge-like substance and spooned it into a smaller holder of birchbark. Then she held it out to him.

"Thank you very much!" This startled her. She frowned. "Thank you," he repeated slowly. Then again: "Thank you..."

But she did not respond. She took a wooden spoon, dipped it into the bowl, and held it out for him. Like her child, he opened his mouth. No point in tasting it; she wasn't going to poison him. But he couldn't stop himself from first rolling it on his tongue. Hmm, rather like porridge, he decided, but made from corn.

She gave him another spoonful which he ate gratefully. How hungry he was! He sat up and gestured — I'll feed myself. She put the dish down next to him and handed him the spoon.

He began to eat, resisting the impulse to gobble it all down at once. Between mouthfuls, he began to look around. Hanging from the first rung of lashed saplings, he saw various cooking implements, and pouches with personal items. A small hand loom stood at one side, behind some rolled up blankets. Two unstrung bows and quivers of arrows hung high under the birchbark covering. Her husband's, obviously.

Just then the flap opened and an older man came through. He spoke simply but tersely to the woman. Thomas noticed his left arm hanging useless at his side. The woman rose and followed him out.

So now, he was alone. But only for a flash. The flap opened again, and a girl crawled in. His eyes widened. Was she the woman's daughter? The sheerest long black hair framed her perfectly formed features, a nose oddly European in size, delicate, between piercing black eyes, about eighteen, hard to tell with Indians. So far he had not heard about the beauty of these people. Thinking back to yesterday, most of them were fairly attractive, certainly not ugly brutes by any means.

He stopped eating as they sized each other up. Who would have thought such a tempting creature lived in this wilderness?

She came around and sat sideways to observe him more closely. He picked up the dish and tried to finish eating without looking at her too obviously. She continued to study him. She didn't think of him as a young man, he figured, but rather as a curiosity. Eye contact such as this could never be imagined with any young lady in England — much less a shy Indian.

She remained seated with her legs at one side, watching him carefully. With difficulty he tore his eyes from her captivating face and nodded into the dish, which was almost empty. "Good." He smiled. Then he repeated clearly, "Good."

This time, she responded. "Good?"

He nodded, and then finished the porridge. All the while she watched him seriously. All at once she said, *"Gdúlg."* She nodded and pointed. "Good."

Thomas glowed. The Micmac word for good? *"Gdúlg,"* he repeated, in a mangled fashion.

Smart, he thought, pretty and smart. Would the others be as intelligent? He'd have them talking English in no time. And they'd make him into a Micmac expert. Maybe even earn a living as a translator? Flights of fancy again. In no time, he had finished the dish and, with his forefinger, wiped the last bit off. He licked his finger clean to get the very last taste and saw her, at last, give the suggestion of a smile.

Without prompting, she took the birchbark dish back, and reaching behind her, filled it a second time, and handed it back.

This time he seemed to catch in that dim light a hint of recognition, as though she might be seeing him for what he was: an attractive young sailor, lonely too, in fact quite frightened, who at the same time wanted so much to become a real participant in this strange and intimidating New World.

He smiled at her again. *"Gdúlg."*

"Good," she replied. "Good."

"Yes, yes, very good..." What next? He pointed to himself.

"Thomas."

She looked puzzled. "Thomas," he repeated.

"Thomas?"

He nodded. Then he pointed to her, and spread his hands in the questioning gesture he'd seen the translator use the night before.

She frowned, and paused. Then she replied, "Magwés."

"Magwés?" he repeated.

She nodded, seeming pleased with the exchange, though she betrayed little.

The flap opened and the translator poked in his head. He motioned for the young man to come out. Thomas hastily finished his porridge and handed the dish back to her politely. "Thank you," he said. "Thank you very, very much."

She nodded, watching his every move.

He grabbed his canvas bag and crawled over to the entrance. Was he at last safe? Or was some final judgement to be pronounced? He hated to leave the comparative safety of this home, this cozy wigwam. Imagine, a rough birchbark enclosure being now thought of as cozy! He rejected the thought and with a last searching glance at her, which told him that she might even sympathize with his anxiety, he crawled though the opening into sunlight.

A delegation of village women and children stood around, watching. The Chief had been talking to two older men, and he now approached Thomas. Thomas tried to read their faces. Inscrutable as ever.

The Chief spoke in Micmac to the translator, as Thomas stood meekly.

The translator turned to Thomas. "Trading-post man.

Maw winjit. Metúqamigsit! Very bad."

"Oh?" said Tom, "a bad man, is he?"

The translator nodded. "English. Bad English. *Mauvais comme un carcajou.*"

That didn't sound like Micmac. He frowned. Spanish? French? But he gathered that the translator was trying to explain the events of the previous evening.

"Bad like wolverine," the translator said. He pointed to the fierce Indian who stood at one side with a woman Thomas took to be his wife. "They have son, Little Otter. Last year trading-post man send son away on sea. Far away."

"Sent his son away? Kidnapped him? To England?"

"Chief say, we keep you. We give you back when Little Otter come back." Heavens! Thomas thought, I could be a prisoner for years. "Chief say, send your finger to trading post. Cut and send."

Oh no! Which finger would they cut off? Oh God, he prayed, let it be the little one.

The translator went on: "But you no from trading post. You from ship."

"Yes," said Thomas. "Ship."

"Finger no good."

Inwardly, Thomas heaved a big sigh. "No sir. No good sending my finger! Trading-post man would not care one bit." Then he wondered how could he help this poor man get his son back. As a Midshipman on the run, or a lowly second footman from a distant castle, he would wield no influence, none whatsoever. He put the thought out of his mind and gestured to the angry man. "I am sorry, very sorry."

This was translated, and then they all lapsed into silence.

Thomas noticed that Magwés had come out of her wigwam. He could not help but cast sidelong glances at her, as she stood watching. She too was studying him, although this time with a different look, which seemed to betoken friendship. When she caught his look, she shrunk back, with what could be interpreted as an attractive shyness.

"Now..." The translator turned to him, "before night, you go." Thomas brightened. They were letting him go. Then he frowned: and what should he do now, alone in this giant forest, with nothing to eat? Then the translator went on, "We help. But you go," and he lifted an arm and pointed.

"Of course, of course I will go. But... why?"

The translator showed no emotion. Then Thomas saw him glance at the angry Indian who stood nearby, four others now gathered about him.

Trouble? Thomas wondered. How far could he get if they set out after him on their own, planning some sort of revenge? Was it actually a trap? He glanced over at Magwés, who was studying the proceedings. She looked worried. Was he about to take the bait and thus be lured off to some grisly end?

He looked at his feet, and nodded. "Yes. I will go away before tonight. And thank you very much for your help."

Now, here he was, once more on his own, on the run, in this untamed strip of the Gaspé Coast.

Chapter Seven

Observing the band during the morning and at their simple mid-day meal, Thomas began to wonder how they managed to survive in this harsh wilderness — overflowing with the "milk and honey" of the Bible, perhaps — but the question was, how to make it all work? All so very alien to him, their way of life, disorderly, even dirty, according to the standards of cleanliness imposed at the castle. No wonder sailors and other whites saw these natives as messy brutes, not worth tuppence. But here he was, facing a wilderness they had adapted to and even conquered for millennia. Slowly over the morning, it came to him that he'd better get rid of any prejudice fast, and learn all he could. After all, he'd be quite alone for the foreseeable future. And they might end up being his only contacts.

Living off the land, the tribe had few of the items that Thomas took for granted, like good steel knives. Working on hides, for example, most of them he knew used sharpened shoulder blades of moose, or scrapers made from the lower legs of a moose or caribou. Throughout the camp, he'd seen scattered remnants of European goods they had traded for: old kettles, a cauldron, some knives, indeed a tinderbox or two, hardly anything new or really serviceable. Why not start by offering them some modest presents? He would definitely need to be taught by someone the rudiments of survival here. Everything seemed so alien, and unfamiliar, compared to the oak forests of Northumberland

Even as a young footman, he had no need to survive apart from the castle. All meals, albeit simple and rarely abundant, had been taken in the cellar kitchens. His mother, the undercook, saw to it he always had enough, though just enough. So what had he been thinking, diving off that ship? The urge to escape, to avoid the forthcoming, and inevitable, punishment emanating from Jonas Wickett, had been so strong, he had not properly looked ahead, apart from knowing the one reason he had joined the Navy was to get here, to this promising New World.

And now here he was, what should he do? How would he actually survive alone? He just had no idea. He had with him a couple of lead shots, thinking he'd buy more, of course, from settlers who all made their own out of lead. But was his powder dry? And if the firearm did work, how much nourishment would he get after the first shots at an animal — skinny enough in spring, he could see now. Wait! Why not ask the band to go trading for him? That way he could avoid all contact with the trading-post owner and his dogs.

He discussed this with the translator, who told him that four tribe members intended to make one of their spring trips downriver to the trading post. They might easily do it today, if the Chief gave permission. Relieved that they were being so helpful, Thomas handed over some money, and thought quickly: a big saucepan, a frying pan, a bigger axe and saw if possible, a hammer and nails, and so on. Powder and shot for his firearm. He also needed blankets, but the translator suggested he get them here from the tribe. The Chief said he could wait until late this afternoon when they'd be back.

So now, he decided, he'd learn something of hunting with a bow and arrow; his pistol might be useful if they got some shot for him, but hopeless in any emergency, the loading being so unwieldy. He confessed this new learning goal to the translator, whom he nicknamed Tongue, much to the latter's merriment. Thomas decided to give them all nicknames, not being able to remember the complex series of sounds that signified their Micmac names. He and Tongue traded names, "Thomas" or "Domas," being easily remembered by Tongue, who told the others.

So Tongue arranged for the young Indian who had tied him up last night to teach him archery. Several gathered to watch the demonstration. His teacher looked as if he had been burned as a child: on the right side of his face near his ear, he carried a heavy scar, so Thomas nick-named him "Burn." Slight of build with wild, black locks of untamed hair and bright inquisitive eyes, Thomas saw in him a gentle quality, almost out of place with his intense and wiry strength.

Burn set up a target, a chunk of wood on a stump, and showed Thomas how to hold the bow, made from ash, and how to place the butt of the arrow against the bow-string between thumb and forefinger, while his middle finger helped draw back the bowstring. The others gathered round, suspecting this might prove quite entertaining.

Burn let loose a couple of arrows himself, and then handed the bow to Thomas. Thomas found the arrow amazingly light. He did his best at holding it and drawing back the bow as he was being taught. But the arrow wobbled through the air and flopped into the underbrush below the target.

The others burst out laughing. Thomas made a face and went to retrieve the arrow.

The villagers were a happy lot, he decided: they laughed at almost anything. The children in particular enjoyed seeing him make faces, something their elders never did. He soon became accustomed to their obvious enjoyment when he tried even the simplest Micmac tasks. He was a prime curiosity, no doubt, with his brown hair lightened blond by the Atlantic sun, his bright blue eyes, his slim frame taller than any man here and, unlike them, the stubble of a beard already showing.

Magwés came out of her wigwam when his lessons began. He saw her watching as Burn showed him again how to handle the weapon. His second try was not much better than the first. Their obvious merriment at his awkwardness and the smothered smiles of Magwés began to irritate him, especially when he saw Burn imitating his hapless actions. All good-natured fun he knew, but he did not appreciate the humour.

That morning, before the four natives had left for the trading post, Thomas had decided to confide his future plans to the translator. The fierce native with the kidnapped son, whom he had nicknamed in his own mind "Fury," had gone off early hunting, and danger from that quarter had diminished, if only for a time. His overall plan had always been to make for an opening in the cliffs to the west, which he had seen from the ship. Tongue confirmed a brook ran there, not used by any band for it was too small for salmon, which spawned up most of these rivers and provided their main spring staple.

All at once one of the trading Indians came tearing into the clearing and dove into the wigwam of the Chief. One little boy started crying and ran to his mother's skirts; others stopped playing with their hidebound balls stuffed with moose hair, and shifted nervously. The little lad, "Toughie" Thomas called him, the one who had gestured with bow and arrow, ran down to the path from the river, let out a crude war-cry and waved his spear before diving into the safety of his mother's wigwam. Three women gathered up their leatherwork and hurried off.

The Chief slid quickly out of his wigwam and called out. Three Elders gathered quickly round him as he gestured, pointing to Thomas.

Thomas watched carefully. He wished the translator had returned from the trading mission.

The Chief called Burn over and spoke firmly.

Burn came over to Thomas. Agitated, he pointed toward the seashore. How might he transmit the news? Something was up at the trading post, Thomas gathered, but what?

At the first sign of commotion, Magwés came out of her wigwam, then dove back in to reappear with his canvas bag. She waited as Burn mimed running on the spot, and pointed Thomas westward. Oh yes, he was supposed to hurry away. Good idea, surely.

Did that mean the trader and his posse were coming? No time to lose. Magwés hurried across with his bag.

Two others broke into the clearing with their bags of trade. Quickly they emptied the containers onto a blanket and sorted through them, while the others gathered around.

Burn barked a command at another youth, about Thomas's size, who came over and began to disrobe, even though the afternoon was quite chill. Burn motioned for Thomas to do the same, indicating they must switch. Thomas was about to object — he had no desire to change into somebody's smelly clothes and give up the linens and cottons that now formed his new identity. But he could see the band was in an uproar, and he'd better rely on their judgement. Keep his boots — but no, Burn firmly pointed to them, and off they came, no matter how sturdy and useful they were, nor how many doubts Thomas had about the ratty moccasins offered in exchange. Waste no time, he told himself, get out of that shirt and fisherman's trousers and pull on the Micmac's leather leggings.

He grabbed the Indian's chamois shirt, pulled it on over his head, and then added the leather jacket. He finally, and regretfully, sat down to tug on the moccasins made from tanned moose or beaver skin, surprised at how light and yet sturdy they were. Burn helped him tie the leggings up to his wide navy belt, all in great haste.

The youth, wearing Thomas's navy boots and dressed in his clothes, headed for the trail back to the river, dragging Thomas's jacket along the ground.

Ah, laying a false scent! So that's why they needed a change of clothing, and especially shoes, to fool any dogs or trackers coming after him.

Meanwhile Burn rushed Thomas over to the trading cache spread out. They grabbed up the nearest pack emptied by the traders and stuffed his canvas bag into it, together with other items Thomas had ordered.

Now the dogs began to bark furiously: the pursuers must be getting close.

Women moved anxiously about, calling their frightened children. Thomas noticed several families gather bundles and hurriedly set off up the river trail. From Magwés' wigwam, he saw the man with a withered arm come quickly out and give a pack to some lad whom Thomas took to be Magwés' younger brother. Her mother then crawled out with several pouches and the three of them set off. Thomas couldn't take his eyes from Magwés who stayed behind watching unhappily. He sensed in her being a wisdom that exceeded his own, especially in these unfamiliar surroundings. Then Burn called out abruptly and gestured. Magwés set off obediently with her family, giving Thomas a last look at the edge of the clearing.

"Magwés!" Thomas hurried over to her. "Thank you very much," he said gravely. She looked up into this eyes, nodded, and then with a long look of concern, tore herself away and was gone.

Burn grabbed the heavy sack from Thomas and, motioning, set off at a brisk trot. Thomas followed, carrying his axe, saw, and a pouch. But almost at once, Burn stopped, bent over, pointed to Thomas's feet and their footsteps. Try to keep them where he trod, Thomas understood. That way it would look like only one of them had gone that way.

Before plunging into the underbrush, Thomas glanced back. The Chief had gathered three Elders and two younger ones as a kind of welcoming party. Thomas waved a "thank you" but the others hardly responded, focussed on the approaching posse.

Burn ran with ease in spite of the heavy sack. Thomas marvelled at his grace. After a few hundred yards, Thomas tried to piece it all together. What had happened? But he had to concentrate more on keeping up with Burn, leaping fallen logs, following as best he could in Burn's footsteps.

The trail turned northward into the interior. Burn stopped. By now Thomas, panting hard, had to acknowledge what great shape Burn was in, though he looked half starved. Burn held up his hand for silence, and listened intently. Thomas tried to stifle his breathing, even his heart from beating too loudly. After a moment, Burn grabbed at Thomas and ran off even faster.

At first they climbed a series of hills back from the coastal cliffs but parallel to them, heading westward. Every so often, Burn would stop to listen. Each time, Thomas strained to hear anything, and yes, he thought he heard — the barking of dogs, was it? But faint. Then they would hurry on at the same unrelenting pace. At one point, after they had been going for what seemed like ages, Burn stopped short so that Thomas almost collided with him. Burn listened, then oddly enough, he turned completely round and led Thomas back down their trail.

Earlier they had passed a swampy lake. When they reached it, Burn stopped and handed the heavy sack to Thomas, who hefted it and again marvelled at the endurance of his young Indian friend. Burn leapt up on a branch and swung himself off the trail. He landed several feet away, obviously to avoid leaving scent for the dogs, and motioned for Thomas to throw him the sack. Thomas did and then leapt up to catch the branches and, hand over hand, manoeuvred to where Burn had jumped. Together they leapt over several clumps of swamp grass, and then Burn stepped out into the water. Thomas followed Burn who steadily and carefully walked around the marsh, sensing the depth. At one point he turned out toward the middle, soon wading up to his waist and then his chest. Thomas hurrying forward, tugged at him. "Why out here so deep?" They were both now thoroughly wet and the spring afternoon was definitely chilling down.

Burn pointed, made sucking noises, mimed being pulled under. Quicksand, thought Thomas, good. Let's hope it wipes out any pursuit.

Wading through these icy waters, Thomas wondered what had really happened. Hadn't his shillings been accepted? Of course, because they came back with the goods. Had the owner of the trading post cheated them? But he had explained to the Indians what the shillings were worth, certainly legal tender, coins of the realm, even here.

And his list had been filled. But perhaps there had been an altercation — had the trader tried to short-change them, to start a fight? He knew the Micmacs did not like the trader.

He tugged at Burn's sleeve as they waded towards the opposite shore, gesturing to ask: what happened back there at the trading post?

Burn pressed his thumb and finger together in the universal gesture for money, for a coin. Then he pointed at Thomas, and continued on.

The three shillings! That must be it. The Kings's shillings. They were new. The Indians had offered them for trade, which now Thomas realized, would have been a first!

Of course the Indians would only trade furs and items of embroidery that he'd seen the women making. What a stir those silver coins must have caused! When they had presented the shillings — and he had specified their worth — any assistant in the post would have alerted the trader at once. He kicked himself for being so stupid. He just could not afford many mistakes like this one. They'd be the death of him.

He knew that yesterday, the marines would have spent the morning searching for their deserter. Furious at losing him, they would certainly have offered the trader some reward for catching their quarry. Once the trader saw those shillings, he would have headed back upriver with dogs in quick pursuit. So that's what caused the ruckus!

Thomas scolded himself angrily: better snap into this new mode of thinking here in the New World. To survive the rigours of this desolate spring, he must be constantly on the alert, especially for British Forces who wished nothing more than his gruesome death.

And here he was again, running for his life. He promised himself never to be so lax again.

The two reached the swampy shore and Thomas, who was freezing wet, could see behind, the distant mound of Port Daniel mountain. The *Bellerophon* must now be sailing off, either in pursuit of the privateer, or hopefully back to the English Channel to fight again. Ahead, the sun was dropping low over the horizon as Burn set off once more at a fast pace. Perhaps he knew they'd dry as they ran. These Indians were a hardy lot. And so would he himself become toughened, no doubt.

How different was this from the forests of County

Durham. Big bushy spruce blocked their way, so they turned to dive through groves of lighter green cedar, which flourished on damp ground, among patches of melting snow. They headed up over dry, sunlit humps with green shoots pushing through dead brown grasses. Now that evening was approaching, one or two warblers from the south were setting up their meagre chorus. Thomas could hear male songbirds calling from the tops of trees. On and on they trotted, through spreads of young birch like the Russian taiga he had read about, and into grandstands of timber, lofty, mighty trunks with little undergrowth, making their trek easier.

Burn seemed to be looking for something. He trotted to the right, and then to the left for a hundred yards, finally plunging through heavy bushes into a blackened area caused by a past forest fire. He pointed ahead and Thomas saw a large tree partially felled by fire or lightning. Under the upended roots, a kind of shelter had been dug.

Burn let his heavy pack fall to the ground, and shimmied like a squirrel up the half-fallen tree. Twenty feet off the ground in its dead branches, he held himself motionless, a statue against the setting sun, listening and watching. He seemed so wise in the ways of the forest that Thomas felt safer. The sun sent bright pink streamers of cloud across the Gaspé sky. His sky, now.

He held his breath as Burn motioned for stillness. Only the faint forest sounds were to be heard. No pursuit? But what about those other Indians, the ones with Fury, might they not come after them? Double jeopardy. Burn climbed back down and shook his head, but still wary. Thomas could see worry in his dark eyes. Not safe yet.

Burn settled himself and motioned to his mouth.

"Oh!" Thomas said, pleased. "We can eat?"

Burn nodded. *"Mijipjewet."* He made a chewing motion with his fingers.

In the fading light, he opened his bag made of cattails, and checked the contents, hastily stuffed in at their departure. Burn found bread and some dried salmon and laid it out on a blanket.

As Thomas was chewing, he pointed and said, "Fish."

Burn nodded. *"Naméj."*

"Naméj?" Thomas prompted again, and repeated, "Fish."

Burn got the idea and pronounced, "Fish!"

Thomas nodded, pleased. He watched Burn take a small piece, then expand his arms to indicate a broad sweep: *"Naméj."* Then he made like one fish swimming, and said, *"Blamu."*

Thomas thought a bit. Fish, yes, *Naméj,* he must mean all of the species, fish. Looking at the actual meat of the fish, which was salmon, *Blamu* must mean salmon. "Salmon? From the river?" he repeated and Burn copied him. "Salmon."

Then Thomas pointed to the bread. "Bread."

Burn responded with *"Bibnaqan."*

And so on they went on, sharing their language, while Thomas struggled to chew and swallow the unfamiliar food. Navy grub had been bad enough, but familiar. At the castle, he reflected, although they were given scraps, he had eaten well: his mother had seen to his favourite choices for breakfast, and even for his simple lunches and dinners. Again he realized he'd be surviving on quite another menu. And not one much to his liking, either.

Finally, Burn patted him on the shoulder, put his hands beside his head and tilted it to one side. *"Elsmasin."*

"Elsmasin." Tom repeated. "Get some sleep? Sleep..."

Burn repeated, "Sleep." But he still seemed concerned.

I wonder what I can do, thought Thomas. Just obey?

Burn mimed, pointing to himself and made his fingers do a walk. He pointed back east to the Port Daniel river. He grabbed Thomas by the shoulder, looked into his eyes, and nodded gravely. A kind of farewell.

But wait, Thomas thought, I can't let him go without explaining, as I did to Tongue, that I need someone to come, in time, and teach me the Micmac ways of hunting and how to survive. A tall order for his sign language, for sure. But he set about it, and after a bit, Burn signified he understood.

Then Thomas put out his hand. Burn looked down. Thomas took Burn's hand, and shook it, and let go. "Thank you," he said. "Thank you so very much, Burn. Thank you."

"Thank you," Burn repeated. And then he turned and disappeared into the dusky wood.

Chapter Eight

Thomas had walked since sunup and still had not found the break in the high red cliffs signifying the brook he had seen from the *Bellerophon*. His Indian moccasins, being unfamiliar, provided little protection against sharp rocks and stumps, and were wet from squelching over swampy ground; his feet hurt and they ached from the cold. He kept on veering back and forth along the edge of the cliffs so as to keep out of sight of any shipping, but now he began to wonder if his brook sighting had been just an illusion. His container of water had long been finished, so he'd better find the brook soon. He felt depressed and worn out.

Then he heard something. He stopped and leaned against a trunk, listening.

Yes, faint rushing water.

He hurried forward and came upon the edge of a valley, a few hundred yards across, which had cut that V-shape in the cliffs he'd seen. He started straight down, then stopped. Slithering down these steep sides would leave scars easily found by any landing party. Here at the brook's mouth is where they'd come ashore.

He turned and headed inland, even though the sun was dropping. It had been a long day, being only weeks from the summer solstice. After all that strenuous walking, he needed to eat, and drink! And rest. But safety first.

The forest grew thicker, with more bushes, making it hard-going. He threaded through thin trunks and between branches of spruce, which scratched his face. No great striding as he once did over the Pennine Fells in western Durham, for sure. But here he was a free man, able to take whatever direction he willed, follow whatever course his conscience suggested. But no time to sit and absorb all that — he just needed to find a place to walk down to that brook.

When he did feel it was safe to approach the valley once again, being a good way inland, he eased down, slipping on the wet leaves and grasses, hanging onto saplings, stepping over tangled branches.

Then, he tripped.

Down he tumbled over and over, his pack flying. He brought up hard against a trunk and lay, breathing heavily. A final indignity. Clumsy oaf! he scolded himself, and lay still, panting. He tried to relax, and then sat up. First, check the pack. The saucepan! He'd tied it on behind. Had it come off during the fall, or much earlier? Bought from the trading post, it could almost be his most precious acquisition: for cooking, carrying water from the brook, storing food, all sorts of uses. He had to find it.

He tried to remember when he had last checked. Taking a break early in the afternoon, he'd found everything shipshape. He had picked a grassy spot on a cliff, chewed on a piece of dried fish, looked out over the grey, sparkling waters of the bay, and then taken a short snooze. Refreshed, he'd checked his pack, adjusted the tumpline on his head, and set off again. Yes, definitely, that had been the last time. But retracing his footsteps that far back would be a terrible drain. Night was falling.

He'd do it tomorrow.

No, better check at least up the side hill. Setting his pack against a trunk, he started back up to trace his tumble. Twice in a couple of days he'd made a mess of things — first the mistake with the shillings and then this clumsy fall. When he reached the marks of his first fall, he stood dejectedly. The pan was nowhere in sight. Wait! Suppose it had tumbled down the hill too? He'd check under each bush, he decided, and then under that low spruce over there. He eased down. Yes, underneath he saw a gleam. The pan. He grabbed it and raised his eyes in prayer.

With his pack and the pan, he clambered down and cautiously approached the brook through the tangled alders growing in profusion along its banks. No trail along this side, although he felt sure Micmac families had passed occasionally, fishing and hunting. So any trail must run along the opposite side, where the flat land was more spread out.

He stopped at a clearing where the brook seemed fordable, about eight yards across. He stepped down into the rushing water and waded over slippery rocks with his heavy pack. Icy, no doubt. But fresh, very fresh, yes he could drink from that. On the other side, he dropped his pack and fell to his stomach. The ground was damp but he lay close, leaned over, lowered his face into the brook and drank thirstily.

He sat back, exhausted and chilled, his clothes wet from sweat. The sky he could see through the trees held few clouds. No rain tonight. He rolled over and opened his pack. He found another chunk of salmon that Burn had stuffed in during the hasty leave-taking. Although he found it tough, hardly edible, he forced himself to eat, allowing himself to take his time while he tried to absorb his new habitation. Here he was, across the sea, landed in what must be the most advantageous spot on earth for a healthy young man. He chewed slowly, swallowing what simple nourishment the Lord had provided, and thanked Him for his blessings so far.

But he knew this was only the beginning.

***

A silvery fish flipped up wriggling into the air on the end of Thomas's fishing line, which he'd made from his mar-line and a pole. He swung the trout, grabbed it firmly, put his thumb in the trout's mouth, bent its head back, broke its neck and threw it on the ground next to the two others. Breakfast, he thought, pleased.

Yesterday, he had not cooked anything nor taken time to eat, apart from some dried meat, spending all his time finding a suitable site for the cabin he proposed to build. At the brook crossing of the previous night, he had made himself comfortable on a bed of moss and fallen almost immediately asleep, only to wake up stiff, tired and hungry, long after the sun had risen. He made his way downstream towards the brook's mouth on a trail made by small game, which the Micmac had oddly predicted to be lacking.

Once on the pebble beach, he breathed deeply. Not a ship in sight. Gulls wheeled and cried overhead. Two crabs made a dash for the water just beyond his toes. Why not join them? He opened his pack and got out the soap that he'd saved from the orlop deck. Hot sun, cold air, and a nippy wind, but he waded out over a sandy bar and plunged in. The icy water shocked him again, blasting him with memories of the awful swim he had endured four days before. But this time he leapt up quickly, and soaped himself all over, including his lengthening hair and the beginnings of a beard. Then he dunked himself under to get the suds off, splashing a few times with shrieks of delight, and trotted up and down, swinging his arms. In an invigorating trice, he found himself dry. He pulled back on his hastily borrowed Indian garb. Much refreshed, he set about exploring a proper site for his cabin.

Upstream from its narrow opening in the cliffs, the little valley widened into a flattened area where the trees grew closer, the stately Balm of Gilead predominated: their large trunks might provide good foundations for any future cabin. After exploring the area all morning, he decided on a site upstream where the valley narrowed into steeper sides. He spread his gear well back from the brook, and took stock. Nothing he had ever done in his life, either in the castle or the Navy, had prepared him for what he was about to do — try to build a home in this wilderness.

On the damp ground still moistened by melting snow, he had noticed tiny ferns beginning to unreel their violinlike heads. I wonder if they are edible, he thought to himself, and on impulse, tried one. Bitter, but tasty. He waited to see if he got a stomachache, and when he didn't, he gathered some to fry with his next trout breakfast.

Ready for a bite of lunch, he discovered that Burn had

added a couple of cakes of bannock from the band's store. He wondered at their generosity, but this would be all he had for a long time — unless he could shoot some game. Would he have to return to get help from the band? That might be dangerous. By now the trader would have received his marching orders from Jonas Wickett. But still, Thomas would have to learn archery, and the use of a spear and, most important, how to lay snares for small animals. Alone, he felt bereft of comfort.

How simple his life had been back home, before he joined the Navy. Although in his early teens, he had advanced rapidly in the employ of the good Earl. He remembered going out shooting as one of four beaters in the extensive household. The day had been cloudy, the grouse holding fast to the ground. This shoot was in honour of the Marquis of Athlone, who came annually to County Durham to enjoy the pleasures of the extensive grounds with their gardens, nooks, alcoves, and even lawns for games of mallets and hoops.

Thomas had motioned for the other beaters to spread out as they moved among the high grasses, beating the underbrush. He'd been on many shoots, and now had become temporary head beater due to the older man's indisposition. In fact, he'd always been interested in firearms, and had taken to cleaning and oiling them for his master. In return, Thomas had been allowed to practise, and became a good marksman, though not, of course, ever allowed to participate in outings such as this.

Finding the grouse not rising, he motioned for the others to stop. Then he saw the Marquis detach himself from the shooting party who were paused for a *wee dram,* and head over towards him.

Was he now in for a penalty? The face seemed stern, but not menacing, although the blue eyes pierced him like a sabre. True, Thomas had noticed the Marquis on his annual shoots staring at him, and had shrunk back, wondering what this man must be about. Other beater boys had told of encounters with noble visitors, stories by no means pleasant. Because of his outstanding good looks, they would joke that Thomas should soon be subject to these vile manifestations. But Thomas was bold, tall, and strong as an ox, and delighted in taking on his fellow workers in various physical contests and challenges. No nobleman so far wanted to tangle with his manifest strength. But could the Marquis now be singling him out for one of those dreaded midnight adventures?

The Marquis began by asking what was happening next.

"My Lord, I suggested that the beaters—"

The tall angular man shook off the explanation and manoeuvred Thomas aside. "I have heard that you might like to leave the employ of our noble Earl?"

Thomas was taken aback. "Leave, My Lord?" How on earth could this visitor know what Thomas really wanted, deep down inside? The only person being party to his secret desires was his worthy mother, assistant to the head cook. Thomas was well aware that the distinguished visitor seemed, over the years, to have singled him out with unusual interest, and often appeared to be discussing him with his mother.

Before he could adjust his thoughts, a pale hand reached out, an envelope in its elegant fingers. "Present this to the Captain Cooke of HMS *Bellerophon*, which as you know is one of the largest and finest man o'wars in His Majesty's Fleet. It is due to pass through Portsmouth Harbour in about three weeks. The Captain is a family friend. He assured me he would give you a try. Midshipman, likely."

Thomas's eyes widened. Everything he had ever dreamed of lay in that envelope. But...

"I questioned his wife recently," the Marquis went on. "She said that Captain Cooke expected to be sent to the New World at some point in the future, though not until that dastardly Napoleon and his ruffians have been beaten."

"The New World?" Thomas found himself at once excited and at the same time in shock. How had this nobleman known? Thomas loved being here close to his mother, in the employ of the Earl. But of late, he had become increasingly dissatisfied. Indentured to a life of servitude by virtue of being his mother's child, he often wondered at this condition over which he had no control. A precocious lad, he would often question these issues of birth, of social practice, and the way in which he and his fellow beings were stratified. Rumblings of new colonies abroad, whose constitutions deemed every man equal, had sometimes been bruited about the castle. But so far no one, not even his mother, could give him satisfactory answers.

And now, he was being offered a new life of freedom. But how had this come to be? He had often prayed, yes, sneaked into the castle chapel after work to kneel and ask his Maker for guidance, even voicing out loud these outrageous longings. Had someone been hidden there and heard them? Ridiculous.

"But you know," the voice turned gentle, "life at sea is harsh. And once you have been accepted into His Majesty's service, the penalty of desertion," a pained look crossed the unlined but aging face, "is a thousand lashes." He looked away. "Death, certain death."

Thomas felt his cheeks burning. No matter what the penalty, he wanted more than anything to get away. First to a new life in His Majesty's service. And eventually, to the New World across the sea. Standing silently behind the guests in the candlelit dining room as a junior footman, he had often heard that wondrous continent discussed. Once abroad, he would manage an escape, thousand lashes or not. His first year at table, Thomas had heard a youthful Captain, the son of a Lord Admiral, regale the dinner guests (duly reported below stairs) with tales of new worlds that were now being discovered and populated across the seas. From that moment, Thomas had set his sights on departure. But how...

"From all I hear," the Marquis went on, "you are most enterprising. I trust — in fact, beg — that you take every possible precaution. I shall ask your noble Lord to give you leave to go. Then, you must lay your plans with a maximum of forethought and preparation."

What was he saying? But this — this was more than he could ever have expected or dreamed. Something about it had the aura of an hallucination. Though considering the previous interest of the Marquis, not so completely unexpected.

As Thomas stared down at the envelope in his hand, his provider went on, "My address is at the top of this letter. If you do ever contrive to make a landing on the far shores of the New World, please notify me to that effect. By that means, I shall know my sea captain has been an honest fellow. And of course, that your brave initiative has matched your own somewhat extravagant dreams."

Their eyes met. Thomas tried to stammer out his thanks, but was taken aback to see the noble Marquis' eyes mist over. Abruptly he had swung his gun up onto his shoulder and stridden off, leaving Thomas with a plethora of mixed and overwhelming emotions. So often he had dreamed of this land, and now at last, he had arrived.

Chapter Nine

The next morning at his fishing hole, he picked up his three trout, each about six inches long, and walked back to the place he had chosen for a cabin. Time to build his first fire. He'd never started fires in the castle, nor had he on board ship. Carefully, he unwrapped the tinderbox, remembering how long it had taken to work the linseed oil into the covering cloths, over and over again, to waterproof them.

And indeed, safe and dry its contents were. Now, to see if he could make it work. He broke off a few dead branches and also upright sticks of bush that would be drier than any lying on the ground.

In the bottom of his tinderbox, he fluffed up the pieces of charcloth, the charred linen, and spread the tinder, a mixture of fibres that kindled easily. He shaved his sticks and laid them aside. Taking the straight sharp edge of the flint and pointing the steel into his tinderbox, he struck the steel hard so the sparks fell on his tinder. He'd been taught to use short, choppy strokes and keep his fingers well back from the edge of the steel; no cuts or nicks here, miles from any medical help.

Awkwardly at first, he tried striking the sparks, which meant shaving tiny pieces off the steel with the sharp edge of the flint: he knew the sparks came from the steel, not the flint. After a few tries, the charcloth began to smoulder and then glow. Quickly he folded in the tinder around the glowing embers and blew gently. The glow spread and, after a bit, burst into flame. His first fire.

The crisp sizzle of silvery bodies in the iron frying pan allowed him to relax. Be ever vigilant, he warned himself, but if the smoke were detected by a sailing ship, it might be thought of as coming from some native family. Would His Majesty's Navy go to the immense time and trouble of tracking him down in this wilderness? Probably not. But he knew Jonas Wickett would go to any length to catch him, and he did not feel safe for a second relying on Jonas's ability to forgive and forget. Other ships would be passing, no doubt. Any one of them might set landing parties ashore in this area, prompted by Wickett's desperation. Don't let down your guard, he warned himself.

And what about Fury, who had lost his son? He and his friends might well come hunting for him, looking to finish him off. If they did, very little could save him. Double reason to be on guard.

Washing down his fried trout and the fiddlehead ferns with a container of icy brook water, he marshalled his optimism and focussed on the enormities ahead. Around him, patches of snow were melting. But another winter would be upon him almost before he knew it. No matter how sturdy a cabin he might build, he had nowhere near enough money to buy stores for those long dark seven or eight months. He had to find an instructor from the Micmac. But would only a spell of teaching prepare him to snare enough game? He had no new powder or shot from the trading post, it being probably forbidden to sell to Indians.

This silence too was new, a silence filled with unfamiliar bird calls or the distant yapping of a fox. How he missed the flurry of footsteps on the winding stone staircases of the castle, or indeed the slap of lines and whine of the wind as the ever boisterous seas crashed about his man o'war. Fine to be negative, he thought, but look, now, for the first time in his life, he had no one else to worry about. He was quite alone: the gurgling brook his only companion. Running as it did down from the interior hills to the sunny bay, it abounded with trout. Solid food for the summer. Why not rejoice in what he had?

A squirrel scolded him overhead. Starving, he thought. Don't bluster at me, mate, just go find those nuts you've hidden. A moose bird swooped low over his head with a squawk and lit on a branch, watching with sharp eyes. Such a bright blue, must be his breeding colours. He longed for some means to identify these new friends. Often on the trail in the last couple of days, he'd heard the most haunting call, sounding like, "Oh happiness happiness happiness." What should he call that warbler?

The moose bird sat gawking at him and his trout. All right, he thought. He picked up an uneaten head and tossed it to the tree. He waited. The bird kept tilting his head on one side and the other to peer at it. Thomas went on eating and before too long, was rewarded by the moose bird flitting swiftly down. With a raucous rattle, it grabbed the morsel and flew off into the trees. At least, he thought, two of us are getting sustenance.

***

Ten days later, Thomas stood back to look at a square of six-inch logs, five layers or so high, twelve feet square, notched at the ends in the manner of military building. It stood well back from the brook, above any trace of high waters that broke over the banks in the spring flooding. The site he'd chosen was also hidden from the brook by a screen of young cedar.

It was getting late in the afternoon, and he wanted to try for another round of logs before dark, but right now he needed to eat. He had fished this morning, as usual, and had left the trout securely held on a twig through their gills, dangling in the stream to keep cool. The last of the bread he'd been given by Burn was getting mouldy, so now he would try to finish that with his fried fish. Amazing how little one needed now to survive. Had his stomach shrunk? He was actually getting to accept this Spartan fare.

He left his axe leaning against the notched logs and walked the hundred feet down a trail he'd made leading indirectly to the brook, still being cautious about discovery. As he walked, Magwés sprang into his mind. Her image had been keeping him company recently, especially when the "Oh Happiness" bird called. Its song brought him back to the Micmac maiden with fierce eyes and sleek black hair.

A dark mound at the edge of the stream caught his attention. He stopped to look more closely. It had not been there before. Or had it? Round and black — it moved! He caught his breath

The mound backed out of the brook. Not ten feet away — a bear cub, about two feet high, with his twig of trout hanging from its mouth.

The cub took one look at him and let out a loud whimper.

From upstream, Thomas heard a roar. The water thrashed as a large mother bear charged up and leapt over the lip of the brook as effortlessly as a buck leaping a fence on the Durham estate. She stopped short, seeing Thomas. The cub was between them. For a frozen second mother and man stared.

The mother bear. And a cub! All the things he had been warned about. Fast and powerful, bears could crack a leg in their jaws, climb trees, knock over a horse with a blow, and they were always ravenous in spring. For a flash, he chastised himself for being careless again, messing up as usual.

Pistol! his mind cried. Back at the cabin. He whirled and tore for home.

With a roar, the mother bear charged after him.

The axe, his brain screamed. He dodged this way and that, yelling aloud to scare her off, yanking his knife from its sheath.

In seconds she was on him. Her claws raked his back, knocking him flat.

Winded, he spun, saw above him this monster out of all nightmares reared on her hind legs. He shouted to frighten her, spun like lightning on the ground to make himself a moving target.

She leapt sideways after him, then pounced. Holding his knife ramrod straight with both arms, Thomas aimed at her heart.

The knife went in. With another roar, she lifted her snout in rage and rose up again to fall on him and tear him to pieces. Her open mouth dripped saliva, her white teeth gleamed.

The end. He saw it clear as day. Nothing could stop her. A juggernaut, a gigantic nightmare from Bedlam, a finish to all his dreams. Wounded, he still whirled over and over, then leapt up and tore for the bushes. But why had she not followed? From behind a tree, he turned.

The animal was circling in a devilish dance, trying to get at something sticking out of her side. The cub pranced, whimpering, beside her.

Then he saw it. An arrow! She'd been hit.

Suddenly faint, he gripped the tree trunk. His back stung with pain. At his feet a pool of blood was forming. Those claws had torn his neck and back open.

The she-bear bellowed and ran northward into the woods, cub following. Who had arrived, he wondered, who had saved him? Not Fury, he hoped.

Across the brook splashed a familiar form.

"Burn! Burn!" he gasped and then, losing consciousness, slid to the ground.

***

Burn stayed with Thomas for almost two weeks. He first boiled a kind of tea out of cedar leaves and poplar bark to help lessen the pain from the claw strikes. Then he took off after the bear, predicting she would not get far. He tracked her a good deal farther than he had first thought, and finished the wounded animal off with his spear. He had butchered the carcass, and stashed it in a tree, for them to retrieve just as soon as Thomas was better.

Burn returned with some meat for their immediate

needs, one reason Thomas had recovered his strength so quickly. He used a tendon to sew up the flap of skin while Thomas bit hard on leather soaked in an herb soporific. Definitely the worst time Thomas had gone through, though in one sense the best, because Burn had saved his life.

Then Burn applied salve from a pounded and crushed herb to keep the flies off and showed Thomas where to find that plant. He also constructed a lean-to for Thomas until he was well enough to finish the cabin's roof with birchbark. Later, they retrieved the meat carcass and Burn stretched the bearskin taut in the sun for curing. He made sure to perform a ceremony of gratitude to the Keeper of Bears for the bounty that had been given them. He smoked the rest, thereby handing Thomas a crucial lesson. Hopefully in this cool forest, hung in a tree, there'd be enough for him to last long into the summer. Thomas did remember well the hams hanging in the cavernous fireplaces in the basements at Raby Castle, where the cooks cured great haunches of venison shot on the estate, along with grouse and partridge. In the process, Thomas learned more about how to preserve the small game he'd catch. He didn't much like the taste of bear, but he had to eat substantial meals to help with the healing process.

Thomas also learned from Burn which portions to use for bait, and how to construct snares for predators. He drove sticks into the ground, notched, with one piece across that would jerk out when the animal ran into it. The secret was to let the game come and go for a while first. After several days, a loop of *babiche* (a strip of raw scraped moose hide or caribou) with a slipknot, would be put in and attached to a bent-over sapling. When the animal dislodged the crosspiece, the sapling would spring up, breaking the animal's neck, to avoid it suffering. Before Burn left, they even caught squirrels, usually the domain of the women, and one snowshoe hare. A few edible plants were appearing in the spring, so Burn taught him which ones to use for what purpose, and applauded his discovery of fiddlehead ferns. In the evenings round the fire, Thomas spent time teaching Burn English words, as he in turn learned Micmac. They were fast becoming friends.

One day Burn mysteriously disappeared only to return late in the afternoon. Eyes glowing, he held out his hand. In it Thomas saw three little stunted plants with odd leaves. Blueberry plants. Yes, a few miles west back in a large burned area behind another river, acres of them awaited the summer sun, enough to provide Thomas with much healthy nourishment. Burn took him there, blazing the trail, before returning to the band.

The next month Thomas finished the walls of his modest cabin. He was about to tackle the roof when Burn returned to alert him of a forthcoming trip. The band had presumed that the French traders in Paspébiac would be safer for Thomas — unless his man o'war were moored offshore again. Thomas dreaded the prospect of seeing a British naval vessel off the Robin's *barachois*. Should he go with them? But how else to get supplies for the winter? He realized that the whole enterprise was more complex than he'd ever imagined, fraught with danger on every count, and nothing for it but to take risks, if he were to survive.

Chapter Ten

A few days later, a great birchbark canoe thrust through the waves driven by four Micmac paddlers with furs and other trading items. Thomas, kneeling amidships, turned to look up at the sheer red cliffs whence came an awful clamour: large black birds — hell-divers, as fishermen called them — wheeled and screamed overhead, while ungainly young, nestled in thousands on ledges, flapped and squawked at the passing canoe. The stench was heavy in his nostrils. It reinforced the apprehension he felt about this foray into civilization.

The paddlers hugged the high red cliffs, letting this shield them from an offshore gale that was blowing. The water was rough but the canoe seaworthy. Thomas could not see across the bay now, but from the deck of his man o'war he had seen both shores and figured Chaleur Bay to be about twenty-five miles across, which naval charts confirmed. Once the *Bellerophon* had sailed thirty leagues past Paspébiac, to the bay's beginnings at Restigouche, where the last naval battle of the Seven Years War had taken place in 1759. Captain Hawker had wanted to ascertain if any American privateers were in hiding up beyond their reach, as the French had done then.

Today, Tongue paddled ahead of Thomas in the canoe. His job would be to negotiate with the Paspébiac trader.

Thomas watched his burly frame with its rhythmic motion, thereby learning the best way to handle a paddle. Thanks to the week with Burn, Thomas had made some headway with Micmac and so was able to carry out a more effective exchange. He discovered the band had decided against doing further commerce with the English trader in Port Daniel. This morning at dawn they had portaged their canoe around the mountain and put out from the beach to the west, to avoid notice.

As the canoe sped forward, Tongue turned and pointed to a low estuary, at the mouth of another river, larger than his brook.

"*Rivière nouvelle*. French name. New river." He laughed. "For native, very old river. *Dlabadaqanchíj*, 'make small potatoes,' which mean river washes stones into small pebbles."

Hard to miss the twinkle in those brown eyes, Thomas thought. Tongue had a way of making everything sound jocular. Nothing perturbed him. "Native family summer here other year. Everyone very thin when summer end!"

"Not enough fish?"

Tongue shrugged. "Maybe family too big!" He grinned.

"Lots of children?"

"Brothers, sisters, uncles, aunts, too big, too big. They go other band." Even as he twisted around to wink at Thomas, Tongue paddled forcefully, always carrying his share of any burden. Odd that such a burly Micmac should be blessed by such intelligence. Thomas actively hoped they would stay friends.

"What about that father in your band who lost his son?" Thomas was glad of the opportunity to bring up Fury who had been on his mind. He hated having to be on guard against such a fierce native who knew the woods and the ways, and could finish him off in a second.

"Still crazy, I think." Tongue shook his head.

"He still blames me?"

"Blame everyone. Never himself. Himself, he send son to trading post with skins. Wrong time. English ship there. He think, he get better bargain. But not better. Lose son instead. Bad thing. Crazy man."

"Oh. He brought it on himself?"

Tongue looked around, puzzled.

"I mean, sort of his own fault?"

Tongue nodded hard. "Maybe go Restigouche, soon. Bad man, crazy. Dangerous."

Thomas nodded. He hoped he'd go sooner than later. The prospect of Fury skulking in the bushes made him almost as afraid as knowing Jonas Wickett was combing the seas after him. Better learn to paddle — who knew when it might come in handy. "Tongue, may I have a go?"

Tongue's lips broadened into a grin when he turned and motioned the others, as he changed seats with Thomas. "You become Indian soon!" he mumbled. "*Gdúlg!*"

"Well, I don't know how *Gdúlg* I'll be, maybe not very *Gdúlg!* Maybe just very bad!" Tongue let out a guttural laugh and leaned forward to pat Thomas on the back. "Well anyway," Thomas said, thrusting his paddle into the choppy waves, "I'm certainly going to try." With that, Thomas focussed on his paddling, his mind somewhat easier. And anyway, he was hoping that up in Paspébiac, he might find a reason to stay for the summer, which would surely give Fury time to cool down.

Meanwhile, his mind went back to the only other time he had landed in Paspébiac, when he'd gotten his trousers. A certain Mr. Robin from Jersey had a cod-drying enterprise in the village, and was transporting the fish to the Old World, for which he needed boats built. When the *Bellerophon* had called in, Thomas had helped load fresh supplies of water and fresh meat.

After supervising the counting of flour bags, he had stopped to watch French carpenters working on a barque, about eighty feet long. A party of marines had been stationed halfway up to the village where they could survey the *barachois,* as they called the sandbank. Seeing no real chance of escape here, Thomas thought ahead. At some point, he'd get away. So what should he wear then? Shielded from the redcoats by the half-built hull, Thomas had pulled out a King's shilling and offered it to the carpenter, pointing to the man's ratty trousers. At first the man had let out a raucous guffaw, but seeing Thomas was serious, he took his pants off quickly, much to the hilarity of his French mates. Covering himself in an apron, the carpenter went back to work while Thomas hurried to his ship, stuffing the trousers under his jacket. Those trousers were now back in the native village, worn by the brave who had traded clothes with him. That visit had given Thomas an idea of what lay ahead. So far as he'd been able to observe, smart young craftsmen might well be in demand.

As he paddled on, he found the choppy waves awkward to move through, but he persevered, and by the end of his last stint, Tongue handed him a compliment. "You good, Thomas."

Thomas turned, and smiled. "Thank you." He paused.

Now seemed a good time to ask a question much on his mind of late. "Tongue," he said, "Magwés, does that mean anything in English?"

Tongue grinned, and looked at him with a sense of connivance. Oh-oh, the old blighter sees right through me, Thomas thought, watching him tap the outer side of the canoe. "Birch."

"It means birch?"

Tongue nodded. He cupped his hands to suggest the girth of a sapling. "Small."

"Oh. Like a sapling? Say, rather like, Little Birch?"

Tongue nodded. "Now, we land."

"Good!"

In the faint light of a rising crescent moon, they beached in a cove shielded by jutting cliffs from Paspébiac. With an efficiency that might have made any company of marines envious, they leapt ashore, pulled their canoe above the high tide line, and scrambled effortlessly up a trail that Thomas could hardly see in this faint light. Even with the short spells of paddling, his shoulders and arms ached from the unaccustomed toil, and his knees pained from the cramped position in the canoe. The four Micmac set about preparing their temporary campsite. Spreading hides, they settled down to eat a snack. None of them seemed to have suffered from their long day of paddling. Such a hardy lot. One day soon, Thomas promised himself, I'll be like that.

***

Thomas found it hard to sleep on the ground with only

one skin beneath him, aching from his day's paddling. But when he did, he slept with the dead weight of a stone. At first light they all roused, and shared with Thomas their simple meal of dried fish and the pulp of berries they had beaten into a kind of brick, preserved in birchbark. One of them had gone to reconnoitre Paspébiac and check out their trader. As he chewed on this simple fare, Thomas tried to repress his anxiety at what lay ahead.

After the meal, they climbed halfway down the cliff in the semidark, easing themselves along a narrow shelf of rock. Thomas saw them tilt their faces to drink their fill of freshwater filtering from the cliff face and splashing onto the beach below. Cautiously, he followed suit, wetting himself in the process. It tasted delicious, as did all the water he drank in this new land. Much fresher than the ancient wells of Durham.

While waiting for their fourth member to come back, they sorted through the skins and prepared bundles for the trader. The tide being low, Thomas picked his way through seaweed and over boulders to get around the point and take a look-see. Different eyes on Paspébiac this time for sure.

As he rounded the point, he spotted, anchored beyond the jutting sandbank, the unmistakable sails of a British frigate.

Now this did present a problem. Should he stop here, wait out the day, and return home with the Micmac? Would the Captain of the frigate have heard of his desertion? Or was Thomas being overly cautious? Surely the whole British Navy would not be focussed on the desertion of one minor Midshipman? But Wickett surely would.

Tales abounded of British Justice, which Thomas disliked as much as he respected its efficacy — the latest one being about a gun captain who had decided, as had he, to settle here years previously. Missing family and home and having saved enough money, he had tried to buy his passage on a British ship, and this being years later, had given his real name. They had seized him and turned him over to the Captain of a naval vessel, who treated him to a merciless lashing. They stopped before he had fully expired, but it was a poor gibbering idiot who returned to the family in Dorset, broken in body and spirit. Thomas had no great desire to put himself in danger of such treatment.

He sat out of sight on a rock and watched the waves rolling in and out: small waves, Atlantic waves, but dangerous in a storm, choppy and unpredictable. What should he do? He'd come all this way to Paspébiac to find a job, the only way to assure himself of enough supplies to get through the winter. Should he just forget the whole risky idea? The French, Tongue had suggested, would be his friends; little fear of them turning him over to the hated British, who had conquered them only fifty years earlier.

But now with the ship in full sight, he had second thoughts. Was it really wise to run the risk of staying? Perhaps he should try to camp here on the bluff out of sight until the frigate left, likely in a few days. But then, how easy would it really be to find a job? Dressed in his Micmac outfit, might they not dismiss him? No, his light hair and skin should mark him as European. Suppose another Navy ship took this one's mooring — wait that out too? But few naval vessels patrolled here; once this went, he'd likely have time to try his luck. But then again, if he stayed until the frigate left and did not find a job, what about the long trek back home with no supplies, no food, no weapons?

Why not go back with his friends and try coming the next time? No, Tongue had told him this was their one summer trip. All right, borrow a canoe and come again by himself. But would they lend him one? A canoe took weeks of building — would they trust him with one over such a distance? Would he trust himself? Well then, pay someone to paddle him. No, he needed his money for supplies. Lucky that scout had gone to reconnoitre: he needed this time to think it all through.

Sitting on his boulder, he cast his eyes over the settlement spread out on the sandbank below the village of Paspébiac. Thriving, he had to admit. On a ship's "cradle and ways" as the underlying structure was called, he saw a skeleton hull taking shape. The Robin's company needed coastal vessels to carry supplies up the St. Lawrence River to Quebec City and on to Montreal. Might he work on the construction of that vessel?

The scout came scrambling down the bank. Thomas watched him talk to the other three in Micmac, and then Tongue came over. "We go."

"Go... But is it safe?"

Tongue nodded.

Thomas followed Tongue back to the cache of trading items. Safe for them, possibly — but safe for him? Tongue never used three words where one sufficed, even though he formed good sentences. So the scout had probably meant that Thomas could come, too. Leaving one man to guard the canoe, they set off up the bank with their bundles, Thomas following with considerable misgivings.

* * *

Thomas strode with his three Micmac friends along a two-wheeled track through woods that were being logged. Piles of trunks lay ready for the sawmill; brush littered the clearings. The sun was rising behind them, but the air retained a late June chill.

After about half an hour, they saw ahead the general store with *G. Gendron et Fils* prominently displayed. His stomach tightened. Suppose the Micmac scout had been wrong, and even now a detachment of marines lay in wait inside. He ridiculed his nervousness. One month alone in the woods with animals as his only companions made him altogether too suspicious of civilization.

The store was built of wood, with whitewashed clapboard sides and a shingled roof tarred black. A veranda ran around the front, with four chairs. They all walked up onto it and went in. Thomas held back — he'd let the others check for danger first. Tongue soon opened the door and motioned him in.

The Trader looked him up and down, and made a remark in French. Tongue laughed and translated. "He say, blond Indian. New style!"

Thomas grinned. Tongue went on to explain that his white friend had come to find work with James Robin.

"Eh, bien, le bureau n'ouvre pas avant sept heures."

Tongue mimed taking a watch out of his vest pocket. "Seven," he translated. Tongue went on in French and the Trader soon went to a shelf and pulled out a large tarred hat. *"Tu vas le rendre après ton rendez-vous,"* the Trader said. "Give back after, *hein?"*

Thomas nodded and thanked him profusely for this additional disguise. He watched the others spread out their items on the counters, and start the long negotiations. He wished he could stay around to help but they knew what they were doing. His views of these Indians, coming from the Navy, were radically changing. Here he was among primitive savages, supposedly not worth twopence, and Tongue could speak three languages. He said that to Tongue, who shook his head, and held up four fingers. "Also Abenaki." He pressed his two forefingers together. "Bit same-same Abenaki Micmac."

Thomas stepped outside and strolled nonchalantly around the clapboarded side of the store. It stood on a bluff from which trees had been cleared, giving him a clear view down at the vast triangular sandbank, or *barachois*, with its houses and warehouses, its fish factory, and some workers' dormitory dwellings. A barque rose above the sand, a simple shipbuilding operation worked on by craftsmen. Try there first, he thought.

White codfish lay drying in long rows on flakes (as they were called) of interlaced spruce boughs with greenery stripped off. Fisherman's wives and children were already at work turning the cod bodies inside upwards now that the sun had risen. Every evening, they were turned back, skins upmost, to keep the night dew from wetting the delicate drying of the white meat. Cod, the main trade of the Gaspé, was controlled by Robin, somewhat as the Hudson's Bay Company controlled furs in the Far North. Robin's codfish were reputed to be of the highest quality, and Robin's ships carried cargoes of them to South America as well as Europe and further on to Africa. But fishing was not to Thomas's liking. Nor did he want to sail off on another ship, though that might be safest. He was not sure what he really wanted to work at, but this was a thriving settlement with lots of possibilities.

So the office opened at seven. How droll! He hadn't thought of time in the few weeks he'd been here, apart from sunrise, sunset, and mealtimes when he'd felt hungry. Before that, for a long six years, bells had told the beginnings and endings of each watch, when to sleep and when to eat. And before that, with the strictly regulated work schedule of the castle, everyone had their specific appointed tasks and the days of the week in which to do them. What a change!

Leaning against the wall, he stuffed his long fair hair up under the new leather hat, waterproofed by tar on top. He still wore his Indian jacket and leggings gathered at the waist, an odd assortment but possibly a convenient disguise. An irregular sight, this young man, taller than anyone around and his sun-bleached hair and beard most unlike the French and Spanish peasants passing.

How best to approach the main office? Then he saw sailors from the frigate disembarking from a longboat at the jetty, and heading for a warehouse to stock up on provisions. Danger for sure. Closer by, he noticed lumberjacks with saws and axes heading back up the road from their bunkhouses to work in the woods.

Should he avoid the road and scramble directly down the bank, taking advantage of the bushes? Or wait for the next group of men to go down the cartroad and fall in with them? Three fishermen came along past the store with nets looped over their shoulders. Go now, his impulse commanded. Trotting after them, he caught up and then slouched along just behind them as a team of horses with a load of flour passed on its way up the rutted dirt road.

So they did have horses! He'd seen opposite the store a team of oxen at work clearing land. How far would he get homesteading without either? One man alone could never clear his land, he knew that. He had to find work this summer no matter what, to allow him to make enough to buy a draft animal.

His confidence was shattered by the sight of three red-coated marines coming out of a Robin's warehouse under the watchful eye of a Lieutenant. They were heading straight up the incline ahead of him. He panicked. As they came up the dirt road, they'd see him for sure.

Chapter Eleven

Striding down the dirt road to the Paspébiac *barachois* with the troop of marines marching toward him, Thomas saw that he had no time to turn and run. As they got closer, he kept his eyes before his feet and as they passed, rubbed his cheek on that side so as to hide his face. But did he catch, out of the corner of his eye, the Lieutenant watching this strange Indian slouching along with the fishermen. Keep up with the others, he told himself, head for their fishing craft, forget the Robin's office. Just follow them closely, look carefree, now move ahead, quick, use the men to block the Lieutenant's view.

Once they reached the flat land, Thomas couldn't resist a glance back. The fishermen themselves had also noticed something was up. On the hill, the Lieutenant paused, and turned to survey the *barachois*. Was he studying this little group? Thomas continued toward their fishing boat, but when they passed one large warehouse, he bolted deftly behind and then paused to take a pee, natural, guaranteed to throw off their attention. He couldn't resist another glance up the hill and was vastly relieved to see the redcoats disappear over the brow of the hill. But they'd soon be back.

Stepping out briskly, Thomas headed down a side pathway that led directly to the administrative office.

He slouched along, trying to adopt the gait of a fisherman, and certainly not the straight-backed posture of a Midshipman of the British fleet. Or indeed, a footman at his nobleman's table.

After what seemed an age, feeling all eyes were upon him, he reached the head office. On the veranda a couple of men lounged, smoking, chatting in French. He shuffled over the platform and knocked on the door.

"Entrez."

Thomas strode in. The Superintendent looked up, surprised. *"Mais je suis occupé!"*

"Excuse me, honoured sir, I am English, I do not understand."

"Busy, very busy!"

"Sire, forgive me, but I have come seeking work."

"What kind of work?" the Superintendent barked.

"I'm young, I'm healthy, I can... work on building your ship?"

"You have a trade?"

"No, no trade. Only eagerness, strength, youth — I am very willing."

"D'où venez-vous?"

"New Carlisle," he lied.

"Ah oui, un des Royalistes."

New Carlisle, the Loyalist settlement, mainly English, was several miles west up the bay. These "United Empire Loyalists" had left their homes in the Thirteen Colonies some thirty plus years before. They were said to be an industrious lot, clearing land at a great rate, having brought draft animals from their homes to the south.

"Yes sir, a Loyalist," Thomas lied. "At your service." He bowed.

"*C'est quoi, ces vêtements?* Why your clothes?" the Super asked.

"On my way here," Thomas improvised, "I was rescued by a fine group of Micmac who found me freezing in a blizzard. I hadn't expected the winter to be so long!" he went on, extemporizing to make it sound better. "When I left them, I had no money to buy better, and so kept these. I find them practical."

"*Plus pratique?*" The Super looked him up and down, clearly not believing the tale. But Thomas sensed that the presence of a young man so able, with British training, had intrigued the man. "*Il faut attendre le chef.* M'sieur Robin, he come soon." He turned when a loud knocking announced the one danger Thomas had been dreading. The marines? He turned pale.

The Super noticed. "*Depêche toi!*" He hurried to open a door behind him and motioned Thomas through. After the storeroom door closed, Thomas crouched behind a case, listening.

"Compliments of my Captain," Thomas heard the Lieutenant snap. "We have been looking for any deserters who might be seeking work with you."

"*Oui Monsieur, je le sais bien. Chaque fois que vous venez,* every time you come, you look. You think every sailor, he want desert. *Mais pas vrai.* Us, we know nothing."

The Lieutenant eyed him. "Very well. My men here will verify that, if you don't mind."

Thomas squeezed his eyes shut.

"*Non, monsieur!* You cannot look into door without permission from my *chef!* He will be here in the afternoon. If you please, you come back at that time."

Thomas opened his eyes.

"You know, of course, good sir," the Lieutenant spat out, "you are under the rule of our sovereign, King George."

"Oui, m'sieur, tout le monde le sait! Why not you come back, see M'sieur Robin," which he pronounced with a heavy French accent. Mr. Robin, Thomas knew, was from the Isle of Jersey where there were Huguenots, and thus English Protestants. *"C'est à lui qu'il faut addressez vos plaintes.* He will 'ear your complaint."

"We believe any deserter who comes here would look for a job from you."

"You have seen this office, m'sieur. No deserter."

"No, but... if one does turn up, please report him to us."

"Ah oui, monsieur," the Superintendent replied. *"C'est mieux peut-être de le chercher parmis les patriotes à New Carlisle.* All English up there, the deserter, he go first that way, I think."

"Loyalists know well their allegiance to His Majesty. But I have been instructed by our captain to make an official visit to Mister Robin to make sure he too knows that his fealty lies with the British crown."

"I assure you, m'sieur," the Super replied, "of his great faithfulness. He is English, and his partners, they all come from London."

Just then the door opened, and James Robin stamped in. "What's all this, M. Huard?"

"Ce gendarme est venu—"

Thomas could imagine Robin's expression by his firm: "Have you a problem, good sir?"

"No sir, no problem now. But there will be if your company tries to shield any deserters from His Majesty's Navy."

"And why would you suspect such a thing?" Mr. Robin asked loudly.

"There are rumours of one being seen hereabouts," the Lieutenant said, "in the garb of an Indian."

Thomas could hear James Robin chuckle. "Should one of your sailors choose to live like a savage, my good sir, I hardly think it any concern of His Majesty. Don't your men have better things to do than search the Indian bands hereabouts for one poor deserter? I bid you, sir, good day."

"Good day, Mr. Robin." Thomas heard the almost contemptuous tone. "You know our vessel has come at your request, to patrol the bay for privateers that might prey upon your ships, carrying on, as they do, commerce between this tiny settlement and His Majesty's great dominions beyond the seas. By tomorrow evening we shall have effected our transfer of supplies and shall take our leave."

"I am greatly indebted to you," Mr. Robin replied. "And in the circumstances, your Captain might care to share this evening's humble repast with me and Mrs. Robin in our abode upon the hill? And now, if you would do me the favour of leaving me to do my work..."

"Yes sir," snapped the Lieutenant. "And I shall convey your invitation to my Captain."

With that Thomas heard the Lieutenant spin on his heel, and march out with his men. In the silence, Thomas could hear his heart thundering in his chest. Why on earth would they go to such lengths, take on such risks, to save him, these French?

"C'est une bande de sans-génie," Mr. Robin spat to his Super as the door shut behind them. He spoke French as well, Thomas heard.

"Des fous, sûrement."

"If we find this deserter, we must treat him with the greatest respect." He heard steps and his door handle turned. *"Si vous le permettez, je vais vous donner une petite surprise."*

"Go ahead."

The door opened, and Thomas rose unsteadily from behind his case.

"Le voilà!"

"Well, well, what have we here?" said James Robin.

"A humble servant of His Majesty, Your Honour." With impeccable manners, Thomas bowed. "I am eternally in your debt."

"Nonsense," said Mr. Robin. "Anything I can do to hinder those wretched marines. They bother us every time they visit. Can't get an honest day's work done — verifying this and checking that. Enough to make anyone wish we were back in the good old days of French rule when, as they say, *laissez-faire* ruled the day."

Thomas followed them into the office proper and stood at attention. This man, his saviour, was the nephew of the great Charles Robin who had founded the company in 1767, nine years before the Revolutionary War. James was not overly tall but had a fine bearing, not portly like his uncle but with sideburns, well-cared-for skin and clear brown eyes, alert to every detail. He was known to be a good and fair leader, though he took all his instructions from Jersey and the family trust.

"Well now, my good man, you look strong, and eager. Have you the British efficiency ingrained?"

"Oh yes sir, I was a Mid—" he stopped, then changed tack. "My former employer in Britain taught me all the arts of shooting grouse, and the manners of a footman in a grand estate."

Mr. Robin laughed. "A lot of use that will be here!" M. Huard also chuckled discreetly.

"Well sir, I shall do whatever you see fit."

"You will?"

"But... if I may state a preference, I'd like to assist your shipbuilding operations. If I may place my poor background into your confidence, I can tell you I was once in His Majesty's service." Thomas saw the recognition flicker in Mr. Robin's eyes. "As a means of discipline but also as a benefit for my character, I was forced to spend a week preparing oakum for caulking. My most disagreeable task."

At this the two men laughed. "So the last thing you want to do is caulking?"

"On the contrary, sir, the first! I promised myself that I would see this knowledge put to good use."

"Precisely the stage we have reached with my nice new vessel. M. Huard, keep this man out of sight for a couple of days, and then once properly attired, please see that he is assigned as an apprentice to our master caulker. I'll talk to James Day. He's in charge. I'm sure he'll agree."

Thomas could not believe his good fortune, and his face must have shown it. James Robin grinned and clapped him on the back. "Don't worry, my good lad. Pioneer life has many ups and many downs. You've made a good choice. I only hope the Good Lord will tend to your safety from now on. This New World has many opportunities, but it contains a great many more hazards. Few are the men who can tough it out."

Chapter Twelve

Thomas climbed the scaffolding of rough boards, and turned to face the smooth, bevelled planks of the ship's hull rising above. About eighty feet long, it rested on its sturdy cradle and ways. The master caulker, a good-natured Brit with rough hands and a florid face, stepped over to him.

"Well, me son, here's yer iron and yer caulking mallet, always double-headed. Head is wood, see, with steel hoops on it, different sizes depending on what you're doing. This one here is right for what we're doing on these lower planks, see?"

Thomas hefted the hammer and took hold of the caulking iron. He'd already looped oakum strings over his shoulder and was about ready to start. His first day on the job. Kind of thrilling, he had to admit.

"Working on the deck is a whole lot nicer, because you're on your hands and knees. That'd be at the end of the summer." He eyed him. "You work outside in. Always."

Any position at all was fine, Thomas thought. He had changed into the common dress of the French settlers here that M. Huard had allotted him in trade for further work, so that now with his full-grown beard, he almost blended in. A compelling disguise, too, should another naval vessel turn up. He could see from the Lieutenant's uncanny prediction of a deserter being here that Jonas Wickett had been contacting other Navy ships as they passed.

The caulker went on. "The first thing you always do is get rid of the rainwater off the deck. It's the one thing you really care about. Causes rot. It's gotta get flushed out with saltwater or it'll finish your whole ship. Anything that is wet with saltwater, it might have other things happen to it, but it won't rot. Rainwater is poison!" He turned. "Now this here oakum — just pieces of old tarry rope spun with tar."

"Sir, I know it well."

"Ya do?"

"Oh yes sir, I once spent days in a little stinking room on a rollicking Navy ship, twisting it. Punishment."

Thomas remembered being assigned the dirty task of picking oakum. He would open the bale that contained the floor sweepings from the factories where they made the rope in the first place: pieces of natural fibre that weren't good enough to go into rope. Hemp was grown in India, that much he knew. When making rope, you want the best fibres to spin. Many fibres were too short. Like with cotton for clothes, one needed the long and staple fibres for rope. So in the end, a bunch of seeds and dirt were part of the sweepings from the hemp factory, all of which found their way into the bales sold cheaply to His Majesty's ships. The Captain or bosun would send his poor miscreant landlubbers, after some easily made mistake, down into the bowels of the ship where they'd pick out the stones and the seeds and take these short little fibres and roll them bit by bit into cords of oakum for use in caulking leaks.

"You get used to it. M'self, I love it," said the caulker. He stood back and watched. "All right young fella, ya kinda poke the loops of this thing with them fingers right into this here seam. Now ya gotta choose the right amount for the opening. Then ya come along with yer caulking iron and yer mallet, and you tap it in."

"I think I can manage that," Thomas said.

The caulker eyed him. Was he giving him lip? "So what you're doing is tapping in cord. You gotta be really cute" — sharp-witted, Thomas knew — "about it. Any fool can haul off and bang the stuff in hard. Won't do to fix it like 'at!" Without further ado, Thomas started stuffing, trying his best to follow directions. "See, the wood has a little bit of give to it. You want to get one row of oakum in there, just the right amount of compression in yer oakum and the right amount in yer wood. It's sort o' hard to describe, but you can tell — if you pay attention, once you're starting to catch on — you can feel how much resistance it's offering, just tap tap tap, it's not like a wall, and the sound changes."

Thomas began tapping. Different from the small oakum room on the *Billy Ruffian*, he thought, out here on the sandbank with a light breeze blowing in from off the bay, and white clouds piling high above the horizon as usual along the coast. Also very different from England where the sky was either uniformly grey or raining.

"They talk about the chirping of the mallet. The sounds change and then it feels right. Easy to know when you got that bit set, and then you move on to another piece."

"Aye aye, sir."

"Now on this here ship, because o' the width of the

seam, we gotta put in another row of oakum after this first one. You try your hand on this first, and I'll do the second, but ya see, maybe you'll pick it up faster than the froggies here."

What's beautiful about it, Thomas reflected later, is that it really is an art.

"Yerss, I'm crazy about it. That's why I came t'be a master caulker. Them two Frenchies over there been at it already two year, and they only just got the hang. You look like you might do a whole lot better. I had t'watch 'em and curse 'em up and down to make sure they didn't mess up."

The master caulker stood looking up at his men, but directing his words at Thomas. "Very distinctive, this here sound of our caulking mallets. You can hear us a long way off."

Most of the men had the strands of oakum close to hand, some in turns over their arm and another couple of turns round their neck.

"This here oakum's the basic staple anywhere, around the maritime industry." With that, the master caulker went off to survey the working party at different levels on this skeleton of the barque.

***

Thomas worked on the ship all summer long, enjoying his job and the camaraderie which had sprung up with his fellow French workers. But now, in August, the approach of autumn began to weigh heavily. Simple calculations showed that at his present rate he could never earn enough to buy the draft animals needed to clear land. And never mind that, what about this coming winter with those heavy snows they all talked about so much? He'd have to take some firm action soon.

He'd gotten enough powder and shot to bring down a moose or two, were he lucky enough to get within range. And should he find a pond or lake where beavers made their domed houses, he might get one to eat. But living alone, a long way from any habitation or neighbours, he absolutely needed enough supplies to tide him through. And find suitable heavy clothes. How to achieve that? His few coins, even if all spent (not a pleasant thought) on supplies, would not suffice to see him through six or eight months.

What about calling it a day and going home for the winter? Gazing out over the apparently limitless bay, images of the castle began to flow: first, his mother sprang to mind. And his promise of a letter. With so many new and exciting goings-on, he had not given it a thought. He could put it off no longer. Then in a flash, he also remembered the golden guinea she had sewn into his shirt. In his rush to escape the Port Daniel trader, he had exchanged clothes with Burn's friend. He must get that guinea back.

Once this job was done, he'd surely make the trip back down to the Micmac band. And meanwhile, he must fulfill his most important obligation, which had been nagging at him relentlessly: write to his mother and his mentor.

The powerful, and painful, scene of his departure rose in all its force in his mind. How well he saw his mother still with the clearest skin, though her hands were now rough and red. Recently, she seemed to be putting on weight and her fair hair was turning grey. She usually worked apart from him in the kitchen while he had his chores outside and in the stables. But his most clear image of her came from his childhood: the lovely willowy woman whom every male visitor eyed with distinct attraction.

Tuesday night after the shooting party for the Marquis, Thomas had confessed his plans and made peace with Goodman, the butler, head of the household staff, and through him with his master, the Earl. The former had already heard of his hopes of the New World, but had cautioned that this might be forever out of his grasp.

The master, in a fit of unusual generosity, had given Goodman a golden guinea for Thomas, with firm instructions that his mother sew it into his shirt where no one would find it. Thomas had also been a great favourite with the staff and at the impromptu farewell gathering, they'd taken round the hat for him — even the scullery maids had thrown in a coin or two. So that when his mother came up to him as he was taking his leave, she held out for him a leather purse filled with money.

He took it respectfully. He could see she was trying to be brave, but not succeeding too well. He was her only child after all. Thomas had never had a father, nor a sibling, so he was all she had. "Now there's always time to say no," she told him. "I've asked Goodman, and he said that you can have your place back at any time. He even told me the master seemed disturbed at the first news of your leaving; but now he wishes you well."

That was news to Thomas: none of the noble family seemed ever to give him a second thought, as was the custom in those days. His mother went on, "Even at the boat, you can turn back if you change your mind."

"I know, Mother." Beginning to get choked up, he found he was already missing the room over the stable where he slept with the other three lads. All his wants, though simple, had been filled. Would it be like that in the Royal Navy?

A long walk down to the main road from this castle lay ahead, and then about four more miles to the nearest post house. The night coach usually came through at two in the morning. Within five days he'd be far to the south in Portsmouth. He had waited a week after the Marquis' unexpected intervention to allow fair notice for his employer, through Goodman of course.

"Now you've brought your warm woollies and your scarf?" she admonished.

"Yes mother, and even my mittens." He forced a smile at his own teasing. "But I am sure, after we have beaten the French, we'll sail to the New World and I shall have no need of them."

"Hush child, of course you will! The winters are very severe over there, have you not heard?"

"I know mother, but by then I will perhaps have gotten a good job, and will be able to buy warm winter clothes." He felt his courage deserting him as he spoke. "They say there is work for every man," he reassured her and himself, "and when you work there, you are free to come and go as you like."

He had been indentured ever since a baby. His mother had often recounted how Goodman had been only too pleased to welcome her and her son. Though how she'd managed to arrange such a fine position as undercook in the Lord's castle, no one ever found out.

"One day, when Martha retires, you'll be cook yourself," Thomas said, though he didn't know why he said it.

"Oh no," she said, teasing him a little, "I thought you were going to send for me."

"Oh yes, Mother, of course I'll send for you. But it may take me a little time to get established."

He could see in her eyes that she knew a little time likely meant several long years.

At this they both found tears leaping into their eyes, and fell about each other, hugging hard. Clasped to his mother's bosom, Thomas felt like a little boy again, no longer in his teens.

"Well you'd better go," she said, trying to clear her throat. "It's a long walk to the post house." He knew she was right, but the moon was out and he should have no trouble. At this time of night no one would be about, none of the usual villains. He clutched the coach fare securely in his bottom pocket.

With the golden guinea sewn in his shirt, the purse from his mother full of change and the few shillings he'd managed to save out of his almost non-existent wages, he felt richer than ever before. His courage rose. He stood taller than his mother now, and looked down into her clouded blue eyes. What concern he saw! Both of them had left unspoken the untold dangers he would face, and the harsh life on one of His Majesty's ships. Had he been a gambling type, like many of the lords and ladies who visited the manor, he would not have given a farthing for his odds of making it across into the actual wilderness of the New World.

"God speed and God be with'ee," his mother said. Resolutely, she turned him around and gave him a gentle push.

He started down the drive. After a few steps, he looked back over his shoulder and waved, and then he turned and looked no more.

***

And so early one Sunday morning in Paspébiac, Thomas found himself seated at the long table in the cookhouse where the workers ate their meals provided by Robin (for a price). Most of the men were away at a Catholic service held in the temporary church building. Thomas remembered those services in the stone chapel by the castle. Built three hundred years ago in the reign of the Tudors, its heavy stone pillars framed a lovely stained-glass window that had escaped smashing by Oliver Cromwell's idiot followers. He loved the design: a knight with a circle of blue glass around the simple face and an upturned sword resting on a stone engraved upon the rock: *SE IPSI FIDELIS — True to himself.* When the castle had been built a hundred years later, the Lord had chosen that motto for his emblem. Thomas rather liked it, and thought he'd use it himself one day.

He dipped his quill pen in the ink borrowed from M. Huard, and by the light of a cobwebbed window, began his letter to the Marquis, his sometime mentor.

My Lord, In remembering your great kindness to me, I have borrowed paper and a pen from the good people here—

He stopped. He was about to write: *in a settlement called Paspébiac on the shores of Chaleur bay.* But then, he thought, don't locate yourself! Suppose the noble lord is contacted by Captain Hawker on his next return to the Old Country. Would he not be forced by his sense of British Justice to betray Thomas's whereabouts? He did doubt that, but in order not to put him in a difficult position, he went on:

I managed to make my way ashore from the vessel on which you so kindly arranged me a position. Now as you see, I have begun to take up a life in the New World. The future is so very uncertain — unlike the Old Country where so much is laid down — so I am unable to predict what will become of me. Suffice it to write that at times I am very happy and at others in despair of ever making the life I intended. The winter promises to be harsh, but the people are good.

At this writing I am alive and well... He stopped again, about to write: *and making a good job of working on a ship.* No, he had better not say that either, as the letter might be opened, and thus betray his whereabouts. Better reveal as little a possible. *In short, My Lord, I am eternally grateful and shall give you news when the events of the future reveal what course I am to pursue.*

Your humble servant, Thomas Manning.

And then he wrote on another piece of paper which he hoped to send with this one:

My darling Mother,
I have not forgotten my promise to send for you, but as

we both know, it may be some time. Be sure that your position in the castle is far better than ever you would find here. That is in no way to say that life is not surprising and full of unexpected joys, but it is also full of remarkable challenges, which your son is endeavouring to overcome with the best will.

Your loving son,
Thomas.

PS: As you might understand, Mother, the times being somewhat precarious, I am not able to divulge a return address. But as soon as I establish myself, it will be sent.

He folded the two papers, sealed them with wax, and addressed them. Now how to despatch them? New Carlisle would be the quickest, and safest, mailing point. But what about here in Paspébiac? No, Robin's ships travelled to Africa and all over Europe, sometimes not even calling in at Liverpool. He didn't want to risk the letters being lost. Perhaps from the trading post in Port Daniel? No, the trader was already his enemy.

So now he had to find an opportunity to go to his compatriots in New Carlisle, no matter what the danger. They would have frequent means of communicating with the Old Country, and besides, he'd love to know just how his countrymen managed to fare in this often brutal wilderness.

But when to go? And how to get there? Trek through heavy woods — no, there'd be a road, well a sort of trail, but a long day's walking for sure. This would mean he'd only arrive at night. Take two days off work? M. Huard would not be pleased. How could he manage that? What about by boat? Far swifter, if the winds were good. But

how to effect that with no regular commerce between the two communities, though he knew an occasional barque made the trip.

Best wait and bide his time. Meanwhile, why not let it be known to the other men on the shipbuilding crew he needed to make the trip? He must fulfill this promise of a letter that he had made, at no matter what risk.

Chapter Thirteen

Four nights later, Thomas was shaken awake. His eyes flew open and he sat bolt upright, ready for flight.

His French partner leaned over. *"Calme toi!"* the apprentice whispered. *"Mon père va à New Carlisle. Demain matin, à l'aurore."*

"He goes tomorrow? First light?" Thomas had by now picked up enough French to understand. But was he ready for the Loyalist settlement? Had he prepared himself enough to take off on this possibly precarious expedition? "In his boat?"

"Oui. On va y arriver à midi."

"We get there midday? Sunday?"

"Mais ça coûte." The apprentice rubbed his fingers and thumb together in the universal sign for money. *"Allez et retours, deux jours de travail pour moi."*

Thomas frowned. "You want me to credit two days of my work here to your account at Robin's?" He'd grown accustomed to the "truck" system, which meant cash was almost never used — all barter. The food they ate, supplies they used, even their simple accommodation, were all paid for by units of work. But this return trip, two days? A steep price, he thought, for just going along in a sailboat that was making the trip anyway. But his duty was clear. He had to post those letters to his mother and his benefactor. This was the only way to get there and

return without missing a day's work. He'd better accept. *"Oui, j'irais."*

The next morning before dawn, Thomas found himself clambering into a fishing boat loaded with several large *paniers* of fish, with the apprentice's father at the tiller and one French companion. Earlier he'd scrubbed away at himself, hoping to erase some of the smell of the oakum that had infused his flesh. He'd even rubbed himself with the leaves of cedar, much to the merriment of the one worker who caught him at it, and who made rude remarks about him visiting some mistress or other. Normally the oakum smell, rather like fine-scented pipe tobacco, never bothered him, but he wanted none of it when he went visiting to find a compatriot willing to send his letter. He'd borrowed better clothes for the trip, too.

They sailed on a rough and building sea but the high clouds carried little hint of rain. The wind direction, as had been predicted, allowed them swift progress under full sail. Going before an east wind, they arrived at the settlement well before noon. One private schooner lay at anchor, but otherwise the jetty contained only small boats and their comings and goings.

Here in New Carlisle, he'd find himself at last among his own. But what reactions might he face? Certainly, in County Durham, no one ever just "turned up" without an invitation, he knew that. But he also knew that in the New World, other practices held sway. Visitors were always welcome no matter what, an unwritten rule. But might notices of his desertion be posted? If so, would they turn him in? Naval ships occasionally called in at Paspébiac, but none had ever pierced, or tried to pierce so far as he knew, his disguise as a French carpenter. But they would stop in New Carlisle, and there, among the British, Jonas Wickett would have certainly seen to it that word would have been left with the authorities. So he did face considerable risk. One place to avoid would be the general store.

Thomas leapt out of the boat and tied it to one of the many bollards. He looked hard at the village settled along the low elevation above this flat meadow where cattle grazed, not unlike the commons at home. He glanced east and saw clouds beginning to rear over the horizon. Should have known, he said to himself. This trip's been too easy so far, and an east wind always brought rain.

He pointed to the rearing cumulus and the fisherman nodded. They might well have to sail back to Paspébiac in short order. Thomas didn't look forward to weathering a storm in this small boat. In any case, they arranged to meet back at the jetty in two hours.

With plans made, the fisherman and his mate hefted onto the dock the first square container of fish. Clambering out of the boat, they set off to trade with the general store.

Now, which house should Thomas visit? A track led through the meadow up to the neat frame houses that bore the style of the Thirteen Colonies: wood frame, mostly two stories high, roofed in black-tarred shingles above nicely clapboarded sides. Two or three were skirted by verandas, or "stoups," which marked houses of means — his target, for sure. But how to approach them? What story to tell, where should he say he was from and finally, how did one send a letter to England? This latter seemed the least important obstacle, for he knew that, in addition to the squadron of four or five ships arriving each spring and another going back each fall, occasional ships must visit every month or so. The schooner at anchor out there might even be leaving momentarily and he'd be in luck.

Thomas strode along the single roadway with its two wheel-ruts, noting horse droppings on the road and sheep dotted among the grazing cows. Wool and mutton — as well as beef and milk — pretty amazing, he thought to himself, with all the harsh winters he'd heard about.

He climbed the hill, wondering how to handle his mission. Beyond the houses stretched a few acres of cleared land with crops ripening in the sun: oats, wheat, and of course, mostly timothy or hay. Well, the farmers have been here since the resettlement orders in 1784 after the Revolutionary War, so they've all had time. And support, he imagined.

He selected one of the more imposing houses, toward the western edge of the village, beige with white trim and a grey flooring on the veranda. As he approached it, he reassured himself that he resembled a fine French worker in his borrowed clothes, not his choice by any means, but then, safe enough as a disguise. He was glad he had decided not to shave just yet. No one, he presumed, would look at his bearded face today and see a Midshipman from His Britannic Majesty's Navy.

He walked up the five wooden steps, crossed the veranda and knocked on the door. It was opened by a gaunt, well-dressed woman, older than his mother, with dark greying hair held up in a bun and a prominent nose that divided two sparkling black eyes.

"Excuse me, ma'am," he bowed, "but I'm from the Old

Country, and I'd very much like—"

"Well, don't stand there, young man, come in come in. Catherine, put on a kettle."

Her daughter rose from a loom in the window, blonde hair in a bun, plain but not without a luminescent beauty, verging on plump but that could be baby fat, he guessed. He put her age at around sixteen.

Her six-year-old sister raced to the kettle, dunked it in a water barrel by the door and lugged it back to the stove. "I've got it, Cathy." Cute as a kitten, full of fun, she had her mother's twinkling eyes.

Catherine stooped to put in kindling and a couple of birch logs to encourage the ensuing flame. Her eyes had risen to Thomas as he came in but now she paid him little attention.

He stood awkwardly.

"Well, young man, you've come to see my husband?" the mother asked, looking him up and down with a curiosity she didn't try to mask.

"No ma'am, not really — well, yes, in a way I have, yes." He almost kicked himself for being gauche. "You see, I have a letter that I would like to send to my mother." He paused, seeing that this registered approval, then went on, "Since I arrived here, I've been in Paspébiac—" He stopped short, aware he must not give too much away. "I was told that M'sieur Robin sends his boats to many African and European ports before they get to the Old Country. I'd heard that you hereabouts are British, so I thought perhaps you might have a quicker way..."

"Well, I'm sure my husband will help. A very thoughtful young son you must be."

A distant rumble of thunder startled him as he blurted out, "I do try, ma'am."

And in the custom of the time, Thomas was invited to lunch. Out of politeness, he deferred.

"No, please young sir, do join us. My husband is due at any moment. I am sure he would be, as we, honoured to receive you."

Learn as much as you can, he told himself, for their life seemed quite idyllic, or at least, very different from his French carpenter and fisher friends in Paspébiac. So he accepted the invitation, forgetting for the moment the weather and what it might do to his return. And of course, he was famished, as he was most of the time these days.

Sipping a good cup of tea, which he realized he'd not had for almost three months now, and surrounded by a familiar language and by manners to which he was accustomed, he allowed himself to relax and take in the pretty dresses, a stylish assortment he'd hardly expected in this distant and savage land.

His hostess seemed to read his mind. "Oh we don't always dress this way, but today has been rather special. Our visiting clergyman, Reverend Mr. Pigeon, comes twice a year, and this morning he took the service."

"It must be a great comfort, ma'am, to have a real church."

"'Tis only a temporary building, down by the commons."

"On the flat land below? I believe I saw it."

She nodded. "So are you a religious man, Mr... ?"

Oh-oh, my name... "I am indeed, ma'am, I went to church almost every Sunday back in the Old Country."

Thomas replied to her first question to give him time to think up an answer for the next.

"Did you now..." she said, as if clearly asking what came next — his name, of course.

"Please ma'am, call me... James," he went on quickly, trying to give himself time to think. His love of the Bible and its language made him grab the first name associated with it: James I. He should definitely not give out his real name; that was just begging for trouble.

She looked at him as though she sensed his prevarication, but introduced herself. "I am Eleanor Garrett, this is Catherine, and that youngster is my namesake." The two daughters curtseyed. "I have three sons, dallying after church with William."

In the ensuing conversations, Thomas mulled over the question of his name. Why on earth was he not prepared? He tried every name he could think of: occupations, Barber, Smith, Taylor, Arkwright, and on to his tradesmen's friends back home: Ainsley, Alderson, Alford — what about that? James Alford. Nice ring.

In due course, Thomas put himself to work carrying in wood. Catherine soon joined him. An able-bodied young woman, she seemed determined to show she was as strong as he. He did so want to begin a conversation with her. Amazing to him that these well-to-do women — actually owning a large house — worked just as hard, if not a lot harder, as the maids at Raby Castle. No room for pretensions and airs, only hard work, he realized approvingly.

The door opened and in walked William Garrett: a broad-shouldered man, not tall but heavy with a definite girth and a solid face, bushy eyebrows, and light hair, every inch a settler.

"Where are the lads, William?" Mrs. Garrett asked.

"Gone fishing with Edmund. Well, they worked hard all week... Now who on earth is this fine-looking young fellow?"

"James Alford, at your service, sir," Thomas dutifully replied.

"English?" William retorted. "You look bloody French to me."

"He's been working in Paspébiac, dear."

"Off a ship, are ye?" William peered at him.

"Oh no sir, I'm from down the coast," Thomas lied quickly. "My family... they've been there for some time."

William nodded, but did not, for some reason, appear quite convinced. And Thomas wondered, why on earth did he ask me if I was off a ship? Trouble ahead?

Now that the head of the household had arrived, Mrs. Garrett and Catherine busied themselves at putting out what seemed to Thomas a sumptuous meal.

"So you work in Paspébiac, Mr. Alford?" William limped up to the table and plumped down at the head of it. He gestured to his leg as he caught Thomas trying not to stare. "Holding Ticonderoga against the revolutionaries, in '77. Grape shot," he stated briefly.

Thomas knew of the many battles around Albany and Lake Champlain in the Revolutionary War. But he quickly wondered how he should answer William's question. He certainly looked like a Robin's man, so no point in denying it. "I do, sir, for M'sieur Robin. Temporarily."

"And so where do you hail from now?" asked Mrs. Garrett.

Thomas had been preparing himself for this question. He knew about another English settlement one hundred miles towards the mouth of the bay, near Gaspé. A place no one would question, he'd decided, and safer than giving away the precious location of his cabin by its brook. "I stay with relatives in Douglastown. They told me there was a deal of work at Robin's, so I made the trip up here this summer."

"Don't know how rich he'll make you!" Garrett retorted. He spoke with a distinctly North Country accent, probably Nottingham, Thomas guessed. He loved hearing it. Made him feel at home, though William was by no means graceful. Well, men from that part of England were known for their abrupt and brusque manner. "That Robin keeps his people on a pretty tight rein, I'll warrant. Those French, they all look half starved. Scruffy lot."

"Now dear, just because you cannot speak their language.... And if I've said it once, I've said it a million times, Mr. Robin is not French, he's a Jerseyman. And a Protestant to boot. They're all Huguenots."

"I believe many of the workers to be indentured servants, sir." Thomas couldn't stop staring at the princely meal. He'd not eaten like this since he'd left England, if even then. All thoughts of storms and fishermen went out of his mind.

"Bloody awful system."

"Dear, it's the same all over," Mrs. Garrett contradicted once more, as she was serving. "You know, Mr. Alford, we all run up bills at the merchant's." She passed him a heaping plate of mutton and local vegetables: potatoes, beans, and peas. "By the way, William, Mr. Brotherton came around again. Heard we'd begun our potato harvest. Wanted to know when we'd settle up for the nails."

"He'll just have to wait!" William snapped. "Old Jarred hasn't even paid us for the wool from our sheep this spring."

"You have sheep, too?"

"What do you think you're eating there, lad," William chortled. And as soon as Grace was said, Thomas tucked into his mutton with as much manners as he could muster. Mrs. Garrett noticed approvingly.

"Aye, sheep, two oxen, can't clear land without oxen, chickens of course, as you can see from that basket of eggs." William gestured to the simple sideboard.

"Now dear, you know we don't eat like this every day. It's a special Sunday, and we thought we'd make it a celebration."

"So you're in luck, lad!" William guffawed. "You picked the right day! Planned it too, I warrant!"

"William!" Mrs. Garrett reprimanded.

"I am indeed, sir, in great good luck." Better and better thought Thomas, drinking his milk. Cows, hens, sheep for wool and mutton, life won't be half bad, once he got going. And then he heard it again: thunder!

"Eggs, that's my job," piped up little Eleanor. "Me an' Cathy, we go to the barn every day."

"Catherine and I," her mother corrected.

Catherine looked down and blushed. Thomas realized his blue eyes had been boring into her across the table. Sturdy, well built, she had a becoming bosom for one so young. And features far more attractively moulded than any serving maid back at the castle. "Ducks, too, as I hear outside," he went on quickly.

"Yes, we all work hard here, young man; you can't go nowhere in these parts bar t'hard work!" William frowned and looked up as another deepening rumble of thunder gathered out their window. The swaying trees bore witness to the wind kicking up.

What should I do, thought Thomas, make a run for the boat? No, they would not be putting out now. He stared at his food, his appetite deserting him. But he soldiered on, "Aye aye, sir. And believe me, we do work, even the French among us, we work all the day long and look to turning out a goodly barque before late autumn." His mind being on the approaching storm, he had spoken without thinking. Oh-oh, now he'd identified himself as working on the crew building a barque for Mr. Robin.

"What'll ye do after the summer, lad?"

This so precisely mirrored his concerns that he found himself taken aback. "Well... get back to Douglastown, I imagine, sir."

"You wouldn't like to come work for me this winter, would you? Logging? I'd see you got well fed. No money, mind, none of us pay in cash. All we do is feed you right and proper, and make sure you sleep warm. And of course a portion of the logs ye cut, if ye're so inclined."

"Winters are long, you know," Mrs. Garrett chimed in. "And very hard. But if you have relatives in Douglastown..." She said it as though she wasn't convinced. Woman's instinct, he thought.

"And even with all our work, young sir," she went on, "three boys harvesting the turnips and potatoes for our cold cellar, two wonderful daughters helping me put up jams, salt pork, dried berries, and heaven knows what else, last winter we had a hard time of it."

"Aye, we did that. Not a family here but didn't feel the pinch. Shut that window, Catherine. Rain'll be upon us before we know it."

Catherine went across to the window, for the wind had indeed grown fierce. Thomas thought uneasily of the predicament he'd gotten himself into. But he tried to maintain his composure. "Rather cold, for August, sir, is it not? Or do you find it normal for the coast?"

"Every year, after one really warm day in July," William chortled, "we say: Well, there goes the summer!"

Mrs. Garrett smiled. "Shouldn't be surprised if it turns quite nippy this week."

"And why else do we work from dawn to dark to get in the last of the hay?" William downed another forkful of mutton.

"Down in the Colonies, of course," Mrs. Garrett went on, "no winter was ever as cold as these up here. Quite, quite unknown in the Old Country, too, as I expect you remember, Mr. Alford, though I myself have all but forgotten. And of course," she went on, eating rather primly, "no one instructed us how to deal with these harsh conditions."

"I'm sure not, ma'am." But he wondered, why did no one think to ask the Micmac, who've lived here through thousands of winters?

Catherine came back from the window and threw him a strange look, inviting, yet distant. As she sat properly apart in her chair, Thomas heard the rain come, gusting hard against the sides of the house. He looked down. Here he was, in a strange village, with a host who had demanded to know if he were off a boat, no means of transport and now, nowhere to stay this night. And a storm in full blow.

Chapter Fourteen

Cold rain beat against the panes and pelted down on the cedar shingles. The east wind, true to its promise, had brought a savage summer storm to the Gaspé. Snug in their farm kitchen with their meal finished, the Garretts seemed to be genuinely enjoying the company of their new acquaintance. But something in the way William kept watching him made Thomas uncomfortable. What did he suspect?

Knowing he was in for an interrogation, Thomas took the offensive. "Sir, forgive my ignorance, but why are you United Empire Loyalists all in New Carlisle? Why not in Paspébiac?"

"No choice. They brought us here and told us any land to the east and west was all taken up by them damned French Acadians. Lieutenant-Governor Cox's doing."

"You were given land?"

"Of course. And we deserved every last acre. And a bloody lot more, I'll tell you that. We fought faithful all through that Revolutionary War. And then, poor Eleanor — both of us spent two year — eighty-three, weren't it luv? — in bloody camps up along the Saint Lawrence, freezing to death waiting for King George to settle us."

"You were kept waiting? Everyone who came up from the Thirteen Colonies?"

"Only militia. Them bloody revolutionaries down

there, scruffy lot, they put some of us in prison, tarred and feathered others, we damned well had to skedaddle. Leave everything behind!" William sighed, and stabbed another large morsel of mutton with his fork. "A lot of fine men and true, we got out fast, came up here. We wanted to stay under British rule, which of course we are up here, ever since Wolfe beat that Montcalm and his French lot of ruffians on the Plains of Abraham." Thomas knew about the *Peace of Paris* in 1763 when France ceded the whole of Canada, all the way down to Louisiana.

Thunder sounded again, this time closer, but they kept on eating heartily. "To get a piece of land, you had to be in the militia — widows too, they were entitled, just like us. Promised each of us a hundred acres, plus fifty for every child."

So that's how New Carlisle had been settled. "Now you own your land?" Just where Thomas had hoped the conversation would lead. "Only those loyal to the King?"

"Bloody right, every last one of us, loyal to King George and he forgot us, he did, high and mighty on his throne while we sat freezing in the snow, waiting for what was rightfully ours."

"But now we're here, Father!" Catherine spoke up.

"Bloody right. And a sorry piece of rock it is, too. I had a fine trade in England. Bloody hard farming here, clearing land, we've had a devil of a time—"

"Now dear, the soil is fine, it is so," she turned to Thomas, "but such backbreaking work. It never stops, you know. In England, William was an apprentice stocking weaver, and he had such great opportunities. It's a very respected trade, don't you know."

"Aye, it is that," her husband went on. "But I could see it coming — the unemployment. I thought, I'll cross the ocean, fight for good King George in the New World, bound to be good prospects. In Nottingham, I'd end up all my life as a weaver — good trade mind, but well, adventure called... Young lad, you know, seventeen years old, so I joined the twenty-ninth regiment, and look what I've got to show for it now."

"Well sir, you have a wonderful house." Thomas was tempted to comment further on it, when Mrs. Garrett mirrored his thoughts.

"No chance of our getting a house this size with all this land if William had kept on with his stocking weaving!"

"Right you are, but then, lass, we worked like hell for every last bit, didn't we!"

"You decided not to fish as they do in Paspébiac?" Thomas asked.

"No choice. That Frenchman, he runs the whole show."

"Now dear, I keep telling you Mr. Robin's a Jerseyman, and a Protestant to boot."

"I know, I know, but he's got that fish trade wrapped up, a man just can't compete! Not that I want to fish, mind, I'm not a seafaring man, got sick as a dog on the boat coming over. No, give me the dry land every time."

"We do sell lumber, Mr. Alford," Eleanor continued. "You see, they need wood in the Old Country, and on the continent too, what with the blockade being over and all."

"Aye, we sell a good amount, sawmill works night and day, I'll tell you."

"You have a sawmill?" Thomas's eyes sparkled. Boards

for his house! Already his mind had been working at the problem. He hadn't seen any independent mills in Paspébiac. One sawed wood for the Robin's company, but no other.

"Aye, on Bonaventure River. Bit upstream from Ezeriah Pritchard. Helped set it up. Nice fellow runs it. Willard Hall. Don't spend my time there, he's got good men."

"We own a share," Eleanor mentioned, wiping the cleared table with a cloth.

"We ship boards over, they send us back salt, tea, china, all sorts of things we need — the comforts of home, you might say." He gave a short bitter laugh, ignoring the wind now buffeting the house. "Well, you don't find any bloody comforts here I can tell you. Things cost so bloody much, hard to make a go of it. I've written over and over again to that bloody man Forbes in Quebec City, no better than Cox I'd say, them 'at's in the government—"

"Now dear, don't get yourself in a sweat—" Mrs. Garrett glanced up as another gale struck the house, thrashing it with sheets of rain.

"No, you're right. No good crying over spilt milk. But every time I see one of them stuffed shirts from the capital, I give them a piece of my mind. And I'm not alone in that, we all do hereabouts!"

Thomas had heard the Loyalists were a fractious lot and now he was beginning to understand. In fact, a good many of them had been so disgruntled that they departed the coast over the last ten years, only to have their lots snapped up by those who remained — at bargain prices. He began to feel more and more happy with his own state, having ended up at that magnificent brook. If he ever made it back... But meanwhile, better grab every bit of information. "How might one go about acquiring land if one were not lucky enough to be in the militia?"

William snorted sceptically. "Thinking of settling on your own, are ye, Laddie?"

Something in William's tone prompted a surprisingly heartfelt flow from Thomas. "Sir, I confess, the land is to my liking. I long to live on it. I long to make it my own, to have a home I can bring a wife to, and with whom I can share everything, to love and provide for her, and for her children, and for our children's children."

Thomas stopped short, embarrassed. The two women, mother and daughter, had grown suddenly quiet and were looking at him with decided interest, nay, even longing. Catherine had been rendered into a statue, hardly breathing. Why had he gone on like such an idiot? He glanced down at his plate. "I'm sorry, I talk too much."

"Aye, talk is cheap," said his host. "The proof is in the pudding."

"Indeed so, sir. Forgive me. But I would dearly love to know how a man might acquire title—"

"To his land? I'll tell you how: go live on it! One day you'll bloody well find it all belongs to you. Plenty of land to be had up the coast towards Douglastown. No roads mind, just damn wilderness. No one there."

"Except the Indians, dear."

"Bloody savages. Gave us a right run for our money, down in Nova Scotia when we threw those Acadians out of Louisbourg. Fought against us."

"But they say they're not a bad lot," Eleanor confided.

"Aye, now that they've started trading with us summ'at."

"Wouldn't you like some more tea, Mr. Alford?"

"I would, Mrs. Garrett, but I should be getting back to the fishing boat."

"Oh they'll never put out in this," Catherine cried, speaking out almost for the first time.

"Perhaps Mr. Alford had better stay the night," Mrs. Garrett suggested nervously.

William looked up sharply, then shrugged as his wife gave him a meaningful look. William seemed to get the message. "O' course, laddie, stay with us. Go back tomorrow. Much too dangerous out on the bay today! You stay here."

***

Gusts buffeted the house as William and his guest surged out the door and set off through the downpour to his barn, several hundred yards away down a rutted and now very muddy lane. William wanted to check on his livestock and Thomas had begged to accompany him, offering to do whatever he could. Night was fast approaching.

When the sons had returned, they had been sent to their room by William, who caught a whiff of rum on their breath. Rain had interrupted their fishing back at one of the brooks, so they had gone to a friend's and found a bottle. Eleanor was shocked, but tried not to notice as the lads, in their teens, were doing their best to appear sober and upright.

Ahead, Thomas saw a grey wooden building, one end of which had been built of squared timbers, notched at the ends, strong, weatherproof, stogged with straw and mud, with one small window. The other and far larger section, for hay Thomas presumed, was sided with wide boards spaced apart, whitewashed, and roofed with black tarred shingles.

To one side and decidedly drenched, a tethered ox looked up as they approached. Thomas saw another, smaller, standing stoically in the soaking rain in a rough corral made of cedar rails.

"Ho Red!" William called as he went up to the larger animal. "Getting a bit damp, are ye?" He untied it, and caught hold of the large iron ring in its nose to lead it into the stable, motioning for Thomas to fetch the other. Thomas slid open the rickety gate of boards and went into the enclosure. His ox, seeing the stable door opened and the other animal entering, trotted out of his corral and followed meekly in. Thomas shut the door as the animal went into its stall, while William tied the larger one to its manger with a loose rope through its nose.

"Lot safer and dryer in here, tonight," William growled. "Don't look like it'll let up afore dawn." He shook the rain from his hat, and strode over to a bin that contained oats. "I lock 'em in here with a big padlock, y'know — like gold bricks they are, though most of the folk here are honest as the day is long."

"Not everyone has a beast of burden, I suppose," Thomas ventured.

"Not on your life! Got this one as a bull calf eight year ago from old Secord Beebe who went off to Wentworth County in Nova Scotia. Fed daily by the wife, by hand, for three weeks."

"Not much hope of clearing land without oxen!"

"Oh well, some have tried. But this…" he slapped his hand on Red's rump, and the ox swished his tail in response, "had to buy milk for it, cost a fortune, and then gruel, but it grew into a fine big ox, as you can see. Great worker." Red lurched to one side as William pushed in beside him to pour the dipper of oats into the manger.

"And the other?"

"Pinch? Aye. Another piece of luck." William went over to give Pinch a container of oats too. "Six year ago, we had a mess of potatoes and a good amount of wheat, you know, ground at the gristmill—"

Thomas brightened at the mention of a place to ground wheat into flour.

William caught the look. "Oh aye, we've had a gristmill going on ten year." Indeed a thriving community, Thomas thought to himself: a sawmill for boards and a gristmill — what else could one desire? It all looked more and more feasible.

"Well, the Tuttles, they were already packing it in, I think," went on William. "Starving they were, so I gave them a barl of flour and a bag of potatoes, then another, worth a fortune that winter, but — though say't as shouldn't — saved their lives."

Thomas nodded. "I bet it did."

"Very scarce that winter. But mind, I had a good piece of land on the hill back, drains well, gets the early sun. Kep' it in wheat that summer. Don't know why, but saved us all."

"Just the sort of good management needed in these parts, I warrant."

"Anyway, when the Tuttles left, they let us take Pinch for nought. I've not heard what happened to them back in the Old Country. Must ask Eleanor..."

"So I suppose," Thomas went on, "that unless you're lucky enough to have neighbours like you, one might have no possibility of oxen. Just too costly."

"Aye, too much for you, laddie, you'd work for that Mr. Robin for ten years before you'd get one. Mind, if you came up here for a couple of winters, I might find a spare calf sometime, depending..."

Now that was an offer Thomas would remember. And his Sunday dinner — how long was it since he'd had a glass of milk like that? Once a week Robin's gave their workers a boiled egg from the farm, their enterprise becoming more and more self-sufficient, but milk, no, none of that. And now that summer was upon them, fresh vegetables had appeared for dinner, but nothing like the feast at the Garretts'.

Right then and there, Thomas resolved that he'd have a house like William Garrett, that he would be a landowner too, a free farmer, with oxen and sheep and ducks and chickens, that he would drink the milk from his cows, eat the eggs from his chickens. He just could not wait to get started.

***

Thomas lay sleeping next to the dying fire. A sound made him open his eyes, and he became aware of a singular presence enfolding him. He looked up and by candlelight saw another face very close to his, closer in fact than any young lady had ever been.

"Sshh," she murmured, finger to lips.

He rolled over. Catherine leaned into his ear, so close he felt the feather touch of her light hair as her cheek brushed his, sending tingles down his spine. "I heard my brothers talking. Laughing and joking, long into the night. One of them even went out into the rain. Apparently at the general store, there's a notice about Navy deserters. They've decided you could be one of them. Of course, there's a reward. They're such pigs. It's only because they're drunk. They would never do such a thing otherwise."

"Do what?"

"Well, Will Junior, the one who went out, he apparently reported you to Thomas Mann, Justice of the Peace."

In spite of the news, he couldn't focus on anything but that mouth, those lips which seemed so tantalizing.

"I'm afraid they could come for you in the morning. Even at dawn."

Thomas tried to absorb all this news.

She leaned above him on one elbow, looking deeply into his eyes. "You have to go, I fear."

He sat up, wide awake. "Yes, I'd better... no don't worry, thank you, thank you." He was all aflutter, less from the danger than from her presence, so close and such youthful fragrance and innocence. She crouched by him in her white nightgown, with the candle she had carried down.

"I know you are by no means guilty of anything, and if you disappear... it will look bad. But I had to tell you."

"Of course." Thomas frowned. She was right: the worst thing was to flee. But what else? Stay and be caught?

"So I have hit upon an excuse. I know the Robin's

barque *Time and Chance*; it leaves for Douglastown at first light, if the wind is right. I can tell my father one of the sailors came in the night and gave you word you were needed back home."

Befuddled, Thomas thought: how resourceful she is, such a quick thinker. He nodded and began to gather himself. But she hadn't moved. He looked up at her, and their two faces, poised, began to merge. He reached out and pulled her close. For one exquisite moment, their lips met. It seemed to him that her whole life went into this touch; for one delicious instant, he felt her being joining with his.

She broke away, flustered, and went to the door. She unbarred it, and held it ready. He gathered his coat and the pouch he wore at his waist, and hurried over.

"How can I thank you?" he whispered.

"You will be back, I hope," she replied, "in better times. And I shall be waiting..."

"Yes yes, I shall definitely be back."

But before he could say more, she had taken him by the arm and, as the wind was still fierce, held the door tightly so it wouldn't slam shut. Quickly, she pushed him out into the rain-filled night.

Chapter Fifteen

The harsh clanging of the morning bell roused Thomas from a deep sleep. Quickly alert, he swung his legs over the edge of his lower bunk as did twenty other workmen, sleepily grumbling in French in their longjohns. He stood up to pull up his trousers, and his eyes went to the window. He could not believe what he saw.

Staring out, he stumbled across the rough boarded floor of the dormitory. The entire *barachois* was covered in white as though a huge down blanket had been thrown across the land and buildings, covering them with a fluffy substance he knew to be snow — his first real acquaintance with the stuff that would preoccupy him for many months to come. The low sun was already sparkling off gleaming folds that now concealed every muddy trail and walkway, piles of boards and refuse, and tufted the fenceposts with tuques — a real delight. So this was what he was in for, in the months ahead.

After his meeting with the Garretts the month before, he had made it safely back from New Carlisle, striking overland. Moving cautiously, he had wanted to avoid leaving footprints in the mud, but he had no other recourse. Rainwater in the ruts gave off enough glow for him to pick out the trail, and he'd soon broken into his Indian trot that carried him out of danger and on to his dormitory here on the *barachois*.

Back again once more in the work camp, he'd forced himself to put aside any memories of the lovely day spent with Catherine and settled into an autumn of hard work. He turned away from the window and, after dressing, joined the others at the long table in the cookhouse adjacent. He spooned down his porridge with its liberal dollops of molasses supplied in puncheons from the West Indies, and listened to the French banter as his companions joked about this arrival of winter, though none of them welcomed it. He now found he was almost fluent so could understand and join in. The room had warmed up: the cook always lit the open fire before the workers got up. Thomas enjoyed the smell of wood burning, the rough sweat of the longjohns, the hot cups of bitter tea. So different from the stench of vomit and rot, the smells of pigs and slithering rats that plagued his ship o' the line. This cookhouse was a simple affair: walls of rough planks with cracks that the workers had, on their own, stogged with moss to keep airtight. Hardly snug, but then, it was never used in winter.

Breakfast was ending when Monsieur Huard came in to make an announcement, a most unusual occurrence. He spoke in French, slowly and firmly. The autumn was by no means over, he said, but in the next fortnight they should all plan to finish their allotted tasks. The week before, Thomas had watched his barque launched with great ceremony. Since then, he had been cleaning the site in preparation for another keel to be laid the following spring. Monsieur Huard announced that he hoped they would all join them again then. During these next ten days, M. Robin and his accountant would be pleased to settle up with the men for their summer's work. Those that wintered here could draw down their past summer earnings in supplies and could, as usual, draw against next summer's work, too. Very graceful it sounded to Thomas, but most men needed the advance and thus would remain in continuing debt to the Robin's company. Next summer they would have no recourse but to sign up again — a situation he was determined to avoid.

Those men returning to Jersey would have their voyage deducted from this summer's earning. There was in fact a schooner, the second to last ship of the year, leaving the following week for Europe, calling in at Jersey after it had visited Portugal, ending up finally at Liverpool. In spite of himself, Thomas quickened: Liverpool was only a hundred or so miles from Raby Castle and he might find himself back home in short order.

What a thought! He could easily come back again next spring. But were he taken back into the household, he'd not leave again so easily. No, once back, his life would be forever servitude. Just what he had come to escape.

The men broke into groups, discussing the new events, and continued as they formed the usual lines at the out-houses. M. Huard came over to where Thomas was sitting, absorbing the news, lost in thought. He now must take firm action about this winter; he could put it off no longer.

"*Eh bien, mon garçon, vous étiez...*" he switched to English. "You have work very well this year. You come back next year, no?" Thomas had of course risen as he approached, and now they drifted toward the weathered door that kept banging open and shut as the men came and went. "You look for place to stay this winter?"

Thomas remembered that M. Huard had known of his

escape from the British Navy, and must have, rightly, determined that Thomas was facing an important decision.

"Well, not really."

"You want stay here, work for me? Very hard, but our men, they know the woods. Not so difficult to learn."

"Thank you very much, sir, but I have a place already."

"Ah, you find place here in Paspébiac?"

No..." Thomas didn't really want to say where he planned on staying because first of all, he didn't know. He'd been mulling over just how to make it through the winter in his cabin, once the roof was truly finished. "But I would be pleased to return next spring, if circumstances were kind. And if indeed I do see the winter through in all safety."

M. Huard was silent, inspecting him, obviously trying to figure out what this new, handsome, and accomplished young man had up his sleeve. Mr. Day, the shipbuilder Robin brought out from Jersey, had spoken highly of him, M. Huard assured Thomas, and had better things in store for him next summer, were he to return. He might work on the larger barque *Gaspé,* a deep-sea craft already half built on another site across the *barachois.*

Reassuring thought, Thomas agreed, and let him know that he might well take him up on that. "Now are there any boats going down the coast toward Georgetown?" Thomas wanted first to get to his almost finished cabin, and decided again to use that distant village as a ruse.

"*Eh oui.* M. Robin, he send boat down, but very slow, she stop Port Daniel, Pabos, Grand Rivière, Percé..."

"*Je veux bien,*" said Thomas. "*J'aime le paysage.* I would like to spend some time seeing the Coast, it's my new home."

"Your new home, yes. And I see *tu parles français maintenant? Très bien!*"

M. Huard appeared well pleased. "But you must be very careful, *mon brave,* the British, they are not — how you say — easy forgive."

And so ten days later, with his knapsack and another large bag, Thomas got into the dingy to row out to Robin's *Goélette*, a coastal vessel heading around the Gaspé Peninsula and on upriver to Montreal. He'd managed against all tradition to wangle some money out of Robin's, as well as trading work for tea, molasses, salt, some tobacco for his Indians, and a bag of flour for himself. To complete his stash, he'd added tools for finishing his cabin and preparing hides, and a couple of presents. The early fall of snow had melted and the weather, though increasingly cold, was fair.

Rowing out to the coastal schooner, Thomas looked back over the *barachois* that had been his home for the summer. Leaving again. No sooner had he gotten used to one life than he had to change it. It had been good, in a way, each day a routine laid down, as it had been on the ship. And at the castle. Maybe he preferred that? No, regulations were what he came here to escape. But he would be leaving the few French friends he'd made, and he'd be much farther away from his compatriots in New Carlisle, the Garretts especially.

Not much chance of visiting them in the near future, nor ever seeing the intriguing young Catherine, unattainable though she might appear at this juncture.

He turned his attention to his next course of action. He felt proud and pleased that he had earned enough for these provisions, but even more, he felt worried about that golden guinea. He must get it back, priority number one. The band up Port Daniel river must be his first stopping place. And of course, he must not be put ashore at his brook. No, getting off at Port Daniel, how could he avoid the trading post? Irony of ironies should he be apprehended there.

As he drew closer to the *Goélette,* a coastal trader, he realized his safety was much more important than any guinea. But what about Magwés, or Little Birch? She had recently come back into his dreams. Was it only because, after Catherine, he'd noticed that few attractive and available women were on show in Paspébiac? M. Robin would occasionally bring round relatives or friends, dressed in their European finery, to see work being done on the boat. They would talk openly in English, certain that no one hereabouts understood, remarking on the scruffy lot making such a fine vessel. Oddly enough, these finely dressed women left him cold. No, Little Birch was of a different ilk. He also longed to see Burn and wondered if the band would like his few presents.

They clambered aboard the schooner and the mate directed them where to stow their gear and on what part of the deck they might sleep. He handed them squares of canvas to prevent deck tar from ruining their travelling clothes, and told them that if the loading went well, they should embark at nightfall and, before sunrise, drop anchor in Port Daniel bay.

A new phase of life in the New World was opening, he reflected, as he lay on deck and watched stars race around the masts as the ship rolled its way along the coastline. He heard all kinds of wonderful creaking and groaning from the rigging of the two large sails that ran fore and aft, not abeam as with his man o'war. But then, this ship could be manned by a small crew, perhaps three or four, unlike the massive numbers needed on the *Billy Ruffian*. Braced for sleep against the railing from which three shrouds rose to the top of the mast, taut and whistling in the wind, he even caught a whiff of his lovely oakum.

He loved the familiar sounds of flapping and fluttering canvas. The helmsman was doing a fair amount of cursing in French, which Thomas was not accustomed to hearing at sea. It brought him back instead to the *barachois* and his fellow workers. He began to miss them already. And as the night wore on, he missed hearing the Navy bells telling the watches, but he knew the cost of a seagoing chronometer would be far beyond any Captain of a *Goélette*. He must measure his time by their position on the shore. In the morning, Thomas focussed on the risks of landing in Port Daniel where he'd face his next obstacle, the trading post.

* * *

The next morning, Thomas scanned the beach and its trading post from the raised foredeck, trying to formulate a plan. A couple of men stood watching the ship; one walked down to the jetty and got into a rowboat. At one of the weathered shacks at the far east end of the beach, another came out carrying some belongings. The trader, distinctively dressed with a broad hat and European jacket, seemed to be staying on his veranda.

Should Thomas wait on board for their next port, Pabos? No. His belongings and presents weighed far too much for such a long trek, and that trip would add at least another week, which could be dangerous in this autumn weather. The early snows had melted, but the nights bore frost, and winter would soon be upon them. Every day was precious.

The man with his belongings got into the rowboat and the fisherman rowed them out toward the *Goélette*. Maybe Thomas should pass himself off as a French worker. He did look like one. Then make for a house at an end of the bank as though he lived there? Squared timbers, no verandas and unprotected by trees, would they be liveable in winter? Their greying walls held little insulation against the subzero weather, so he doubted settlers wintered there. To his left on the long hill of Port Daniel mountain, signs of cleared land indicated that perhaps year-round farmers did live somewhere. But three fishing boats moored by the jetty made it more likely the beach inhabitants were summer fishermen.

The rowboat was drawing close. Time to decide. Were the two men French? Should he test his disguise? But if they were French and he spoke to them, his accent would give him away. But speak English and they might well suspect who he was. But why would anyone associate Thomas with that lone deserter of a year ago? So try English.

The boat came aside and a rope ladder was thrown down. Thomas moved across to the traveller clambering aboard, an older man, clothes impoverished but a beard trimmed for travel. "Any Englishmen here?" Thomas indicated the shacks.

He shook his head. "Mostly French. Trader might be both. But I'm leaving. No work, no chance of a life, I'm headin' fer Montreal."

Thomas nervously descended the rope ladder into the small boat, and took his heavy bags as they were handed down. How would he ever get past the trader?

"*C'est frette, hein?*" the rower remarked. "*Ça commence, l'hiver.*"

"*Ah ouais,*" Thomas blurted out without thinking, after his summer among the French. "*Ça commence, bien sûr.*"

No reaction. His *joual* had worked. When they reached the jetty, Thomas tried to stop the noise made by his hammering heart — would it not alert the whole community? He grinned at the thought and stepped boldly up onto the jetty — only to find the trader looking right into his face. The man reached to intercept the bags. "Staying a bit?"

Thomas grinned and shook his head. "*Non non, merci, j'apporte avec moi.*" He shouldered his bags firmly.

The trader grunted, and turned to see his goods plunked down rather too heavily on the uneven boards. He walked over to supervise.

"*Merci, hein?*" Thomas called and hefted the double bag onto his shoulder so it hung front and back, swinging the third over his shoulder. He set off up the jetty and turned right onto the beach. So far, so good...

Waving farewell at the boat, he kept heading for the group of houses at the east end where the English traveller had emerged.

He glanced back. The trading post man stood watching. Well why not? Any newcomer would be a matter of interest. This place was so small, he'd want to know everyone's business. Thomas felt his heart sink. Trust in the Lord, he said firmly to himself, He's done pretty well by you so far.

Reaching the last shack, he headed around it to appear to go in the back door, as did most owners here. Once hidden, he stopped and leaned again the wall. Dare he sneak a glance back now? Better not. Quick, just take off.

He found a trail back near the river. Making the best time he could with his unwieldy and heavy bags, he soon found himself panting heavily. He stopped to listen. So far, no sound of pursuit. The trail circled the eastern side of the river estuary before turning northward into the interior. His mind began to whir. Would he ever find his gold guinea? How would the band respond to seeing him again? Would Fury be there, waiting? And Little Birch? The answers all lay ahead up the wooded trail.

Chapter Sixteen

Thomas kept moving as fast as he could along the trail upriver toward the Micmac encampment. He made sure to stop every so often and listen. Doubts still plagued him. Were the trader and his friends gathering at this very moment to set out after him? He wished that it were not so late in the season: he could well do with a screen of leaves. With his heavy bags, he pushed himself hard. He'd be safe once he got to the band.

Or would he? Would they be of the same mind as before? Had Fury altered their perception? Adverse sentiments spread easily in one's absence, especially among a tight little group. And he'd only been with them two days.

All at once he tripped and his bags went flying. Damn! He lay, winded. What had possessed him to be so careless, messing up once again? As he picked himself up, he glanced over to see a line stretched across the trail. Aha! A signal. A sapling had sprung up, clacking against a trunk, making a racket. Good, he thought, no one will surprise my Micmacs.

He started to gather up his things when he saw a form sprinting down the trail, bow and arrow at the ready.

Thomas waved cheerfully.

The Micmac stopped, lifted his bow, arrow fixed to the bowstring.

"Wait!" Thomas shouted. "It's me, Thomas." In Micmac he called, "Friend."

The man lowered his bow slightly.

Thomas rose, and spread out his arms. Was this a member of the band? He didn't recognize him. But he felt sure the man would remember him.

"Last year..." What was Micmac for that? He went on in their language, "me come, live at brook."

A slight recognition flashed across the usually stoic face. *"Epchilàsi!"*

Welcome, Thomas knew, and smiled. He nodded. "Thank you," he said in Micmac as the man came forward and, in spite of Thomas's protestations, shouldered two packs.

"How is everyone? Lots of fish?" Thomas asked, in what little Micmac he had picked up.

"Gdúlg." Good, Thomas remembered, and they set off together up the trail. He noticed that the snow, all but melted in Paspébiac, could still be seen here melting; the ground he had fallen on was damp, and the trail moist beneath his feet. On the back of his pack, Thomas had hung two saucepans and a large kettle for Little Birch, with a smaller one for himself. But when should he give it to her? Would it be appropriate, or against Micmac etiquette? Indians were decidedly strong in their protocols. He wished he'd stayed longer on his earlier visit to learn more. Maybe just give it to her family, he decided.

Coming into camp, he had the strange feeling of, well, arriving at a familiar and welcome site. Everything was nicely worn in. On a kind of rack made of sticks held up by horizontal poles twenty feet off the ground, waterproof baskets of meat sat, drying.

Clever, he thought, animals that climbed trees could not reach them. Smoke drifted up from a couple of the oblong huts; he suspected haunches of game were being smoked for the long winter ahead. The pathways were now swept clear, worn smooth by many feet, the wigwams cared for, their birchbark nicely trimmed and sewn. No longer did the camp seem so haphazard, disorganized, and yes, even dirty. He now understood the reason for things being where they were, and felt at ease with these living arrangements, so alien to him at first. He was surprised that he remembered so much, and how the intervening months had brought him a kindlier, and more appropriate, view of how they all lived.

The Chief rose from his conference logs at his arrival and, with courteous nod, retired to his wigwam. Thomas found himself peering at the home of Little Birch. Out she came, carrying dishes to wash. She stopped, struck motionless.

The two stared at each other for a long moment. Thomas felt his pulse race. Then she hurried off.

Burn had suddenly appeared and taken in their look. Animosity flashed in his eyes, which shook Thomas. Quickly it disappeared and Burn came across to welcome him.

"Burn, how are you?" Thomas asked and reached out to shake his hand, heart pounding from the sight of Magwés. But a villager came over from the Chief's wigwam and indicated that the Chief was now ready.

Thomas got down on to all fours to enter the wigwam for the obligatory ceremony. He crawled in to sit before the Chief as he had done previously in very different circumstances. At least now, he knew the procedure. Tongue come in to translate.

The Chief took up the decorated pipe, and Thomas produced the tin box of tobacco purchased from Robin's general store. He handed it to the Chief.

Once the tobacco had been inspected, smelt, fingered, and inserted into the hollowed stone of the bowl, the Chief solemnly lit the pipe and inhaled. Slowly, he blew out a cloud. Thomas watched. Then he spoke to Tongue.

"Good tobacco," Tongue translated. "Chief thank you."

So far, not bad, thought Thomas. He accepted the pipe and this time made a point of pulling in the smoke. Tongue and the Chief watched carefully, hoping, Thomas supposed, for another outburst of choking and spluttering. But the incident passed.

Thomas let silence fall as he gave back the pipe. How on earth do I bring up the subject of the guinea? he wondered. The Indians were not given to small talk, he knew. No time for "How's the wife" sort of blather.

Tongue spoke a phrase, and then told Thomas, "I say him: you work Paspébiac."

Thomas nodded. "Tell him I helped build a boat. Very big. Eighty feet long."

Tongue did so. The Chief nodded.

Now what? thought Thomas. How soon can I ask him?

In the ensuing silence, the Chief reached back into his own possessions.

Thomas waited. He was burning to find out about his main source of wealth.

The Chief turned back with something cupped in his hands, as if they imprisoned a young bird.

Thomas frowned. What could this mean?

The Chief opened them to reveal — his golden guinea!

The Chief spoke a phrase. "He keep this for you," Tongue translated.

"Oh thank you, thank you!" breathed Thomas, delighted and relieved. "However did he find that?"

"Young Longbow find in jacket. Give to Chief." Tongue seemed as pleased as Thomas. "Big value?"

"Oh yes," said Thomas, "very big value. Thank you."

That was easy, almost too easy. Then he realized that all Micmac lived by a strong code of honour, and would easily recognize the importance of the coin. And now, his mind turned to the other presents — how to properly present them to Little Birch and her family. Having experienced life not only in Paspébiac but also in the Garrett home in New Carlisle, he saw how desperately the band needed even basic necessities. His own few gifts would hardly make up for what really he now saw as their extreme poverty.

He looked up to see the Chief staring soberly at him.

He tried to smile. What was coming?

The Chief spoke to Tongue.

Thomas waited.

Tongue reached out and touched him. "Chief ask, you stay winter with us?"

What? Stay with the band? It had never crossed his mind. No, of course not, he could never stay with the band.

Then he thought, with the Micmac he'd be more likely to survive. Within range of civilization and near the trading post, if the worst came to the worst, he'd be able to get supplies and so not starve. So this offer perhaps he should actively consider. It might even turn out to be an interesting challenge. He began to warm to the idea. Look how much he'd learn: of the woods and herbs and medicines, of the deep snow and how to travel through it, how to snare animals and find the great game on which everyone's livelihood depended. From them, he'd borrow the heavy clothes that he now realized were so desperately important in this ever-increasing cold. So much to grasp and conquer! So much to learn. Who better to teach him than these people who had done it for millennia?

Although he suspected other motives, he was torn. Now the Indians were used to long pauses, but finally he told himself: get on with it!

He threw caution to the winds. "Yes," he said, looking into the Chief's wise eyes. "Yes! I will stay."

The Chief spoke again, and Tongue translated. "You go back to cabin, get things, come back, stay winter."

***

Once outside, he resumed a halting conversation with Burn. The time had come to give his presents. Now? Or this evening round the fire in each wigwam? But how would he be invited in? Some chatter alerted him to women coming down the trail. Behind them trotted Little Birch.

She stopped short, an involuntary hand at her mouth. Then she bowed her head, put her eyes before her feet, and hurried on to her wigwam.

He glanced up to see Burn studying him. Oh-oh! Had he been so maladroit as to break the Micmac code of behaviour? And then a ghastly thought struck him, could Burn be interested in her too?

He motioned for Burn to come over. "Burn," he said rummaging in his backpack, "I have brought you something." Heavens, he went on, I'd hate to have him angry; I hope this will make it right. He pulled out a cloth, unwrapped it, and handed Burn a gleaming steel knife in its leather sheath.

From the look on Burn's face, yes, it did wipe everything else off his mind. He positively glowed. Thank heaven, Thomas said to himself.

Next Tongue. He asked Burn where he'd gone. Burn, knowing a gift might be forthcoming, hastened to find him. When they returned, Thomas huddled with Tongue, while Burn and others gathered to look.

Thomas pulled out a quill pen, ink, and paper.

Tongue looked perplexed. Oh-oh, thought Thomas, I presumed too much. He may be a great translator, but he may not even know how to write. So he put down the paper, slowly took the bottle of ink, unscrewed the cap, and then, dipping the pen in the ink, wrote a sentence in English.

What a reaction! Tongue took the pen himself, dipped it in the ink, and began to write too, but with symbols that Thomas did not understand. He nodded to himself, as Thomas explained, "You can learn words in English, Tongue. And in French too. Then you will be able to send notes to everyone."

Tongue beamed, and nodded. "You will learn me your language writing."

"I certainly will, Tongue!"

Next of course came Little Birch.

It was not until that evening, after other formalities, that Thomas got a chance to ask Little Birch if he might meet her mother, who had been the one to feed him first. Magwés went to find her, and soon she came out of her home and motioned for Thomas to join them. He sat down in front of their entranceway, as the family gathered: Little Birch's mother, whom he nicknamed Full Moon because of her round face and sad eyes, her uncle with one arm, and her little brother, Brightstar, Thomas nicknamed him.

Now try your best not to look at Little Birch, he warned himself, and focus on her mother and her uncle. The gleaming copper kettle came out first, and did cause even more of a stir than Thomas had first imagined. They'd had another, but it had been repaired so many times as to be almost useless. All the same, Thomas noticed a heaviness about the family, which his presents did not lighten.

***

The next morning early, Tongue asked the Chief if he could go along with Thomas to his cabin, to practise his English. And of course, Thomas would better his Micmac. With the coming winter, a splendid idea, Thomas thought.

Tongue, carrying a couple of the packs, led Thomas through the heavy forest, threading through open stands of first-growth timber, and then across clearings, around dead falls, avoiding swampy land. Here close to the coast, the land was mostly undulating and flat with a few gullies made by ancient brooks. Tongue followed the paths laid down by deer and other animals, the same hardly discernible trail that Burn had followed the previous spring.

At long last they reached the lip of the bank above the camp. Instinctively, Thomas paused, listening. No intruders. Thomas led the way down. He found his heart beating as they crossed the brook, and he could see, through the leafless trees, his half-finished cabin.

Tongue stood silently, taking it all in. "Very good," he said at last.

"You think so?" Thomas hurried to his door and opened it: signs of activity from his little furry friends and some dead leaves were all that greeted him; no one had visited during the summer, that much seemed clear. Quickly, he trotted up the trail to where he had buried his tools. Also intact.

Could the woods be more friendly than he had surmised? Not a little pleased, he showed Tongue around. The stocky linguist nodded his approval, more than usually impressed by these endeavours. His tribe never built cabins.

They quenched their thirst from cool brook water in a cup Tongue fashioned out of birchbark he folded ingeniously, and then shared a simple evening meal, eating at first in silence.

After a time, Tongue said, "Band make ready now, for go."

"Go?" Wonder what that meant? thought Thomas . "Go where?"

Tongue lifted his arm and pointed north.

"North? You mean right into the interior?"

Tongue frowned. He must not have understood "interior." "Into the deep woods? Far north?"

Tongue nodded. "Many days' walk."

"But what for? I thought you stayed at the mouth of the river."

"No. Sea freeze, river freeze. Must follow game. *Dià-mugweyek.* Hunt moose. *Matues,*" which Thomas knew was porcupine. "Sometimes caribou. Trap animals."

"Oh. Furs? For trading?"

Tongue shook his head. "For wear, for clothing." Tongue made as if to shiver. "Very cold winter. And for eat."

Thomas certainly did remember hearing of the beaver furs and hats in London, so *à la mode* a few years back. But here, fur was a sheer necessity. And again, he realized that his own clothes must now be a priority. The heavy coat he had bought from one of the departing Robin's carpenters would hardly suffice, though it had been a gesture in the right direction. "How long do you stay there?" Thomas gestured north.

"Four moons maybe five."

Oh Lord, thought Thomas, what have I let myself in for? Five months? In the depths of winter, miles from anywhere, no trading post at hand. In fact, nothing but open space. Icy woods. What would they live in? Surely not birchbark wigwams? He'd freeze. Would they have any spare clothes to lend him? He began to have severe doubts about this unknown future. His cabin looked better and better. But no, he had promised, and now he would live up to it. Those desolate hills in the interior so far from civilization, with all their dangers, would have to be faced, no matter what the risk.

Chapter Seventeen

The next day, Thomas and Tongue worked on winterizing his cabin and stowing tools and any other belongings in places not easily found. Thomas was also worried about the roof of his cabin. With no knack for stitching birchbark, he placed rocks to keep the bark in place, though he had no great expectations of that lasting.

At dawn the next day, they both started back to the band's encampment, Thomas with mighty misgivings. But jogging easily through the woods together, Thomas cheered himself by noticing the difference now in his conditioning from that first trip. He covered the ground with ease, chest no longer heaving, arms and legs firmer as he ran rapidly and surefooted through the woods. Being a sailor, he'd had no opportunity to get in shape for such unanticipated activities.

On approaching Port Daniel, they took care not to follow any perceptible trail and even struck northward above the camp so as to approach from upstream, away from the mouth of the river and its trading post.

When Thomas reached the camp, the Chief determined he should move in with Burn's family to get better acquainted with the Micmac language, and to learn how to set snares and hunt with bow and arrow. That way when they all trekked into the interior, he'd be more prepared.

Burn's father, a square body atop two bow legs, spoke little and glowered a lot. Thomas nicknamed him Big Burn, instead of trying to pronounce *Weliedulin*, which meant, "he who builds canoes for great rapids." His wife seemed docile, never complaining, moving about her job silently, but with a sadness in her eyes. Although known as the master canoe maker, Big Burn had turned to fashioning bows and arrows, now that the winter was at hand. He seemed to accept his guest, teaching him how to shape the black ash or mountain maple into the shape of a bow, notching both ends for the string, and how to protect it with hot grease, polishing the grease deep into the wood. When not teaching him, he would send Thomas by hand signals to cut wood for their fire and tend to other jobs.

The weather had grown definitely colder, snow was falling, and Thomas kept wondering when the band would take off for the uplands, and what he should do, if anything, about more winter clothes. Should he try to buy them? How does one scrounge a sweater according to Micmac protocol? He worked hard learning archery from Burn, for all agreed that his powerful firearm, although essential, took too long to load in emergencies. Thomas had bought some powder in Paspébiac, and only a few lead shots, for it was made mostly at home by the settlers.

Burn and several other young men made no bones about their impatience to get going. So the Chief, by common consent, sent Burn with two companions to report on the game situation in the interior. Meanwhile, families kept to themselves, making preparations for the trek by day and telling stories in their wigwams at night.

With clouds gathering and snow flurries falling, Thomas wanted to spend time with Little Birch, but she was among those working hardest. Was she avoiding him? Hard to tell. He contented himself with his archery, at which he was improving, happy to know she was close at hand. Did she feel the same way?

Before Burn left, he had mentioned to Thomas that their food supplies this autumn were not as ample as they might be, and the band prayed nightly to the Creator for plentiful game during the dark winter months — and for strong hunters to harvest it. To make matters worse, Burn and his friends, having travelled fast, returned three days later with a negative report. The dilemma remained: stay here longer, or leave at once. Thomas was worried: unsettled feelings among these usually relaxed Micmac did unnerve him.

The next morning when the sun broke out of early clouds, the weather warmed up and a kind of late St. Martin's summer (a warm spell) fell upon them for an all too brief period. The Chief convened a meeting and called for a modest banquet.

The camp exploded into action. Fires were laid and Thomas set to work with his tinderbox — deemed a marvel and loved especially by all the children. The women filled two hollowed stumps with cold brook water to which they added corn, roots, and a porcupine fortuitously killed two nights before. Stones heated in fires were placed and replaced in the stumps to cook the soup that, with other foods, would be shared by all that night.

While women busied themselves with these preparations, the Elders sat on logs around a fire to begin the traditional conference to set the time of leaving.

The banquet was enjoyed with great gusto by everyone save Thomas, who still had trouble with most of their rough foods, except for some tubers that he took to be Jerusalem artichokes. Burn had not been assigned any tasks for the preparations, having travelled long and hard. So now he lit a pipe in honour of the occasion and motioned for Thomas to join him. They sat on a couple of stumps at one side and talked in English and Micmac, watching the conference, called a *mawogmkejik*. Thomas again marvelled at how the Elders all spoke slowly, with consideration for each other, and with dignity.

At one point, Little Birch came to stand beside them. Thomas rose to give her his stump, but no, that was not the Micmac way. She paused only for a few minutes, without speaking, and then went on to help the women.

"Next spring," Burn leaned over to Thomas, "I throw her stone."

"You what? Say it in Micmac? I didn't understand."

Haltingly in English and in Micmac, Burn explained their custom of how a man proposed to a woman. He entered the tent of the family, and after certain set preliminaries, tossed a stone in her lap. If she accepted it, that meant she agreed to be his bride. If she put it aside, it meant she was not ready, or she didn't want him.

"And that's it? What about the wedding ceremony?"

"No ceremony, this band. Couple live together. But first she must accept stone."

Burn went on to explain that a young man could not toss the stone into her lap until he was considered a full member of the tribe, and had spent time with the family, too. "After winter, if I okay, Chief say me, I ready. I live with family and I throw stone for sure."

What a mouthful to swallow: Burn and Little Birch. Why hadn't he really grasped that sooner? Of course, the perfect match! What had he been thinking? He himself came from a totally different culture; a marriage with her could never, ever have worked. Put it out of your mind right away, he sternly admonished. And anyway, had he really thought of marriage? Of course not, it was just that, oh yes, he was so very drawn to her! She was everything he could ever want in a young woman. But he had never gotten as far as thinking about marriage. And now, she was lost to him forever.

Stop that, he commanded, you're just torturing yourself. Change the subject! He looked over at the Elders. "How long will they talk?"

"Until all agree," Burn told him.

"Don't they take a vote?" Earlier on, Thomas had explained the system of democracy to Burn, who considered it laughable.

"No. No, not our way."

Well, thought Thomas, I wonder how the British Parliament would function on this basis?

Night fell and the central fire threw a rosy glow on the bronzed features of the Micmac Elders. Smoke from their pipes curled upwards and their eyes reflected the roaring fire as they spoke in turn, seriously, each giving their own opinion. Cedars provided a scented backdrop, while white and yellow birch soared upwards, seeming to carry their deliberations into the starry sky where they'd be heard by Niskam, the Creator. Dwarfed beneath giant trees, their conference below seemed capable of making the most weighty of decisions.

Behind Thomas, as he sat watching, the river continued to ripple and splash over rapids, which acted as a natural barrier for canoes and made this a convenient portage point. But he heard no night-bird songs like the British nightingales that sang near the castle. Finally, Thomas found himself getting sleepy, long accustomed to going to bed with the sun and rising with it. Burn too gave a big yawn. "Will they decide soon?" Thomas asked.

Burn shrugged. "Maybe they discuss all night and to-morrow. Maybe only one pipeful."

"They've already had several," said Thomas. "I think I'll go to bed."

Burn nodded but remained seated.

After Thomas had been asleep for a while, he was wakened by a gentle nudge. He sat up, wide awake in a flash.

Burn was taken aback by his nervous reaction, but then murmured, "Leave in morning."

"Tomorrow?"

Burn nodded. Thomas began to worry, would Burn and his father make a good team to be with? The father was not the jolliest companion for the long and confining winter months. No worries, if the game were there, the band would soon find it and survive. He went back to sleep.

On the morrow by first light, Thomas was helping pre-pare supplies for travel while Big Burn's wife cleaned out the wigwam. Most of the band had already dismantled their wigwams, bundling up the birchbark for travel, and now were busying themselves with last-minute details. The Chief called Thomas over, and with the help of Tongue, introduced him to Little Birch's uncle, *bàsêk neutpidnoqom*, Micmac for the arm that dangled use-lessly. In his late thirties perhaps, he had a face like Full

Moon's, rounded, with large gentle eyes, but the features possessed a haunted look, caused perhaps by his disability. He lived with Full Moon in their wigwam. Thomas promptly nicknamed him One Arm.

The Chief pointed to One Arm and said to Thomas, "You go with him."

Tongue translated.

"You mean, travel with him, to help him?"

"No. Live. His family."

"His family?" Thomas had never thought for one instant the band would be separating into families, as Tongue seemed to be indicating. "Don't we all go together? All the band?"

Tongue explained, patiently and haltingly, that in winter, each family went to a separate territory. In it, they were free to lay out their own traplines and to hunt without interference from other families. That way, no family would have to travel more than a couple of days on each trapline. And the Chief partitioned out the territories annually, rotating the assignments to make sure no one family got all the good game areas year after year, nor another continually having a hard time of it.

"So we separate?"

"Yes. You go with family of One Arm."

With whom? Thomas stared.

Tongue saw his confused expression. "Big Birch, he die. Need hunter and trapper for family. One Arm good, but no two arms. Need two arms for trap, for snare, for bow and arrow."

But that therefore meant with Little Birch! He would be spending the winter with Little Birch. What a deal of confused emotions this aroused.

Later, during the evenings on the trek, Thomas heard the story of Big Birch, which explained that sense of heaviness he'd found among the family when he had first returned. Big Birch had not really been a seagoing man; he was much happier spearing salmon in the river, at which he was superb. His Micmac name, *nedawiwskewn*, indicated that. But in order to pull his weight with the band, he had consented each year to hunt seals with them. This year there had been a large influx in Port Daniel bay due to unusual cold currents.

He had been assigned to hunt with another young fisherman, and late this summer, they had gone out alone. With a storm rising, his young partner had managed to harpoon a large male seal. Rather than let it escape with their line and harpoon, they decided to land it before the waves built to full force. In their light canoe, they aimed for the cove around Port Daniel point, but as the seal dove and tugged them along, the treacherous shoals and sharp rocks of the point damaged the canoe. Only too soon, it sank. The young man made it to shore, but Big Birch, unable to swim, had disappeared.

Now Thomas found himself with a severe dilemma. He wanted to do his best to care for Little Birch, but now she was spoken for, the dangers of any relationship with her seemed to outweigh the benefits. And he realized he'd be with just one family: a man with one arm, two women, and Brightstar, nine or ten. Was this so much better than being on his own at the cabin? True, he'd be able to learn the lore imbued in them over centuries of experience. But would that be sufficient to save all five of them? Other families might be hard put to feed themselves, let alone give any food to this family. Only his own strength, his own health, his own gun with its limited powder and shot, and the hunting instincts of One Arm, would see them through.

And most important of all, now that he thought about it, the odds were not all that high that this cobbled-together group — with its addition of one inexperienced young white man — would even make it through the winter alive.

Chapter Eighteen

The band moved off more or less together, the families travelling within half an hour of each other. At the first fork of the Port Daniel river, the band separated, two-thirds going up the right fork, leaving the family of One Arm and a couple of others to take the west fork. Several families owned dogs that trotted along with them, though oddly enough none pulled sleighs. It was their last farewell, and they all waited for each other to assemble here.

Thomas said goodbye to Burn and his family, shaking his new bow high in signification of his "present" from Big Burn, the arrow maker. He actually saw the glimmer of a smile on the old man's face. When it came time to say goodbye to his good friend Burn, he saw a change. Burn looked at his feet, almost tongue-tied and evidently in pain. Thomas saw him throw a glance at Little Birch, who was standing off, having no part in this. Thomas thought fast, and then said, "I will do my best to bring her back to you safe."

When the full import of this got through, Burn seemed relieved, but still clearly confused and hurt at the idea of Thomas spending all winter with the woman he had been thinking of as his future wife. But what alternative had they? Burn was certainly needed by his own family, and they were not yet betrothed.

After they parted, Thomas trudged with his new family through the afternoon as snow began to fall in big fluffy flakes that caused Brightstar to caper about excitedly and Little Birch to lift her face to the sky with pleasure. It seemed to make the going easier. They all had snowshoes strapped to their backs, although Thomas had not practised with them yet: the snow had not lasted long enough nor was it deep. The further into the interior they went, the deeper it would be and the longer it would last.

Thomas wore Big Birch's *muksins*, or moccasins, soft boots of sealskin lined with hare, suitable for walking through the snow, and probably waterproof. He was now dressed for the winter, thanks to the clothing that Full Moon had passed on from her late husband, Big Birch. She had cleaned and prepared the clothes, and gave them in a small ceremony the morning after they left with the band. Had Full Moon suspected something between him and Little Birch, and put this idea forward herself to the Chief? Possibly, if she thought it likely that Thomas might make for himself a solid and bountiful life as a settler, free from starvation or other dangers. But Thomas doubted she'd looked ahead that far. He was just an unfortunate white man who had been assigned to help, and she'd be sure to doubt just how much help that would be.

For his undershirt he wore the softest deer hide. His next covering was a woven wool shirt, and outside that, a heavy jacket reaching down like a morning coat almost to his knees, which all Micmacs wore. This one had a hood whose fur lining and trim were made of wolverine that, Full Moon explained, did not frost up from the breath. He counted himself inordinately lucky to be inheriting the clothes of one of the more prosperous members of the band.

As they struggled back on the trail with their winter loads, Thomas found his sense of chivalry battered. He could not bear the sight of his Little Birch pulling the *toboggan*, the Micmac means of transporting heavy loads that always fell to the women. This carrier made from slats of wood, smooth on the bottom and curved at the front, slid easily over snow, but Little Birch had to drag it over the ground wherever snow had blown clear. Her mother struggled with an equally heavy one, while the three men carried big unwieldy packs on tumplines, a belt that passed around their foreheads. Both women wore traditional peaked hats with flaps to protect their ears, which Full Moon had woven in heavier material than their summer headgear.

The first night, the families camped together at a pre-arranged site, having located the remnants of a kind of base camp. Thomas duly lit the fire while the women prepared the food. One Arm, amazingly dextrous for one so handicapped, made the site habitable with other husbands, cutting boughs for the beds and laying out the furs on top. Male members of the families went off with their bows and arrows to try to find small game for the evening meal, although they had brought a stash of dried salmon.

Thomas felt clearly a new distance between him and Little Birch, for they both knew they would be sleeping and eating in close proximity for a long time. She must, he reasoned, be as concerned as he was. After all, would she not know Burn's intentions? That other young Micmac, slim, gentle, accomplished and intelligent, would make her a good husband, in spite of his disfigured face. Thomas made up his mind to be as prudent as possible. But as he sat across the fire from her, he just could not stop his eyes from straying to her extraordinary features, the clear planes of her cheeks and forehead, her emphatic cheekbones and almond eyes, all shaped through millennia of wilderness living. He had to force himself to look down and concentrate on trying to stomach his tough dried salmon.

On the second day, the various families parted. This is it, thought Thomas, as he watched the others move off down the west fork, which would parallel the coast before plunging up into more distant highlands. His adoptive family struck due north from here — the five of them, alone against the Gaspé winter. Little Birch caught his look of concern, and explained the whys and wherefores as best she could. She had taken to communicating with Thomas, speaking slowly, using her hands a lot, scattering in the few words she'd gleaned. Another family had been asked to relinquish the area they were heading for, as the Chief thought it would be a better source of game. Thomas took this to mean that his family were least likely to survive. Probably true, he thought. He already found it surprising how much work they did on so little food. His stomach had shrunk, but that did not stop him from being always hungry.

At the same time, Thomas felt a welling up of confidence. He was used to being up against impossible odds, and in fact welcomed the duel that destiny had set for him. He resolved to be the winner at any cost. After all, Little Birch was now his responsibility, though all too short-lived. Through the falling snow, with flakes clinging to his eyelashes, he watched her struggle on ahead with her *toboggan* following One Arm, who led, searching out the easiest paths. Brightstar followed, then Full Moon and finally, Thomas brought up the rear.

He also could not forget the look in Burn's eye when they parted. Were Little Birch and Burn truly meant for each other? He tried not to let his *joie de vivre* disappear. Keep optimistic, he told himself, especially now, facing a long winter of deprivation. Her image had meant so much more to him during the summer than he had imagined. Why had he not guessed that someone as pretty and accomplished as she would already have been spoken for?

Late in the afternoon of the second day, they came upon a hill whose north face lay covered in deep snow, so they all stopped to put on their snowshoes. Brightstar came over to help Thomas, who was struggling with winding a strip of well-oiled leather round his ankles, so that he could fix on his snowshoes.

"I wish I'd had time to practise all this," Thomas confided.

When they rose to go on, he kept stepping on his own shoes and tripping. Big Birch's giant racquets, three feet long and over a foot wide, were made up of ash bent into a U-shape at the front, curving back into a long tail. In between, a taut rawhide webbing had been stretched, with a hole for the toes at the crosspieces. At first, Thomas found them hopelessly awkward, though he saw Brightstar capering about with great agility.

The first hundred yards up the steep hill, Thomas fell twice, his pack flipping over and items spilling out. Brightstar laughed and pulled off his beaverskin mittens to help him reassemble the pack.

"I'm sorry," he said in English "I just don't seem to know how."

After his second tumble, he took care to watch the others and swung his legs wider, taking bigger strides, placing each snowshoe carefully, one after another. By the time they stopped for dinner, Thomas had actually begun to enjoy this new way of walking. Picking his feet up high made his thigh muscles ache but he had added another skill, he realized with a glow of accomplishment.

One Arm was leading, following instructions of the family who had used this territory previously. But he was not finding their next stopping place. He called a halt anyway, and set up camp for the night. Thomas used his tinderbox to start a fire and One Arm prepared the bedding, with Brightstar chopping boughs for a lean-to, in case it snowed in the night. The women prepared the simple meal, heating snow in a tin pan for the bitter tea they made out of the needles of white spruce to help them avoid colds or sore throats.

At noon on the third day, rising early and pushing on hard, they crossed the final foothills and dropped down into the semi-flat swamplike plateau that was to be their territory. With no adequate drainage, the giant trees of the coast did not grow here: only stunted spruce and fir. Just the kind of territory moose loved.

Heartened, they pushed on until late afternoon, and then rested while One Arm searched for the camp, or at least some trail blazes. He found the trail to their west and led them over. Although exhausted, they kept snowshoeing in the light of a low moon until long after sunset. At last they arrived at the site, a round depression in the ground among shorn trees fixed with old frames for skin-stretching. In winters, the Micmac practice was to dig down a couple of feet and then over the birchbark to pack snow around the base for insulation. On a rise, and sheltered by a low set of craggy rocks, the site did seem at first primitive, but liveable.

Worn out, the little family just chewed dried seal meat and fell into their hastily unrolled hides without even making a fire. Thomas lay thinking, so this is it: winter in the Gaspé woods with an Indian family — only our combined wits and the acquired learning of generations to keep us from an untimely end. He made sure to offer up a proper and heartfelt prayer; he'd need all the help he could get.

***

The next three weeks proved even more difficult than Thomas had feared. Game was indeed scarce; Burn had been right. The family had to dip into their store of dried meat, a dangerous practice this early on. The days had grown much shorter as they approached the winter solstice, but they still seemed inordinately long to Thomas. He and One Arm had to make the most of the available light, leaving before dawn and coming back as dusk was settling, choosing the best layout for their traplines. They travelled most of the snow-covered territory, checking for hare and otter runs. A couple of times, they stayed overnight, a new and rather exhilarating experience for Thomas. They would first dig a kind of shelter in the snow under the branches of broad spruce, making a windbreak should the weather turn nasty in the night. No question of having a wash or hot tea in the morning: just mark the place as suitable for a bivouac, chew a bit of dried salmon, and off you go. He marvelled at his new-found stamina. They did come across several runs of small game, but oddly enough, no moose yards.

What a desolate landscape this plateau was, deep in the Gaspé Peninsula about thirty or forty miles back from the river. Stunted pine grew throughout the ever-present swampland of frozen mud and ice-covered ponds. It was a bleak environment, enlivened only by the tell-tale signs of a few animals. Some streams on which ice had not yet formed might be suitable for drinking. One Arm seemed to know which water was good, just from the look and taste. They came across three larger lakes, which One Arm said might hold fish. One contained a beaver house, and One Arm pointed it out, remarking the occupants could provide nourishment once located — much easier with a dog to smell them under the ice, but theirs had died the year previously. Thomas learned more about making snares and where to set them. He even learned to set large deadfall traps for prey animals: cougars and lynx that lived on the small animals active in this hostile environment. The caribou roamed farther north, the provenance of the Chief, being the best hunter, who took his family deeper into the interior. It was an unusual spring when he did not come back with a good store of caribou, to feed the band until salmon began their annual spring drive up the rivers.

That high distant caribou terrain hosted bands of wolves, which scared Thomas. His British upbringing and those medieval tales of the supernatural awakened an instinctual dread of any encounter with a wolf. He passed his fears on to One Arm, using his best Micmac, but One Arm brushed off such superstitions. He was much more concerned with the omens that criss-crossing snowshoe hare and tiny vole tracks seemed to provide, together with aspects of the stars and such like divinations. Nevertheless, Thomas was glad they'd been assigned this arid wilderness where wolves seldom came.

Their territory comprised two plateaus separated by a slight rise connected by a shallow ravine through which ran a stream. It gathered into a lake and later trickled down through more hills to the west, finally ending up on the coast, perhaps forming the Nouvelle River. After they had laid out a basic trapline, One Arm went immediately to the lake. Thomas saw him sitting, well-wrapped in the beaverskins that he slept under at night, his line down a hole he'd cut in the ice. Thomas found this sight hard to comprehend: he'd never heard of fishing that way. One Arm came back that afternoon reporting that he had found but little sustenance: two trout. Under the deepening ice this winter, for some reason the fish seemed lethargic, with no appetite for bait.

A blizzard snowed them in for three days, during which Thomas worked hard with Little Birch on her English, and she on his Micmac — one thing both enjoyed, and from the time of their setting off, a nightly exercise. The family again ate into their reserves of food, and Thomas wondered if the plentiful game predicted for this region would ever appear.

One Arm had, with Thomas, laid down traplines and set baited snares. They visited the line every two days so as not to let their catch be eaten by other predators. This time as they were on their way home with little to show for their efforts, One Arm signalled Thomas, speaking in Micmac. "You find wigwam, alone?"

"I think so," Thomas said, not at all sure.

"I go find moose," One Arm said in Micmac. "Moose make space." Thomas did not understand. One Arm explained: "Flat area. Moose tramp snow flat. Maybe three four moose together. One man moose, also women moose."

"Ah yes, a moose's yard!" Thomas had heard Little Birch explain the feature on their trek. When the snow got deep, these monarchs of the forest fed in a circle that expanded as they ate, and thus made a flattened area often as large as an acre, or more, to give them mobility to fend off wolves. They took care to avoid deep snow in which they might flounder when attacked. Micmac hunters always looked first for the moose yard, where the animals made easy targets for an arrow, or if a hunter got close enough, a spear. You never threw a spear, you only used it at close quarters.

"I come back later," One Arm said. "You go now. Bring back meat."

All they had snared wouldn't last long, Thomas thought, with only two weasels hanging round his neck. But then again, the women might make some sustenance out of it. The situation, Thomas recognized, was getting more worrisome. "Maybe on the way back, I'll find a hare to shoot."

One Arm nodded, and set off to reconnoitre. Nervously, Thomas watched his form disappear among the stunted spruce and then set about finding his way back. Fortunately it had not snowed, so all he had to do was follow their snowshoe tracks.

Alone, he was able to focus on the landscape and marvelled once again at the changing beauty the snow wrought. The straight, black shadows of the birch, mingling with the gentler outlines of spruce boughs, fell across the undulating humps and hollows of the snowdrifts, where the wind so casually piled them before going on its way to distribute more tuffets and hollows and hillocks. He passed a lake that had not yet frozen, leaving centre patches of black water rimmed with grey, encroaching ice. The ever-present wind wove drifts around bushes, wiped the earth clear at the base of trees and built banks at obstacles. The untidiness of autumn had been erased, leaving all pristine and pure.

He got home before evening. He'd found no snowshoe hare tracks, but did mark a rabbit run they'd missed on the way out. The women prepared the weasel in a broth made from its carcass together with some cattail roots. All four took care to spoon up only their tiny portions of flesh.

The next day, the family waited anxiously for One Arm. In the meantime, Thomas helped the women scrounge some caribou moss, which they then boiled for a few minutes in water, rinsed, and boiled in new water until it became a kind of jelly. Mixed with a little meat or grease, it made a somewhat nutritious dish. This lack of food began to mire Thomas in a kind of despair, the first he'd felt for a long time. He even noticed a haunted look on Little Birch's face. She always ate less than her mother, and he was worried about her and her endurance.

One Arm did not return for two days. Late in the day,

Thomas and Little Birch kept trading looks, but no one wanted to voice what they felt. Finally, Thomas said, "I think I should go look for him."

"No, we must wait. He will come back, I know it," Little Birch said, which provoked an outburst of fear and worry from her mother.

Thomas looked from Full Moon to her daughter. "Well, it can't hurt if I just take a short tour. Be dark in a couple of hours. He must not stay out another night."

Resolutely, Thomas got into his outside clothes, and pushed aside the heavy skin hanging as a door. There, through the lightly falling snow, he saw a dark form — One Arm!

Exhausted, with frost-starched eyebrows, he staggered forward. Thomas helped him into the wigwam, where the two women helped take off his outer clothing. Little Birch stoked the fire to prepare some warm but thin soup they'd made from bark.

They waited for him to relax. When he was finally able to sip hot liquid, he gave them the bad news: not one moose yard.

They sat around the fire in their cave shelter, acknowledging that things did look bleak, almost desperate.

Thomas tried to put on a brave face. "Maybe tomorrow, the weather will change."

"Not just weather." Little Birch looked gaunt. "Glooscap has taken away game."

"Why don't we go back to the summer encampment," Brightstar offered in Micmac. "We could trade some goods, maybe,"

"What goods do we have?" Full Moon asked.

"We would never make it that far," Little Birch told her

brother sharply. "Not enough to eat, trip need energy. Our things are too heavy. Too far."

"Could we try another hunting area?" Thomas asked.

Full Moon shook her head. "It happens many times in winter. One family go short. But they never go to place of other family, unless dying."

"Do we want to wait that long? Until we're dying?" Thomas frowned.

On and on they discussed it, as the fire began to burn down, each one taking their turn. Finally, One Arm held up his hand.

They fell silent, knowing a decision — the purview of One Arm as the eldest male — had been made.

One thing only left, he said. Perform the age-old Micmac ceremony for summoning a moose.

Chapter Nineteen

They all took a nap before the ceremony. The two women lay abreast at the back of the wigwam, One Arm and Brightstar slept apart under their caribou skins, and Thomas closer to the entrance under his beaver covering, Big Birch's legacy. Beaver pelts were the warmest of all coverings, but it took almost a dozen beavers to make one blanket, so Thomas considered himself extremely lucky to have inherited such a prize, if for only this one winter.

After a spell, One Arm roused them. While they were getting ready, he prepared his materials for the ceremony: sweet grass, tobacco, a pipe, and so on. He asked Brightstar to stoke the glowing embers in the central round of stones.

Thomas saw that Little Birch and Brightstar were not dressing and frowned. Little Birch caught his look.

"He is supposed to spend a day in a sweat lodge to purify himself first, but he cannot here. And also he must fast, and I did not see him eat, so that is all right."

"But aren't you coming?"

Little Birch shook her head. "Women not allowed."

Thomas paused. "But I have to understand what is going on, what the ceremony is all about. I cannot do it without you."

Little Birch shook her head.

Unaccountably, Thomas surged with anger. Perhaps he had not eaten, or the harsh conditions were getting to him, or he'd had enough of "fitting in" with customs he neither sympathized with nor understood, but his anger gushed out.

"No sir, One Arm, she is hunting with us, she works as hard, and I say, she is coming out to translate!" He glanced at Little Birch. "Translate!"

Little Birch stammered out the gist.

One Arm looked round abruptly. "Not find moose if she come," he answered.

"There is no way that Little Birch will spoil this hunt," Thomas heard his voice rise in spite of himself, "she's a good person, she cares for the game just like you do, her spirit will help, not detract. If you want me to hunt with you tomorrow, she stands nearby and translates."

Full Moon was watching, perturbed, and shrank back. Little Birch was taken aback by this new side of Thomas she had not seen.

Thomas stared resolutely. One Arm stood, almost dejected, and then nodded. "She come. We try that way."

Breathing hard, Thomas put on his outside garments, and crawled out with Little Birch following, soon forgetting the confrontation in his stimulation at participating in this first Indian ritual. The moon's crescent hung above eye level in an almost clear sky, and clumps of disfigured spruce added an ominous gathering of black sentinels.

They stood in a circle, Brightstar, One Arm, and Thomas with Little Birch behind. They remained quiet as One Arm joined them, his pipe lit from a brand in their fire. He also carried a whisk of stiff grasses. Then he came round the circle, and blew smoke over them, whisking it to "smudge" them.

She whispered to Thomas, "He purifies us, before we begin."

Thomas took this in with due solemnity; in fact, he had decided to give himself fully, asking his own Lord to deliver him into the spirit of this age-old ceremony. Nothing else had worked; maybe this would.

Facing the hanging crescent of moon, One Arm began to intone a low song in guttural monotone, consonants and vowels moving out one after another. Little Birch leaned in to Thomas. "First he prays to Grandmother Moon, asking her to bring us a moose." After a pause, she went on, "He says we are helpless, we have no food, and we ask Grandmother to provide for us."

Her uncle raised his one good arm, keeping his sung invocation going. Finally, he stopped and went back into the wigwam. While they waited in moonlit silence, Little Birch whispered to Thomas, *"Nugum,"* Grandmother Moon, she is our mother of the first creation of the Micmac, with Grandfather Sun. Our months, they are like the moon months, twenty-eight days, thirteen months in one year."

One Arm came back out, and moved a short way apart from them with his lit sweetgrass smouldering. Facing the moon, he passed the sweetgrass back and forth before him, crooning again a phrase over and over.

"What's he saying now?"

"It is not allowed for me to speak that," Little Birch told him.

After a pause, Thomas whispered, "Why doesn't he just call a moose. I've heard you can do that, just call a moose and they will come."

She smiled. "That is only in the autumn, when woman moose, she want baby moose, she call big moose. So hunter pretends he is woman, calling for big moose." She saw Thomas's look, and dropped her eyes, embarrassed.

"Oh sure, Magwés, even we English know what to do when a woman wants a baby," he teased.

She shook her head at his irreverent chatter. "So in winter, no moose come when you call. Only in autumn."

"Look there." She pointed up at the Big Dipper. "See seven stars?" Thomas was acquainted with Ursa Major from his days in the Navy. "Those seven stars, they are seven hunters. Every autumn, they chase bear. They kill him, and his blood, it falls on *Gitpu,* the eagle. So *Gitpu* shake his feathers, and blood falls on trees. And that is why leaves turn red in autumn."

"Maple trees. Really?" Thomas liked it when she spoke of Micmac lore. He determined to ask her for more stories. So far they had been too busy, just focussing on each other's grammar and vocabulary every night.

One Arm had brought out his drum, which he handed to Brightstar. Thomas had not seen it before. Brightstar began to tap it slowly with a curved bone, light taps alternating with heavier ones to produce a Micmac rhythm. Soon One Arm, with the help of Brightstar, took some tobacco from his pouch. He bent, and holding a pinch of tobacco in his closed fist, thumb uppermost, he began speaking.

"What's he doing now?" Thomas asked.

"Now he prays to *Migmuessu,* the spirit of the woods. He makes offering of tobacco: first the earth, the good land which gives us game, and then the four directions."

Thomas nodded, intrigued, as One Arm straightened

and held his hand out before him, intoning again.

"Now he offers North, for hunters, for brave ones." He tossed the tobacco, and then turned west. "Now, for the gift of patience and wisdom." These concepts Little Birch was able to get across in a number of extra words, whispering so as not to disturb One Arm. "Now the south: the snow, the hunters who understand the woods."

Thomas nodded, feeling so privileged to be part of these sacred mysteries, as Little Birch went on, "Now the east: light, energy, spirit seekers, those who know how to pray."

They fell silent, waiting. "What happens now?" asked Thomas, unable to repress his curiosity.

One Arm went back to the fire, and came out with his tuft of sweetgrass now lit and smouldering. In rhythm with the drum, but not singing, he began to speak again, smudging the air before him, all the while turning slowly in a circle. Then he lifted his one arm, faced eastward out into the woods, away from the wigwam, and smudged in a circle at arm's-length.

"Last part of ceremony. He pray to spirit of moose, the head spirit, the one who give the moose to the hunter, or take them away. He say, we are coming to find you. Creator will give you to us, and we ask Keeper of Moose for very fast kill, so we will not cause pain." They watched in silence as he continued his prayer, tossing sprigs of tobacco in the air. "Now he say to spirit of moose, we will use all parts, skin, meat, sinew, we reverence you, we pray to your spirit. Please, you must come save us."

In a final gesture, One Arm took something out of his pocket and held it up.

"That is piece of moose horn. Watch." One Arm took his sweetgrass and as Brightstar held it up high, he smudged the moose antler, and then the two of them put its leather thong around his neck. Then he extinguished the sweetgrass, and stood staring out into the woods.

Thomas found himself relax inside, he could stay here forever under the crisp stars, waiting, waiting for the moose to show. The four of them cast shadows over the snow, like ancient markers written on a sheet of time.

One Arm turned. "Now we sleep. Tomorrow, we find moose."

The four of them went into the wigwam in silence, and lay down. Thomas stayed awake for a long time, absorbing the gentility and reverence that the Micmac bestowed on the game which fed and clothed them. He determined he would do the same.

* * *

The next morning Thomas opened the heavy flap of the sunken wigwam and crawled out into a blast of brilliance, as the sun poured out its glistening light over the snow. He had to squint, shade his eyes with mitts to see anything. One Arm came out behind as Thomas knelt to tie snowshoes on his feet shod in fur-lined moccasins. Little Birch came out and handed Thomas his pistol and pack. The two went off with the sun for company and starvation as their guide.

All day Thomas and One Arm zigzagged back and forth across the territory, searching for tracks. Its swamplike condition at this altitude resembled the muskeg of the

Far North above the treeline. After an early morning burst of optimism, Thomas felt himself flagging when they found no tracks. As the day wore on, he grew even more tired, more than ever before, including his long night watches on the ship. Dangerous, he thought to himself. Both of them were in dire need of nourishment. And he kept waiting for the recriminations due him for insisting on Little Birch being at their ceremony. But though he must have felt it, One Arm never let on.

Thomas walked behind, lifting each foot more and more slowly, in the biting frost and blinding light. Earlier, One Arm had learned from some Inuit how to fashion eyeshades from whittled wood with a centre slit. They fastened behind the head with *babiche*, a strip of hide. But he hadn't brought his today. They had been daubing their cheeks below the eyes with soot, to make a black band from one ear to the other as partial protection.

To make matters worse, huge storm clouds had been piling up in the east. Thomas kept his fearful eye on them. In late afternoon, it clouded over and heavy snow began.

"What do you think, One Arm?" Thomas asked in Micmac.

One Arm frowned. "We go trapline. Rest there. Wait for Moose. From trapline, more easy find way home."

Thomas followed as the older man headed west, unaccountably finding his way through stands of spruce, occasionally stopping to scent the air. Thomas could hardly see him ahead through the large, lazy flakes that were covering up all distinguishing marks. A couple of times, he even tripped. Hard to get any sense of depth with air, land, and track ahead so very white, no sun piercing the overcast to create the shadows that define a trail. Amazing, One Arm's sense of direction, Thomas thought, as he brought them unerringly back to a section of trapline that, after a few moments, Thomas recognized.

Getting his axe from his pack, Thomas chopped the lower branches off a large spruce, some ten yards away from their snares. The two of them hollowed out the snow, piling it into a wall, and curled up next to it in the snug burrow, for all the world like a nest of the game they were trapping. Thomas unrolled his beaver covering and together, they fell into a sheltered sleep.

The wind blew up into a blizzard in the night. Not really the life he'd seen for himself, he grumbled, nor for Little Birch. If only he could have taken her off to a better life in his soon to be shipshape cabin. If only Burn had not laid claim to her. If only... Stop that! he commanded. Put her out of your mind! You've got enough problems of your own right now.

At dawn, Thomas woke with a nudge from One Arm. *"Diàm."* His round face had broken into a rare grin.

"Moose?" Thomas could hear nothing.

One Arm motioned. Then Thomas heard it. A movement, from the direction of their snare. A branch swished. "Yes, moose!"

One Arm nodded, and quietly they got out of their rolled hide. One Arm took his spear down from the branches; Thomas began to load his flintlock. What a process, he thought. How could the infantry ever fight wars with this unbelievably laborious instrument?

"I will go out, take a shot."

"Albàsi!"

Careful for sure, Thomas thought as he crept from

their hidden refuge, One Arm following. The moose stood in a deep drift just in front of the clump of spruce where they had set their snares. The animal was panting and looking, Thomas would swear, as if perplexed.

The moose saw them. It stared. Thomas marvelled at the mighty breadth of the antlers, over six feet across. Later in winter, they lost their gigantic horns and grew a new set. Now, the moose appeared regal, magnificent. And tremendously lethal.

The beast brought down its head, uttered a lowing sound, and gathered its huge brown body, almost a ton, six foot at the shoulders, a large hump tapering back to a small haunch — so much larger than any bull Thomas had ever seen.

Breathing what he thought might be an appropriate prayer to the moose spirit, Thomas raised his firearm.

The moose charged.

Thomas waited until it got within ten feet and pulled the trigger.

At the same instant the moose flipped, its foreleg caught in the snare that One Arm had set for small game. As it went down, the shot missed the chest and struck somewhere in the back, causing no serious damage.

The spark from the trigger-pull always took a good fraction of a second to reach the tinderbox, flash down into the breech to ignite the charge behind the lead shot. That fractional second's pause caused Thomas to miss.

Quickly! he yelled at himself, get the powder out before he gets up. He dropped his gloves to the snow and opened the powder horn. Don't get the powder wet, don't let any snow get in — so little time — measure it, tip it in, quick, quick! He tried to steady his hands as he poured the correct measure into the breech and then glanced up. The moose struggled to its feet.

Thomas reached into the deep pocket of his coat for another ball. The moose bellowed and backed up, it's foreleg bleeding. Quick, get the wadding for the shot, push it down the barrel! But his fingers were freezing. He fumbled with the wadding, nearly dropped it.

The huge moose readied for another charge. With horror Thomas saw the sapling attached to the snare had broken off. Hurry, he urged himself while One Arm struggled past through deep snow. With one good arm, the hunter raised his spear to await the charge.

Thomas grabbed his long ramrod to tip it into the opening of the barrel.

Before he could tamp down the shot, the moose charged.

Thomas pulled out the ramrod fast, but the moose bore straight down at him. As it passed, One Arm thrust the spear into the animal and caught it in the neck.

The charging juggernaut slowed just enough. Its massive antlers struck Thomas, smashing him backwards, sending the flintlock flying, goring his face and head. But he was alive, though stunned.

With an amazing agility, the animal stopped and tossed its head sideways to rid itself of the protruding spear.

Bleeding and dazed, Thomas reached for his firearm. The moose ignored his spreadeagled body and turned its attention to the other hunter, now defenceless at one side.

It whirled to face One Arm as Thomas tried to sight down the blurry barrel.

Head down, the moose lunged at One Arm. It tossed

the man to one side with its great horns. Then it whirled to finish him off when Thomas pulled the trigger.

Miracle of miracles, the snowy gun fired.

The shot struck the moose in the head and with a quiver the animal fell sideways. The whole of its one-ton bulk pinned One Arm to the snow, the massive antlers twisted so they gripped One Arm underneath.

It lay, kicking and quivering in its death throes, gouging One Arm more. Thomas breathed a quick prayer and struggled up. His forehead had been gashed and blood ran down into his eyes and face so that he could hardly see. He forced himself to wade through the deep snow, and with failing strength tried to shift the quivering beast off his friend. To no avail.

He stood panting. Strange gurgling sounds issued from One Arm's throat. The weight of the animal seemed to be choking him.

Thomas reached out again to wrest the beast off One Arm's body. But its weight and twisted neck pressed relentlessly into One Arm's chest, suffocating him.

With a flash of insight, Thomas grabbed the foreleg thrashing in spasms and, with a last burst of energy, used that leverage to roll the animal over and off his friend.

Then he lay back, panting hard.

One Arm raised his head, blinking, losing consciousness.

The body of the giant animal finally gave up the ghost, and was still.

All three forms lay without moving.

Then somehow, Thomas forced himself up and moved over to help hoist One Arm into a sitting position. His curious croaking sounds lessened.

Knocked the wind out of him, Thomas decided. In Micmac, he murmured, "You'll be fine."

Everything now happened in slow motion. The sun's heat warmed them, and they began to collect themselves. One Arm crawled on hands and knees to their hideout under the spruce where he retrieved his pack. He returned and, still in pain, wiped Thomas's face, cleaning his wounds on face and neck. He fashioned a bandage from a strip in his pack, and bound the gash. He also used his *únbesun,* his store of native medicine, to lessen the pain.

"But how are you?" gasped Thomas.

One Arm confessed his chest hurt badly, some ribs perhaps broken, but otherwise he seemed intact. With luck, they would both make it back to the winter wigwam.

That store of meat saved their lives. But before they ate, they repeated special prayers to the Keeper of Moose: We are sorry for taking your life but we needed you to survive. And with the winter solstice behind them, although the days were still too short to travel the trapline, they rested and nourished themselves.

Until the magic happened.

Chapter Twenty

Little Birch and Thomas had been occupying themselves with their evening language lessons when One Arm went out to relieve himself. Full Moon was decorating a special blouse for Little Birch to be used, Thomas guessed, for her "stone ceremony" in the spring, an event Thomas preferred to forget. One Arm came back in, unusually stimulated, and spoke hurriedly to Little Birch.

"Thomas, we must go out now," she ordered, in what was fast becoming good English.

"Out? But it's so nice by our little fire." Full Moon had thrown herbs onto it to scent their winter wigwam, snug in its heavy blanket of snow.

"Come, Thomas," she commanded, getting herself dressed. Reluctantly, he tugged on Big Birch's heavy outside jacket of caribou and out they went.

Thomas headed first to where they usually relieved themselves. "Hey, it's really cold," Thomas called back. "What's going on?"

She waited until he came up to her and, taking him by the hand, pulled him along. "*Maliaptegen! Ditti!*" she scolded affectionately in her own language, as a form of intimacy. She went on, "You are like a moose bird! Much too curious!" She forged on ahead.

He followed her snowshoe tracks up a low crest. "Keep your head down," she called, as she broke into a clearing.

He obeyed, and when he came close, she said, "All right, you can look up."

An astonishing sight greeted him: the whole northern sky shimmered with an aurora borealis.

"*Waqadaskl*. They are dancing," Little Birch said, her eyes alight with the same shimmer. She looked over at him.

Thomas had never seen such a display. The spectacular curtain of light wavered up and down, a greenish background, with streamers of red and purple flickering above a filmy curtain hung surely by some impressive Micmac deity to dazzle them both. "Little Birch, I can't believe it."

She seemed pleased at his reaction, and moved against him, to shelter from the light wind. They stood as one watching this amazing display, dancing, it seemed, only for them.

"When I was a little girl, we would whistle at them. Legends say if you did, they would come down to snatch you away. So we would whistle past the door hide, just open this much," indicating with her hands, "and very fast, drop the covering to hide and stay safe. So exciting!"

As she spoke, he found his arm go round her as it might a little girl.

Under her bundled clothes, her lean body began to press firmly against his. His arm tightened. She looked up into the sky, letting her head fall back onto his shoulder.

He breathed in her presence in this clear, icy night, and moved his cheek closer to her soft hair, flowing free above her heavy jacket. Tall for a girl, she was the perfect height for him. Then she turned to look up at him. "You like?"

"'Do you like them?' is better," he said, lapsing into his teacher mode, and then kicked himself for being such a pedant.

"You have seen them before?"

"Never like this in the Navy, too far south I guess, but sometimes this winter coming home late from our traps. But not so vivid. I never dreamed..."

"Dream, yes," she said. "When Grandmother Moon makes love to Sun, we say her spirit plays in sky. Spirit of sun and moon, playing together."

"Playing?" Yes, that's the word. "I think they are laughing, too. And dancing."

"Yes," she said, "laughing, their spirits are laughing and dancing."

What pleasure could any Englishman have, in London town or on the turrets of the Raby Castle or in any county fair, that could compare with this? Even a flare from a neighbouring man o'war, a rocket he had seen occasionally in the Navy, bore no resemblance. The whole sky was laughing and dancing. Silver freckled the snowy landscape as the moonlight shimmered with the joy of the dance.

She seemed comfortable leaning against his chest, looking up at him. Both his arms went round her, and now he stayed looking down into her dark eyes, alight with fun and the reflection of the lights. He could feel his heart hammering, and heard her breathing grow deeper, quicker, as though she had been running.

She must love this phenomenon, he thought, enveloped in her beauty and in the moment — when from some inexplicable depth, at the same moment they both leaned closer. And their lips met.

A rush of blood flooded his lungs and his heart. He clasped her ever so tightly as though they would never part.

They stayed in the embrace for what seemed an age.

She broke away, panting a little, putting her hand to her forehead.

What had they done? Broken some taboo?

"I must go in." She tore herself away, and strode down toward the wigwam. Thomas looked back up at the northern lights, thoughts churning.

How could he ever face Burn? No, he was just being foolish. Confused feelings flooded over him: was this not just a momentary passion? No, not at all, she was a truly gorgeous woman, so clear, innocent, purposeful, so direct, she would make a wonderful wife. To Burn! — don't forget that, he reminded himself sternly. He and Little Birch must forget this and resume their roles of brother and sister. And when they are married, he went on to himself, I will still visit them, they will come to my cabin, I will share my meal with them as I would share everything with her, my life, my hopes and — wait, there I go again! Don't overdo it — nothing happened, in fact. Nothing!

But yet he knew that something had happened to his soul, and it would probably never change back.

* * *

In the ensuing days, the encounter left them both confused, as Thomas tried so hard to quell the wholesome appetites of his young body. Thankfully, their hours were

full: Thomas kept going out for two or three days along
the trapline with One Arm. The small game was back for
some reason, or coming to life now that the days were
getting longer. Little Birch worked with her mother at
preparing the skins the men had gotten, and either smoking or hanging the meat to freeze-dry high in the upper
branches of the one tall spruce that grew nearby.

Thomas was determined to forget what was happening
between him and Little Birch, and worked ever harder
on their languages in the evening. Brightstar, with his
child's inquiring mind, loved listening in and was picking
up a lot. One Arm chimed in from time to time with
questions, and answered Thomas in his concerns over
certain traditions and taboos, but only when translated
by Little Birch. Thomas soon realized that if he were to
talk to One Arm, it would have to be in that man's own
tongue, though through no fault of his own. He just did
not have Little Birch's quick mind for words.

For the life of him, Thomas found it hard to get to the
bottom of how their language worked. He couldn't see
the structure in Micmac. And then one day he hit upon
it: "Little Birch, could it be that Micmac is a verb-based
language?"

"Thomas, you ask such big questions."

"Sorry. What I mean is, you all talk mostly in verbs.
Walk, for example. We walk either fast, slow, happily, angrily. But you have a different word for each of them. You
put the adverbs into the verb. That's why I'm finding it
so hard."

"No, Thomas, you are doing really well."

"Yes, but when you say hit, or hurt, how you hit or hurt
changes the verb each time, like 'with a sword' — you

put the tool into the verb. It makes for such long words."

"But it's so simple that way."

"I guess it is, to you...

"Why do you bother with all this, Thomas, you are doing very well."

"But even summer or winter, they're verbs, too: 'When it is summer...'" Thomas sat back and ran his hand through his hair.

"Thomas, let's go on with our learning words. You're putting me to sleep."

***

The next fateful week, Thomas was out on the trapline with One Arm, and they stayed the night. One section had yielded almost no game, so at dawn when they struggled out of their bivouac, One Arm went off in search of new animal runs, letting Thomas head home with three carcasses round his neck: one muskrat, and two squirrels, their stiff frozen bodies swinging and banging against his waist. He gave One Arm his loaded flintlock since he could not, with his one arm, work a bow and arrow.

Thomas trudged down the shallow ravine that connected the two levels of swamp, tramping beside its stream running under thinning ice. They had felled a tree over it at the start of the season, and feeling carefree, with enough game around his neck to feed them, he hurried over the log, slipped, and fell splash! right into the icy water.

Not more than three feet deep, but freezing cold, the

stream doused him and made his clothes sopping wet, his legs, arms, chest. He struggled up, cursing. How many times would he make mistakes before learning to be as error-free as this wilderness absolutely required?

Chilled, freezing, in fact, he just clutched his game, waded out of the icy stream and started home as fast as he could. The weather was mild compared to the subzero weather they'd faced during the winter, but below freezing and certainly cold enough to do him damage, chilling him more as he went. Keep moving, he told himself, but then tried to forget it, apart from berating himself. Why ever had he not been paying attention? He could have cut a staff to help him cross, but the previous ice had always been thicker. No good giving himself another lecture, as he'd done every other miscue: the mistake of the shillings, falling down the cliff, careless about the bear, on and on. Mistakes here could be life-threatening. But he still had no idea of the enormity of what had taken place. Slowly, the heat drained from his body.

Only three or four hours to home, so no red flag went up, no great danger sign flashed in his brain, apart from knowing he had to get there as fast as he could, because the sopping wet clothes sure felt unpleasant.

Soon, his mind began to wander as his legs and feet and toes started to hurt. He was so hungry, having had little real protein — only one trout caught the night before in a lake. As his body chilled, he grew more and more fatigued.

On he trudged down the gorge and soon came out into a goodly wind on the plateau that held their winter encampment. Only a couple of hours more. But his brain was not functioning properly. Everything was so white.

Of course. But which way now? Where in fact was the camp? No blazed trail here: always easy to find one's way back from this close. Or was it? Should he turn left or right? Everything looked different. He could not sight the one tall spruce by their camp. Nor could he climb a tree: they were too small, and he felt too weak.

He struggled on, trusting his instincts. But he was losing all desire to walk. And then, it came to Thomas that perhaps if he had a nap, he'd feel better, and then he could set out again.

Yes, how nice to sink into soft snow. Wouldn't he feel so much stronger after a short rest? No, he'd better keep going. Have a sleep when he got home. Curious, "home" being now a primitive birchbark dwelling in the wilderness. His mind went off on tangents again. How far he had adventured! Home had always been a room in the loft above a stable with other footmen, none of whom had been promoted to head game beater. But he had. And now here he was, in a snowy wilderness far from civilization, with a native family. How curious! As his mind wandered, his footsteps faltered. No focus.

So maybe he should rest. He'd not heard of the white death by freezing, which every Micmac child is taught. The lore of the Indian was plain: never, ever, surrender to the sleep which lurks in every subzero wood: that relaxed and pleasing sensation of sinking into oblivion, with grace and no struggle...

Yes, he did need a rest. Just for ten minutes, a little snooze, and then up and at 'em again. How nice indeed, to curl up right here and now by the path, and just... let yourself go.

He walked a few more steps and then, at a convenient

snowdrift, Thomas knelt, curled up, and knew no more.

***

Thomas lay in a dream-lit consciousness where nothing made sense. Strange haunting images travelled across the back of his mind. He wandered the earth and found himself back in the pantries at the castle, where he gorged himself on cookies, and then feasted on a huge caldron of soup.

His mother drifted by, fair and slim as she had been in his earlier years, caring and tender. As she passed by, floating back and forth, she caressed him, her hand passing over his brow.

And then he was out with the hunting parties, among the lords and gentlemen, handling a shotgun with the best of them. Conscious of rain falling, he again felt so very chilled, yes, freezing to death, but then he wanted to stay with the hunting gentry so that, chilled or not, he might enjoy their company. Then, oddly, he found himself in the huge kitchen by the open wood stove, with the cook opening the door so that the peat fire blazed up and his mother cradled him, long before he seemed to have reached the age of walking. He lay in her arms, allowing the warmth of the fire to seep into him. And then he felt her move, shift a little, and his consciousness grew faintly solid, and he seemed to be rising to the surface of some deep lake. Was that day breaking above? Who was really holding him?

The shifting of his mother's body rocked him like a shallow boat, but then he forced himself back into the dark waters that shaped his awareness, hovering in the warm deep liquid between the stillness of death and a kind of half-consciousness.

For who knows how long this continued, when again for the second time, he felt his mother's arms move and he began to be aware these were not her arms enfolding him. He tried to keep half-awake so as not to disturb the immensely comforting feeling she gave him, although it was more and more appearing not to be his mother, but another body.

A dream? Well, not too bad either. And then he slowly willed himself into a temporary consciousness, and was now definitely aware of a body on either side of him, naked as he was, holding him tightly, surrounding him. More dreaming, he told himself, and was about to sink back, when he remembered all at once, the ghastly nightmare. Could it be true? No, only a dream, but what was it? Find out, go back, face the horror, stay in the dream, stay half-dead, half-awake, and feel, surely, yes, was that not a slim leg across his stomach? And there, by his left side, another, large, fleshy, and warm, yes, what a lovely dream for sure!

Such a change from his shocking nightmare, conscious of struggle, and struggle without ending, it seemed. How nice that it was all over, and he came to be in this bizarre dream, clasped by bodies on either side. He allowed himself to sink back into the embrace of warmth, when the ghastly nightmare returned in full force. He'd fallen through the ice.

What a nightmare! So how on earth did he find himself here? Piece it together, he told himself. Don't give a flicker of recognition, don't open your eyes, don't wake, rest here, eyes closed, breathing regular, and piece it together.

He now felt clearly on either side of him, two naked bodies, holding him tight under the beaver-skin blanket. He lay still, trying not to let his breathing show surprise while he figured it out. On the right, that inner thigh lying crooked on his stomach — Little Birch? And the heavier fleshly leg pressed against his left — her mother Full Moon? Nothing erotic in their postures. Again, the touch over his brow that he had dreamed being his mother — the hand of Little Birch caressing him tenderly from time to time.

And then it came to him.

Little Birch had received a premonition, a kind of vision. She had insisted on Brightstar and her going out on the trail to look for Thomas. One hour from their wigwam, they had come across his body. Together they had tried to wake him, lifting him with many exhortations. But he was not conscious. They half dragged, half carried him the desperate half-mile to the wigwam. But how? And then, in the time-honoured cure he had yet to learn about, they undressed him, placed him under skins and hides in the wigwam, and got their naked bodies next to his, in the only accepted way to bring a frozen person back to normal. Slowly, surely, this therapy had warmed him back to life.

He luxuriated in the feel of the hard body of Little Birch, her tender flesh, her small soft breasts pressing against his chest, and the larger breasts of her mother Full Moon, nestled to his left.

Their arms held him as if he were a baby, tightly but not too tightly, their breathing measured as his, and he once again fell asleep, as they were. And so, in this kind of treasured heaven with his two most favourite people, he drifted off again, wondering at the same time what would happen when he woke up.

Chapter Twenty-One

The melting ice that Thomas had fallen through signalled the approach of spring. The days grew warmer.
Thomas would sit, munching his smoked meat or cooked
porcupine in broths of bark or needles, all of which he'd
finally learned to stomach and even enjoy. He'd watch
the melting snow gather into drops and trickle down
branches onto gnarled trunks, then glide on down the
glistening bark to melt the soggy snow beneath. Small
game had begun to emerge from hibernation, and their
snares were often full.

Thanks to the intervention of Little Birch and Full
Moon, Thomas had fully recovered from his brush with
a frozen death and was functioning normally. The bond
with Little Birch had grown stronger, now that she had
been instrumental in saving his life. But at the same
time, Thomas kept himself distant, though his whole
body ached to know her.

One evening, One Arm said in Micmac, "Soon, we go
back to sea."

Thomas looked at him, askance. Over those many
evenings around the fire when Thomas had worked so
hard with Little Birch and Brightstar, exchanging words,
surely One Arm should have picked up this simple expression.

"Whenever you say," Thomas replied in Micmac.

And the sooner the better, he thought, much as he wanted to remain forever near Little Birch. This awful gulf between them was driving him crazy. Once back in his cabin, the pain might become endurable. But would she ever cease to occupy the central point of his being and thought?

He somehow perceived that she too might feel just as close to him, but he couldn't be sure, even as that very fact disturbed him. Was this leading to some climax that neither of them anticipated? He longed to explain his detached demeanour, but then again, she was perceptive. And how else could they both behave?

Two nights later, One Arm announced, "After next trapline, we go." He too seemed eager to leave for their summer base.

A cold snap coincided with their departure, which would make the trek back easier, firming up the slushy snow that had made their last tour of the trapline difficult. They'd been collecting all the snares and traps, to avoid harming animals after they left, and come back with moccasins and clothes sopping wet from the thaw. Little Birch hung their things to dry on a horizontal pole in the peak of the wigwam. These last days of preparation had been especially difficult: dismantling swatches of birchbark and bundling it for the trip home.

Fortunately for Thomas, plodding along the trail with his big load occupied his whole energy. Their ample supply of moose meat had been smoked in a structure he and Brightstar had built under One Arm's instructions, digging a trench in the snow and constructing a makeshift smokehouse. So this meat overburdened them all, especially Little Birch, who had piled her *toboggan* high.

Leaner, more muscular, and accustomed to eating little, Thomas still found the long trip home almost unmanageable with his heavy load. He had to stop often between meal breaks to rest and catch his breath. At night they all fell exhausted under their hides with no thought for anything else.

At the main forks of the river, they greeted another family coming down the east fork, who proceeded to give them the bad news: One of the band's finest hunters and his little son had stumbled upon the lair of a cougar with newborn kittens. When their bodies were finally found, not much remained.

"Mountain lions are rare," Little Birch told Thomas. "But not unusual. Very shy, they only attack in special cases, like this one."

"Do I know the family?"

"This family gave us their location this winter. That is why my mother is very upset."

Thomas frowned. "That's just awful. I don't think I met them."

"Oh yes. Little boy, he was one who waved bow and arrow," she gestured, "when you make faces." Oh no! He'd admired the little boy's ferocity and his daring; he remembered him clearly. What a shock. "Two daughters and mother, they go other family. She say both nearly starve. But they are safe now."

They stayed at this base camp to perform a private farewell for the departed. For Thomas it was a lesson well learned: the quirks and hazards of this land brought forth inestimable bounties but so often claimed you before your allotted lifespan. Now more than ever he wanted to rescue Little Birch from this precarious, though enriching, life with the tribe. But how?

They set off once again and, at long last, legs almost giving out, Thomas staggered into the clearing of the band's summer home. He let down his heavy sacks and, in a trance of exhaustion, sat on a stump to stare at the abandoned skeletons of wigwams. Hardly inviting. Most were denuded of their bark by families who took their coverings into the interior; normally clean interiors and round hearths were littered with the detritus of a receding winter. Piles of dirty snow lay in hollows where previously, sprightly paths had borne witness to the pitter-patter of moccasins.

But as so often in the Gaspé, spring had turned its hand to providing a splendid day for their homecoming, billowing cumulus hovering high over the river mouth. Some of the band had arrived, as evidenced by one wigwam in perfect shape and another being finished by a woman sewing the birchbark seams with a bone awl and thin roots of spruce.

Little Birch came up and let her *toboggan* lines fall. She sat beside him, as worn out and depressed as he was by the amount of work facing them. He smiled at her and she gave him one of those looks he loved, wiping sweat from her brow, though the air was chill.

They turned to see Full Moon arrive, drop her *toboggan* lines, and just sit on the ground, staring. Worn out.

"Wigwam first, I think," Little Birch murmured.

Thomas shook his head. "Tomorrow, Magwés. Today we rest." A couple, facing the future, exhausted but determined.

"Lucky, no rain tonight."

"Yes." She knew a lot of English after the winter of lessons and practice. And he knew Micmac, although when alone they spoke English. Thomas had an idea she might become the second translator to the band, when Tongue was out hunting or otherwise busy.

"Now we have a nice moose skin for our beds," she murmured, congratulating him.

"A moose skin, yes." He remembered that battle. Just the sort of excitement he'd prefer to avoid in the future.

The future... yes, what of that? Should he leave at once? No, better wait and help them get sorted out. Well then, why not just stay and live all summer with Little Birch and the band? No, if he stayed he'd only be participating at the one event he had a horror of ever seeing through: her wedding. How he wanted to get Little Birch away. Life with him would be hard too, yes, but dreams, he had dreams of what it could become. Dreams he wanted to share with her. No, stop thinking like that!

At the same moment, they both looked up to see Burn appear in the opening of his completed wigwam. He froze.

Little Birch drew away from Thomas and tried to regain her composure. Their positions had been so natural. But now Thomas felt covered in confusion. What should he do next? He took a second to gather his thoughts.

He rose and walked — well, staggered, really — over to Burn as his legs refused to respond to his brain's commands. He greeted Burn warmly, and said in impeccable Micmac (which might help, he thought), "I have brought her back safe. Now she is all yours."

He put out his hand to touch Burn's shoulder, and then turned away. He didn't want Burn to see the pain start into his eyes, although on reflection, he knew that

Burn must have seen it and sympathized.

That decided it. Go quickly. Stay tonight, perhaps, but then leave first thing in the morning.

***

The walk back to his cabin took Thomas a whole long day, with no awareness of where he was. He walked by rote, stepping around windfalls, threading through the trunks of maple and fir and over swampy ground, for the snow had not yet melted. He didn't even think ahead to his cabin. He was just lost in darkening thoughts. Forget her, he told himself, just use every ounce of willpower, concentrate on what is before you. And a whole lot did lie ahead.

When he arrived at the cabin, he found his new home had lost much of its appeal. The birchbark roof had blown off. Winter had strewn soggy leaves and blown dead branches all around, and a tree had fallen across his path to the brook. He sat on a stump, put his head in his hands, and stayed like that for a long time.

Forcing himself at last to get up, he circled the twelve-foot-square cabin. A well-worn hole in the back indicated that an animal family, perhaps a skunk, had wintered there. No cleaning for him tonight. All he could do was pull the bedcover from its peg and spread it out. He walked down to the brook, got a long drink of water, and filled a saucepan in case he woke up. Without eating, he lay down and fell into a tormented sleep.

The morning after, hardly refreshed, he opened his eyes. First day back in his precious cabin. Alone. That word, which had enlivened his former days, now sounded like a knell, promising only a long, lonely summer. But then the sun rose, the ever-present brook clucked and chuckled its way down its nobbled streambed, and one or two birds called from up the brook. Thomas began to take heart.

He gave himself a real talking to. Look what a lucky man you are! Freedom to do exactly what you want — bounded only by the confines of an unpredictable world that can surprise you at every turn. What more could he ask for?

Over the next three weeks he rediscovered some energy and even the will to set about making everything shipshape. He fixed the roof, built shelves, fashioned a chair and makeshift table. He travelled the brook, drawing maps and testing for the best trout pools. After months under the expert eye of One Arm, he now was able to spot more game runs, possibly a muskrat hole or two, certainly a mink run — and even a thicket whose brambles heralded a family of hares. No snares now, let them raise their young, he thought. He could feed on trout, which were ravenous in spring and rose to his fishing line with comforting regularity. Time once again for fiddlehead ferns, and he now knew how to select and boil bark for tea; so for the moment he managed to function.

But the image of Little Birch kept thrusting itself into his thoughts. Whenever he forced himself to consider his own survival and to prepare for the summer ahead, concern for her stifled his plans.

Yes, the summer. What should he do?

Work in Paspébiac? He liked caulking hulls with

oakum, but that was not getting him ahead. Stay here and begin clearing his land? But alone? How long would it take to get Little Birch out of his mind? This being his first encounter with someone like her, he had no idea. What about never? He shuddered at that thought.

Just then a distant crack of a branch rescued him from spiralling thoughts.

Who could it be? He carefully loaded his flintlock and cautiously left his cabin, making his way in a roundabout fashion to the edge of the brook where he could observe without being seen.

Scrambling down the hillside, came a familiar figure. "Tongue!"

Tongue was delighted to see him, as was Thomas. The translator had not arrived back from the wintering grounds before Thomas had left. Thomas took him round the site, and finally they sat with a cup of bark tea.

"How are they all?" Thomas asked. "Did the Chief get back all right?"

"Very good. Much caribou meat."

"Little Birch is fine?"

Tongue merely gave him a significant look.

"And Burn?"

Another significant look.

"So did you come by canoe? When are they taking furs to Paspébiac?"

"Now, I think. Canoe leave from Port Daniel."

"Really? They want me back there?" Made sense, he supposed. Ice still floating on the bay might make landing with furs at his brook dangerous.

Tongue seemed itchy to get back, so Thomas gathered up whatever he might need for the summer. He'd come back later for anything he'd forgotten.

It being noon, he set off with Tongue, but not without misgivings. Did he really want to face Little Birch again? Had she accepted Burn's proposal?

They made good time, Thomas by now being accomplished at trotting through the woods for hours on end. About halfway along, they stopped to drink some water and have a chew on the dried moose meat Tongue had brought.

Shall I bring all that up? Thomas asked himself. He glanced over at Tongue, only to see the older man looking back at him somewhat quizzically.

"So Little Birch got the visit from Burn?" he burst out, at last.

Tongue nodded.

"Burn gave her a stone?"

Tongue nodded.

Thomas remembered Burn's account of how couples got married or rather, pledged their troth. The young man visited the family of the girl, and then at one point tossed into her lap a polished brook stone.

"So they are together?" Thomas didn't want to meet the eyes of Tongue and feigned disinterest.

Tongue waited, not saying a thing, until in desperation, Thomas raised his eyes. Tongue seemed to be enjoying all this, much to Thomas's irritation. Finally, he spoke. "For a long time, she stay looking at stone."

"Yes?"

"Yes." He gave another maddening pause. "She turn over and over in fingers."

The old beggar is playing with me, Thomas thought, getting annoyed. "Go on." This was certainly no joking matter.

"Then..." Tongue mumbled.

Thomas waited.

Tongue waited.

"Then?" Thomas found himself demanding again. Tongue, the devil, was making this so hard.

"She put stone down."

"She put it down?" Thomas could scarcely believe his ears.

Tongue nodded. "She not accept stone."

"She not... But I don't understand."

Tongue looked at him. "*Aqalasiéw*, white people, pretty stupid."

Thomas grinned. Yes, dumb, no doubt. Well, well! He was elated, thrilled, he didn't know how to behave. But poor Burn... "So how did Burn feel?"

"Burn leave. Go up coast, to other band. Listuguj. Next day."

Burn gone. What a shame. He must have been devastated. Oh well, thought Thomas, better get on the trail. Who knows what she'll do when and if I try?

Chapter Twenty-Two

After dusk, Thomas and Tongue arrived back at the band's encampment. The Chief welcomed him without much ceremony; perhaps after his killing of the moose, he'd been almost fully accepted into the band. Thomas also sensed a heightened interest around the camp. He didn't see Little Birch anywhere; to ask after her just now would not be the thing to do.

The Chief and his wife offered him a covering, and Thomas went off to sleep not far from the flowing Port Daniel river. He made himself comfortable on a bed of leaves, and lay down to sleep.

But sleep he could not.

Toward dawn he got up and, as silently as he could, made his way along the shore. He sat down on a log, and waited until dawn glimmered with faint light in the cold spring air, and then finally lifted the darkness off that fateful day when he would, or would not, toss the stone into Little Birch's lap.

What should he do? Suppose she said yes? What had he to offer? Nothing. Some land, but he had no legal title yet. Could it be taken away from him? Of course. And more, should he snatch this child — this woman — even if she agreed, away to a life of loneliness? What indeed was the right decision? Would it really be better for her to come live with him, a long day's walk away from her family and her band? Well, she could easily walk back whenever she wanted. No, he wouldn't let her go all that way alone. Why not — she knew the wilderness better than he did. But suppose they were to have a child? If she were pregnant, she couldn't walk all that way. He would have to find a way of bringing her. So perhaps he should stay with the band and live with her there? But that was precisely why he wanted to toss the stone into her lap — so she wouldn't have the rigours of another winter in which, let's face it, some died and others might starve to death. But who's to say the two of them wouldn't starve to death in his cabin, if they stayed?

Round and round these dizzying thoughts went. Of course, exactly these misgivings, cast in other moulds, he guessed, would preoccupy every would-be groom on the night before he asked for his loved one's hand. However hard life was going to be, together or apart, the decision would never be easy. So he asked in his heart for God's guidance, as a shaft of early sunlight caught the tops of the giant Balm of Gilead overhead, heralding the need to make a decision.

He stooped, took off his moccasins, and began to walk along the riverbank, half in and out of the icy water, looking for a suitable stone. He had one in his mind: it had to be, of course, very smooth, and just the right shade of grey, verging on green if he could.

Being a salmon river, it had a stony bottom and pebbles lay in profusion under the clear running water. But how cold! His feet and ankles could only bear it for short bursts; his hands and forearms ached when he reached to pluck out one jewel of a stone after another, examine it, and toss it back. The pain was good, somehow, a kind of expiation for any past sins, purifying him before he'd make his final gesture.

There, in deeper water, lay the one he thought might be perfect. Pulling off his leggings, he strode out and, leaning in, iced himself in the very snows that once covered the interior and now flowed down to join the Chaleur Bay beyond and later, the great Atlantic on which he had ridden his man o'war for long and painful years.

He picked it out of its jewel-box bed in the trout-filled waters, and splashed his way back to the bank, shivering powerfully. Yes, perfect. Small and smooth and the right colour. He waved his arms around to restore circulation and dried himself and put on his trousers again. Once upon a time in Britain, this hunt might have been a trip down a tawdry alley to a money-lender, where he'd pick out a pawned golden band from many lying on much-fingered velvet. But now he saw this as the perfect ritual — such an appropriate way to approach and entrap the one creature he loved beyond all others!

A kind of electricity enlivened the campsite as he returned. The women moved sprightly to and fro, tossing glances his way. Children stopped in their games, Thomas noticed, and two little girls put aside their little dolls of fir that danced on stiff birchbark as they tapped it. They too seemed waiting for something to happen. Perhaps a feast? He walked over to their hollowed stumps and saw them filled with river water in which the carcasses of tasty muskrats, two squirrels, and some of his moose meat simmered. Fresh fires had been laid and started nearby. Another thing we never worry about here, he reflected, is wood — always as much as we need, while in the Old Country he had to make forays with other footmen to find fallen branches, for the Lord of the Castle was against cutting any of the stately trees. Every morning, too, he used to carry stacks of peat from behind the stables to stoke the kitchen fires, but they hardly compared to a roaring birch or maple log.

Still no sight of Little Birch. He wondered what she was doing. He noticed that on the conference logs, the seated Elders were throwing glances in his direction as they smoked. Children were trying to follow his every move, without appearing conspicuous. A fisherman came from up the river with an alder branch on which gleamed many trout. Thomas saw him pause and take it all in, presumably forming a scene in his mind's eye. Yes, something was definitely up.

At long last, Tongue approached him.

"Good morning, Tongue. What's happening?"

"You are welcome to the wigwam of One Arm."

Thomas rose with all solemnity, trying to still his hammering heart.

Knowing he was the centre of attention made it a lot worse, and to be frank, he didn't like it. He would have preferred anonymity at this crucial juncture. All at once, he had an impulse to run away, grab his sack, and tear back to his cabin. But no, the invitation had been made, and the invitation had now to be accepted.

Solemnly he walked across the clearing to the wigwam of One Arm, dropped to all fours, and entered.

He was almost afraid to look up. When he did, he saw straight ahead of him, One Arm, and to his left Full Moon, while next to her, what a transformation! Little Birch wore the very same blouse he had seen Full Moon decorating in the winter, with a skirt made of the finest calfskin, painted with intricate patterns, and her feet in new moccasins. Her sleek black hair was held back with a carved comb, and her hands lay folded in her skirt which, with her crossed legs, so unusual for a Micmac woman, lay open like a basket. Full Moon also wore clothes he had not seen before, her finest he presumed, sewn with intricate designs, her hair freshly washed and gleaming black. One Arm wore one of those European jackets that someone in the band had loaned him. Brightstar had been shooed outside, but hovered around the entranceway with other friends, pushing, prying, giggling.

Oh my gosh, he thought, where did I put my stone: in my pouch, which I left outside, or in my pocket? He felt such a fool. He surreptitiously reached in his pocket, and grasped it. He hung on to it to give himself strength.

One Arm lifted the embroidered pipe, and handed it to Thomas. He remembered that Little Birch had told him smoking tobacco means the smoke will rise, and your thoughts will go up to your ancestors, giving your uncles, your grandfather, especially Big Birch, news of what you are doing.

Thomas took it. He noticed that Little Birch had not looked up. Solemnly he unwrapped what little tobacco he had left, and inexpertly put some into the stone bowl of the pipe. Then he tried picking up the tongs, fumbled the lit coal, dropped it onto the blanket, then hastily brushed it aside. He tried again, as Full Moon smothered a smile. Don't mess up too often, he told himself.

One Arm reached for the pipe, and handing it to Full Moon, deftly with iron pincers made from old barrel-hoops found on the beach, took another brand from the fire, placed it on the pipeful. Then she handed it back to him, and with his good arm he lifted it to his lips, and pulled heavily. Then he blew out a vast great cloud of smoke in the direction of Thomas.

Thomas spluttered and coughed. Full Moon lifted her hand to her face to hide the broad grin that broke over her. Thomas dared not look at Little Birch.

One Arm now handed the pipe to Thomas, who took it, careful not to inhale too much. He drew into his mouth a pipeful and blew it right out again.

"You are welcome," One Arm said, with a strange formality.

"*Pjilási!*" repeated Full Moon. They had been together all winter long and gone through all manner of experiences, but now she seemed as nervous as Thomas. Only Little Birch did not stir, still looking into her lap.

They stayed like that for what seemed an age. By now, Thomas had grown accustomed to the peaceful stillness of a Micmac ceremony.

Finally, he reached in his pocket and took out the stone. Full Moon and One Arm stiffened.

He held it in his fingers, looking down. He turned it over and over, then massaged it gently between finger and thumb.

They waited.

This better work, he thought. With a sigh, he breathed on it.

One Arm and Full Moon traded looks.

Unaccountably, he lifted it and looking up, pressed it to his lips. Probably all against conventional proposals, he thought, but why not invoke his own Lord. He needed all the help he could get. For the first time, Little Birch stole a glance at him. He saw in her eyes a flash of wonder.

She quickly looked back down again.

Well, he thought, the moment has come. Leaning forward, he threw the pebble into the basket-shaped lap made by the wide deerskin skirt of Little Birch.

At first, she did not move.

For what seemed an age, she stared down at his smooth river pebble. Her eyes then lifted and seemed to search his face intensely. "I love you," he repeated in his mind, "I love you, Little Birch," over and over. "Little Birch, I love you, I always will, I'll care for you always."

"But," he said in his thoughts, "only accept this stone if you are sure."

She picked up the stone and stared at it. His heart rose and then sank. What was she going to do? Put it aside or keep it?

Full Moon could not repress a gasp — the suspense was obviously killing her, too. One Arm put his hand on her shoulder.

Then Little Birch lifted the stone to her mouth, just as he had done, and also pressed her lips against it.

An upsurge of blood suffused his every artery. She was accepting him. Her two hands clasped the stone, she turned her gaze on him, and he knew in one breathtaking moment, the one dream of his life had come true.

***

The next day they set off for his cabin. He had spent the night out of doors as before, under a canopy of interlaced branches, dreaming of their future together. What had he done? What had she done, indeed? Would they be happy? Had this been the right thing? Oh go to sleep, he kept telling himself, leave yourself in the hands of the good Lord and He will protect the marriage.

She had stayed in her own wigwam for the last time. It was a ritual he appreciated, for he wanted his own cabin to be the site of their first night as man and wife.

Now that he knew from practice the best route to his brook, he led Little Birch northward into the woods first, then along a highland route about a mile back from the shore, so that no English trader would come across their trail. He needed no interference from Port Daniel settlers, even though it was now almost a year since he had deserted.

As they walked along, Little Birch kept pointing out different plants that she said they would use for food or for medicine: "*Gamùjamin,* I think you call raspberry: survival food, you eat shoots in spring. Yarrow and camomile, good for tea. This kind of cedar bark, you boil in water, twenty minutes, we drink in fall and spring. Makes skin smooth. Also for no fleas. Bears use it for nests." On and on she went.

"Little Birch, you know so much!"

"We all do."

"No, you more than others."

"My mother says I have a gift of healing. My grandmother was a *Buowin,* a healer. They say her spirit lives on in me. I like these things."

It was as if, in the company of the wiser and more experienced woman, she had spent her time observing, learning by watching. Now she was a properly married woman, out on her own, she could, and did, take charge. He felt that she was doing all this to reinforce her own growing sense of herself, becoming thereby more assured and self-reliant.

***

At the end of the day, Thomas and Little Birch reached the lip of his "Hollow." He stood beside her as she peered down through the bare trees, absorbing the scene. Then he led her down the side hill, and when they came to the brook, he stopped.

Thomas watched her reactions as Little Birch saw for the first time, through leafless trees, his modest cabin. Her new home, he could see her thinking.

"Come," he said in English. She hitched up her pack and headed for the brook, but he steered her aside.

"This way." He led her upstream through a screen of alders, pushed aside a young cedar, and showed her the bridge he had made by felling a tree. He had lashed another to it to make a bridge, high enough to avoid the spring tides, and had flattened them with his axe to make it safe. He would never forget his plunge into the icy waters this spring.

He crossed, and she followed. They stopped at the edge of the clearing, and she let her pack drop to the ground, looking around at the homestead.

"Do you like it?" he asked, almost fearfully.

She said nothing, just took it all in. He put down his pack, and gently took her hand. She moved to lean against him, and the two of them stood looking across the clearing at what would now be their new home

A thousand joys mingled in his mind and in his heart. How on earth did God ever bring him to such a happy day? A home, and now a wife.

Had he remained in England, he might have spent decades to get this far. All day as they had walked together along the trail, he had marvelled at this wife — someone he could truly love who in her blood carried thousands of years of this land and its nature. If he could divine her feelings at all, she did love him back, too. He knew the next few days would bring a raft of changes, a plethora of problems. But somehow, he felt optimistic that they would conquer them all.

Leaving their sacks behind them, they walked over to the cabin. As she was about to step in, he stopped her.

"An English custom, madame!"

She frowned, and looked at him.

He swept her off her feet in a grand gesture, surprised at how light her body was in his arms. "Trust me." He stepped up onto the flattened log he'd put down as a door stoop and carried her into her new home.

He put her down. She smiled, and then turned to look into the gloom, as her pupils adjusted to the interior.

"Do you like it?" he asked, after a bit.

She nodded tentatively. Then she stepped out to circle the logs, inspecting the four ends, and checking the moss he had stogged in the cracks. She pointed to the roof. "I will stitch this birchbark. My first job."

She came in again. He hadn't moved. She went to the back wall, checked under the eaves, saw a mouse nest and pointed. He smiled. In the walls of the cabin, he had drilled holes and placed pegs, whittled from cedar. Then she knelt by the hearth he had laid for their indoor fires and smoothed her hand over the brook stones, flat stones, red and earthen grey, stones that had been washed by a thousand springs and frozen by a thousand winters. Then she sat back, thinking.

Thomas went to sit in the open doorway, looking out. She joined him on the stoop. He absorbed each detail of the forest in the approaching dusk. The moss on the trunks of the maple trees, the bare bushes, the tall pillars of birch, some in bud, across the brook. The sound of the brook surrounded them, as it would as long as they lived here. Such a comfort he thought. After a time of silence, he felt her touch.

"Food," she said. "We must eat. Can you start a fire?"

"Oh yes. *Welàgewei.*"

"Supper," she echoed, and smiled. Their first meal in their new home.

Impulsively she hugged him, and then they kissed, a deep long kiss of happiness and peace.

They ate their supper silently, Thomas savouring every bite in a glow of intense happiness. He kept studying Little Birch's face as she ate shyly, looking into the fire. Was she thinking of the night that was fast dropping upon them? Was she wondering how it might all go? Had she not heard stories among the women, of their nuptial bed and what it might be like? Might she be afraid?

He studied her face, so archetypal, all the planes and features in tune. Her black hair fell in waves (he had asked her to let it down), a frame for the perfection below. Her lanky body, in an almost angular frame, still seemed so intrinsically feminine. To possess such a creature was beyond all comprehending — unbearably exciting, considering what was fast approaching.

She looked up. "Home." She nodded slightly. "Different."

"Yours, now," he replied. "And my heart too. All yours."

She looked down. Not used to such demonstrations of affection, he imagined, she didn't know how to take it. He'd have to be more careful.

She gathered the wooden dishes and mugs together, took them outside to clean in the brook water. He stayed in and set about preparing a better bed for their first night in each other's arms. He cut fresh cedar boughs, which scented the cabin with a delicious evergreen smell. Next came moss, and then the bearskin to cover it all. A rabbit-skin blanket would be all they'd need over them tonight, he thought, with the door shut, and no wind.

Dusk began to settle and it was getting cold, but Little Birch was adamant that they make safe their only store of meat, the portion of moose the band had given them. She took him up the brook, and selected a fine poplar from which to stretch a line across to another. In the centre she hung the stash, to prevent animals getting to it.

"Why so far away?"

"Animals, they always smell this, they always come, we don't want them around our cabin. This for us, that for them."

"Fine by me, Magwés."

He climbed down and saw that she stood, rather uncertainly, waiting. He went across and took her hand in his and put it to his mouth. He pressed his lips against her fingers, trying to say with his eyes: it will be wonderful.

Then, with her hand still in his, he led her into the cabin and closed the door.

* * *

The low flame of a tallow wick on the floor softened all reality, creating the mood he wanted. Avoiding any swift motion, as though she were a doe, easily frightened, he removed his jacket, and then his woollen shirt, and finally his undershirt. Unbuckling his belt, he let his leather chaps fall to the floor.

Keeping her eyes on the floor, she made no move. Thomas stepped forward, began gently to unlace her bodice. She shook her head and then, promptly and efficiently, got out of her clothes and folded them neatly aside. At last, she looked up at him. Naked, they stood facing each other.

His eyes began to rove her exquisite body, every feature so perfect, when to avoid that, she stepped close, and pressed her body against his. Almost at once a crazed passion seemed to envelope them both, and his arms went round her.

He began kissing her cheeks, her neck, smoothing her wild black locks, as she began to explore him too, her tiny fingers moving down onto his manhood, caressing it, as she kept pressing her lips against his. They melted onto the bearskin and inexperienced though they were, began to make the finest love, Thomas was sure, ever seen or felt anywhere on earth.

When the moment came to enter her, his body begged for completion but he restrained himself, becoming tender and gentle, moving all the while as she accepted him into herself with building ecstasy. As the two became one, he felt he was embracing the embodiment of all natural things, all creatures born that inhabited this wilderness world, she was for him every brook and shimmering wave and churning rapid, the brilliant stars and shafts of sunlight, as the two of them moved in great waves on the bearskin covering. She was the happiness bird, the wolves and caribou, big game and small game, all the landscape of this wide sprawling New World, and for her part, she accepted him as her new partner, explorer and adventurer, a mystical embrace, man coming from the sunrise and woman facing sunrise, in a song of the earth, a union that bore so much promise.

Chapter Twenty-Three

Two mornings later, Thomas got up at dawn, making as always the most of every daylight hour. The May air was crisp but not too cold. He let Little Birch take her own time getting up and began to saunter back to the trail, after he had relieved himself. Why not check on their store of meat, he thought, guided by some premonition. The snow had all but departed now; this was his second year in the New World. How much he'd learned, he said to himself, when suddenly, he heard what sounded like the scrape of claws.

The hairs rose on his neck. He drew the knife from its sheath which now, like a Micmac, he always carried. Blood pumping, he stood listening. Then he inched forward, placing his feet like a member of the tribe, one after another carefully over the branch strewn ground. Then he saw it — up the tree where his moose hung, a tawny colour.

Could that be a lion? Not here for sure. But the body, he estimated, must be at least four feet in length. He crept closer. A cougar? Maybe, but they lived back in the interior, like the one that killed the Micmac hunter and his son. Inching up, he saw it was playing with the rope above the dried moose. Ferociously hungry, poor thing, Thomas surmised. What to do? Yell and frighten it off? Run back for his gun?

Then behind him, he heard a distinct mewing. Kittens? He turned. Her litter. Three cougar kittens feeling sorry for themselves, now that Mum was not around, and complaining loudly. Oh-oh, he had placed himself between her and her kittens. Not good!

He drew back, and as he turned to run, the kittens saw him and mewed louder and started spitting. Go fast! He tore past the kittens, who shrank back. He caught a glimpse of the cougar hitting the ground under the tree and bounding after him.

He turned to face her, and thrust his arms out, stiff, the knife clutched dead ahead. He let out a wild war-hoop as the leaping cougar flew through the air. His knife caught her in the neck.

The yowl gurgled in her throat as her claws tore at his arms and neck. Her blood mingled with his, as she jack-knifed away to snarl and spit at this foreign object stuck in her throat. He managed to roll aside, but then she came at him again, blood streaming from her neck.

Weakly he braced for her next onslaught. But the knife had done its job. She was done for.

But so am I, he realized. Dazed, he tried to staunch the flow of blood spurting from his right arm where her claws had shredded it, and from his neck and side.

The kittens ran off into the bushes, frightened by the thrashing death throes of their mother. Those kittens... He almost felt like kneeling in prayer by her writhing body, but she was snarling, blood gurgling out of her throat as she tumbled over and over. He lifted his eyes to Niskam. "I'm sorry, I'm so sorry..."

Finally, she lay twitching on the pine-needled moss.

He became aware of the warm liquid running down his

left side. He felt his neck with his hand, and then saw from his arm his blood pulsing out in spurts.

"Thomas! Are you all right?" Little Birch came running up, calling his name. She stopped dead, aghast. "Thomas!" she screamed, and ran to him.

"My arm."

"Yes yes, I can see." She knelt quickly, pressed her thumb next to the slash to stop the flow. "And your neck. Press there." She put his hand on the flap of skin where more blood was issuing. He pressed, though he now was feeling faint.

"Try to walk. We must get back to the cabin. I have my things..."

Thomas nodded and tried to get up, holding his neck, while she clasped his arm. They staggered down the path, her holding him up with surprising strength. He made his feet cover the ground as fast as he could.

"It's stopped a bit," she encouraged.

"But for how long?" What a fine mess, he thought, bleeding to death just when everything was perfect. Ironic! This day of all days, the start of his married life.

He was losing consciousness. Hurry, he said, and let the hand drop from his neck.

Awkwardly they made it to the cabin when he started to black out. She helped him down onto some leaves. "Do not let go." She placed his hand on the neck again. "Hold your arm here, with hand. Press. Press hard. I get pack."

Alone for a moment, he could see that no matter how good it was to make life, it was still so easy to lose it. It had taken him a full year to get this far, and in a few seconds, that mother cougar might well end it all.

Little Birch came to crouch beside him. She set to work with a strip of moose hide and a stick to tie a tourniquet round his arm above the wound. She placed a pad under the strip over the artery, which effectively shut off the bleeding for the time being.

She wiped the blood off his other cuts as best she could, and then settled herself with a precious bone needle and fine tendon. "I will stitch this." She set to work on the flap of skin that had opened on his neck and from which more blood ran. But first, she took from her bag some tiny dried leaves. "Chew these." A soporific? Thomas stuffed them in his mouth and chewed hard. The pain did lessen.

Thomas succeeded in stifling what would have normally been cries of pain as the needle thrust somewhat roughly into his tender neck flesh. He looked down at the cut on his arm. In spite of the tourniquet, it kept leaking blood.

When she had finished stitching his neck, she tied a bandage round it and inspected his arm. *"Gesipemgewei,"* she mumbled to herself. But Thomas heard, and knew what it meant: very sick indeed.

The prognosis was not good. Damn, who'd have believed it? He sank back, and left himself in the hands of the Good Lord, and of course hers. His thoughts spun round and he felt weak. Was he delirious? He thought of the kittens, who would now surely starve. Maybe they should go find them? If only... If only he got through this. Alive.

"Your neck is better, I think. Most bleeding stopped. But blood still runs down your arm, when we loosen the tourniquet." She sat back, clearly worried. She had reached an impasse.

"Cauterize," Thomas murmured weakly.

"What is that?"

"Burn the cut."

"Burn? How?"

"My knife. It's steel. Make it red hot. In the fire. Then put on cut. Stops blood."

"Oh. I have heard, yes."

Quickly, she put kindling on the fire, and rose. "I come back." She took off fast up the brook.

No idea, Thomas thought in a haze, that she was such a good healer. So much to learn about her. If I live to find out.

She came back from the dead cougar in what seemed a flash with his knife, which she thrust into the building flames.

He turned his head, saw his knife in the fire, and tried to get his brain around what was about to happen. He'd seen surgeons on naval ships cauterize wounds in battle. He'd heard the screams. How would he stand the pain? Not so much the pain, he worried how he'd stop himself from screaming over and over, when that red hot knife pressed into his open wound. Indians did not cry out. Stoic, they bore all sorts of pain without complaint.

What would she think of him? His screaming would be involuntary, something he just could not control. And would burning the wound actually staunch the blood, save his life? What if it did not work?

Fainting, he called, "Magwés." Again a bit louder, "Magwés."

She turned. Thomas gestured. She came and knelt.

"I am afraid," he whispered. "I know I will scream. I won't be able to stop."

She looked at him, in pain herself, but her mind worked fast.

"I am not an Indian, Magwés, I will cry like a baby." In spite of himself, tears came into his eyes. "You will lose respect."

Little Birch rose. "I must go. Find plant. And Thomas, you are never coward. You killed moose. All the band knows this. They respect you."

"But Magwés..."

She spoke the words which he longed to hear and which soothed his rattled brain: "Whatever happens, I will never, never leave you."

Thomas watched her go off. What herb was she looking for, what native medicine, and what could it do? He turned his head back, and watched the tops of the leafy trees above him. Curious moment in his life, he thought: this could be the end. He might live no more. Did those plants above know what he was about to go through? Would these branches continue to wave for a month, for years, for generations, here in this leafy spot? Would other generations of young men like himself, come across the Atlantic to make a new life for themselves? Would many things be invented — how recently had they discovered the power loom, the cotton gin, even a steam locomotive for a railway. What might the future bring to them both. But a future he might never see. And in such a way, he forced his mind from his plight and onto more prescient thoughts, waiting for the worst to happen. But she would be searing his flesh for his own good, to keep him going, keep him strong and well. Quite an initiation.

He prayed out loud: "Dear God, help me through this.

Be near me at my hour of need. Protect me from cowardice. Give me strength to be a man, to be an Indian, for they are the strongest, help me be like them. Help me, Lord."

With a piece of hide, Little Birch covered the handle of the knife whose blade glowed red, and came forward. She gave Thomas another type of leaf, and motioned for him to stuff it in his mouth, with chewing motions.

He did so, chewing vigorously.

She then gave him some leather, and said, "Open your mouth, hold in your teeth, and bite hard."

Oh Lord, thought Thomas, hold this tight with my teeth? Before he could think, he popped the evil-tasting ball of hide into his mouth, and at that moment, he was stricken with the most unimaginable electrifying pain shooting through his whole body as the glowing knife pressed into the open wound. He stiffened as though struck by a jolt of lightning and opened his mouth, but thanks to some godlike intervention, no sound came out as he writhed in torment and then the pain pierced his very existence so that he blacked out.

***

The next morning lying under their rabbit skins together in his cabin, Thomas awoke. He was conscious of his neck being stiff, which he attributed to his spasms of pain last night more than to his arm that hurt, yes, but not unbearably.

The morning chorus of birds surrounded the camp, as though they were all so pleased to be here on the Gaspé

Coast, the bright New World which Thomas had taken on as his personal challenge. Each one seemed to be rejoicing in the rise of the sun. He imagined the Micmac camp: a few of them would be up and about, the women going for water down at the river, little boys sleepily stretching, the Elders coming out for a smoke on the two logs while awaiting food. A great happy family no doubt, quite unlike the hustle and bustle of the manor house, where everyone moved obediently at their appointed tasks under the watchful eyes of layers of authority. So yes, he realized, he had become very accepting of his tribe, however primitive they had at first appeared to his Old World eyes.

Even the happiness bird he could hear this morning, calling out to him: happiness, happiness, happiness — and he *was* happy, knowing that the major pain had passed, the bleeding was stopped, and he would recover.

She stirred beside him, and her eyes flew open. "You all right?"

"Yes, Magwés, more than all right."

She leaned over and kissed him tenderly.

"You saved my life. Again."

She rose to a sitting position. "You will get better now."

"But Magwés," he mumbled, "how did you stop the blood from that gash on my back?"

"I shut the little pipe."

"You mean, the artery?"

"Yes, I took tendon from leg of moose," she reached in her medicine pouch to show him, "you must first grind tendon, there is a little covering—"

"A sheath, sort of?"

She shrugged. "Well, you grind, and it comes very fine, for sewing."

"You did?"

"My grandmother did this, but she showed me. You tie it around little tube. It stops blood."

"You mean I'll wander around with a chunk of moose tendon in me?"

She giggled. "No, Thomas, the body, it makes the tendon," she gestured, "part of body, your body, like new, it goes away."

"The tendon gets absorbed?" Thomas could hardly believe his ears. If only the surgeons on ships knew about that, they wouldn't have to use the thread that sailors found often irritated them long after the wounds had healed. She was clamping an artery shut better than any ship's surgeon. Amazing how these "bloody savages" could devise their own healing methods, far from any so-called civilization. "Magwés, you're a miracle."

She smiled. "Maybe. But I learn so much from you, from watching you, seeing what you plan here to build for us."

Later, they discussed this mysterious appearance of the cougar, so rarely seen this close to the actual coast. The tribe's shaman would claim the spirit of Burn had come back in this form. She smiled when she said it. Tough young lady, thought Thomas. He preferred to think that the mother cat had been hungry this spring and was after their store of moose. Then, afraid for her three kittens, she had attacked him. Oh yes, those kittens: *"Gajueijíj,"* Thomas asked, "kittens" in Micmac, "What about her litter?"

"Very tender," she said, a word of approbation he had used after their better winter meals. "We will have one for lunch today."

227

What a thought! Hard to take. But then, this was a hard land, you had to be tough to make it; no place for sentimentality. Kittens could be loved in the Old Country, where people had carved out a living for millennia. But here (no pets save for the odd dog) survival came first — just hard work, hard caring for each other. He felt confident that, with this tough new partner, they would make it together, against all odds.

Chapter Twenty-Four

Two weeks later, Thomas leaned back against the wall of their cabin, almost healed "This will be perfect next winter, I just feel it."

Little Birch looked at him. "It is perfect..." She frowned. "But next winter? Next winter we go with the band, no?"

"Well... I thought we should stay here." Thomas realized he had yet to reveal his vision of their life together, it had been so real to him, he'd felt she knew it already. Obviously not. Had the time come to explain it?

In fact, the new joy of being together, working together, and with time for play too, had filled their days. Little Birch found a new freedom, she had told him. Micmacs were fun-loving, enjoying laughter and games, but somehow women in the band always had more responsibilities than leisure. Although Little Birch now worked harder than ever, she felt so much freer somehow, finding that idea hard to translate, for in Micmac there was no such concept. Their whole lives, in a sense, were free.

Stitching the birchbark roof, making meals, preparing hides, helping him drag logs, decorating a shirt for him, she had been working tirelessly, and seemingly happily. She checked his arm regularly, making sure, by means of the herbs she knew, that it healed well.

And he had begun to feel his old self again. Moving slowly at first, he had finished up clearing space around the cabin, then cut wood into small lengths and stacked it for next winter's fires, fished, snared, worked at fixing up the cabin interior, and then had begun in earnest to explore this new territory of his.

"You see, Little Birch, I don't want you to go through another winter like that again. We must prepare more to be like settlers, living the way they live, and farming."

She said nothing, just looked down.

"Is that wrong?"

She shook her head. "But you know what we call this brook."

"No. It has a name?"

"Every brook and every hill we have given a name."

"So what is this?"

"Shegouac."

Thomas frowned. "But that means, empty."

She nodded. "Well, it means not much game. And so, not good to stay for winter."

"And you knew this all along?"

"Yes."

"But you didn't tell me."

"You like this place. You like your brook."

"But...

"Not woman's place to speak things. And I like it now."

Thomas nodded. He knew better than to start an argument. But that night, he realized, she might be dead right. For the time being.

So what would they do this winter? He was determined not to let her go through all that again. And he certainly didn't want to face it.

"Maybe we will soon begin to farm," he said. "Like real settlers."

"Yes."

"We can plant some corn between the trees. Wheat, maybe. I can clear more land."

"Down here? But Thomas, this land is wet. No sun morning and late day. Many small brooks. This land maybe not right for farm, to me…"

She was right. The Hollow, as Thomas now called it, did tend to be swampy. One area, probably a couple of acres, where the valley widened between the cabin and the brook's mouth, was flat and, looking far ahead, Thomas could see that the land would be arable. But hardly the place to make the magnificent farm he envisioned. So perhaps she was right.

***

A few days later, he came back from exploring to find Little Birch sitting in the sun in front of the cabin, working over some hare pelts she was cutting into strips, about an inch wide, and twisting them into a furry rope. From that, she would likely make a coat, or a small blanket.

"I have an idea, Magwés," he said. "Come."

She rose obediently and followed him up the west bank of the Hollow and out along its lip toward the sea. He brought her to a high point where, through a screen of new leaves, they could see blue waters about five hundred yards ahead. Before them, the hill sloped sharply down to a flat area that ran level to the cliffs. Up here, a great vantage point, Thomas thought.

"What about up here for our location? To build our real house? It's a great vantage point."

She looked at him in surprise. "We do not need a 'real' house. Our home is bigger than the Chief's wigwam. It is enough."

"Suppose we have a family?"

"Suppose?"

"Well, if we have a family, that means we will need more space. Bedrooms."

"Bedrooms? Don't settlers sleep where the fire is?" She shook her head. "You will have to explain all that."

He would have to, he could see that now. "And we will need a barn, for animals." So much to explain.

"I see." She frowned slightly, and then moved away from him, making her way down the slope towards the flat area.

From the way Little Birch was checking the ground, sensing the trees, the growth, and looking about, Thomas began to wonder, why make the house up here? He followed her down, and they met at the foot of the hill.

"This is better for your special house, Thomas, more sheltered from north wind."

"But the view..."

"We will have a view here. When you cut those trees."

He saw the wisdom of her remarks. The area she had selected was indeed level as it spread towards the cliffs and also westward, which he had explored. Room for a barn, and four or five acres in front for an eventual garden, with acreage to spare for feed and animals. The ground seemed fertile; lots of sun, once it was cleared. He could claim four or five acres westward, then run his property line back, even a mile or more, past the west fork of the brook. Good water for cattle back there and down in the Hollow. Lots of woodland and pastureland, which one day he would clear.

"You are right, Little Birch. It's good here." He turned to her, eyes shining. "You are just wonderful."

"No Thomas, you are amazing, you have many ideas. I just help you."

On these trips of exploration, Thomas preferred bringing Little Birch, who knew the forests and plants. She found berries and roots to eat, herbs for healing, all of which had Micmac names, not much help to Thomas, but he tried to memorize what they looked like.

"And you don't want to hunt with the band this winter?" she asked.

Thomas shook his head.

"It was hard, but not all winters are so hard," she said.

"Little Birch, my customs are different, I want you safe in a warm house, no fear of hunger, I want to keep you warm and our baby warm, by a fire we have filled with wood; I want us to have a settler's life, with our own land, and our barn full of animals. We can still hunt and fish and snare, and build a canoe, we will even fish in the ocean too, of course, but I want to stay in one house all year, winter and summer. We shall grow food between the trees, and when they are cut down, we shall plough and plant crops, and work with oxen, and our children will help us."

He could go on and on, he had developed such a strong vision, and the more he spoke, the more he wanted to speak, and the more Little Birch got caught up as she tried to visualize it.

"All right, Thomas," she said at last. "I trust you. If you

want to make your farm and you want your life this way, I will help."

And he took her and wrapped his arms around her, and clung to her as though she were life itself.

Chapter Twenty-Five

At midday a few days later, Thomas was up at his new house site clearing brush and cutting trees, when he heard a call from Little Birch down by the brook's mouth. It sounded urgent. Worried, he grabbed his axe and set off at a trot down the rough trail that dropped steeply to the broad brook's mouth.

He pulled up short. A long war canoe had beached with what looked like a form lying in the centre.

Tongue was conversing with Little Birch. She turned as she saw Thomas and hurried over. "Our Chief is sick. His stomach. They brought him here."

The band's four best paddlers stood by the waiting canoe. In its centre Thomas could see the Chief, lying on skins. They were hoping, Little Birch explained, that Thomas with his knowledge of white man's ways, might know what to do.

"Here? Now?"

"Yes, you must look at him." She went on to describe some preliminary symptoms.

"Magwés, they don't need me, they need a surgeon. If your *Buowin* cannot cure him, they'd better take him to Paspébiac."

"But Thomas, no one listens to natives. We need a white man."

"You mean, they want me to go with him to Paspébiac?"

"If he must go, then you must go. I will come too."

Thomas paused, frowning. He wondered how safe it would be? But no time to waste! "Wait here."

He set off for the cabin, only to find her trotting beside him. He would get some things, but so would she. On the way, Little Birch explained that the *Buowin*, their healer, had done all he could to no great effect. The Chief, known to be exceptionally stoic, nevertheless evinced great pain. When Thomas arrived, he grabbed his pouch and, on a hunch, his golden guinea. When she was ready, they trotted back down the path.

The paddlers pushed off and forced a pace towards Paspébiac. Thomas began by questioning the Chief through Little Birch, who had become a better translator than Tongue. Before long, Thomas decided that his sickness was what befell a cousin of the Earl of Darlington: gall stones. Thomas knew the gall bladder could get infected, and eventually kill. It required an operation, and one that certainly only the most experienced surgeon could perform.

He explained all that to Tongue and Little Birch. They passed this on to the Chief as the Micmacs paddled on, in precise and beautiful rhythm. With the east wind behind them, they made exceptional time. Thomas soon spotted the point where they had landed on their last trip one year ago. But this time, they headed right out past — and into the full view of a British man o'war. Three masts, square sails, and this time, yes, his own *Billy Ruffian*.

He froze. "Magwés, that's my ship! It must have come back from Europe this summer." Long forgotten images of Wicked Wickett swarmed all over him, icing down his spine and chilling his heart.

"Oh no!" She knew about her husband's desertion and what punishment it could bring: one thousand lashes on each of ten ships of the line. Very little left of his body after that. His soul would have long departed.

What should Thomas do? He tried to collect his thoughts as they paddled around the spit of land to the jetty on the west. His nemesis being back had not crossed his mind, occupied as he was with the Chief and Little Birch. Would Jonas Wickett have already come ashore to search for traces of him hereabouts? But he would have to find a surgeon fast.

Better chance it and go straight to Monsieur Huard. Ask his advice, even though he'd be sure to get reprimanded for not passing on his whereabouts, and not accepting that shipbuilding proposal for him to work here this spring.

She looked round at him, gesturing: what should we do?

"Keep going," he said, and she frowned. "The Chief comes first."

They pulled up at the jetty and the paddlers moved the Chief quickly onto it, laying him under canvas on soft bags of flour awaiting transfer to the *Bellerophon*.

Thomas checked, and saw no signs of any redcoated marines. He set off for the administration office to ask M. Huard's help. When he entered, he found no one but a young assistant. "Where's Monsieur Huard?"

"Who is asking for him?" the youth demanded bluntly, with an odd French accent. From Jersey, Thomas imagined. Clearly, Thomas with his beard and odd Micmac outfit was not someone this young man wanted to deal with at all.

"Thomas Manning, at your service," he replied smartly, but then paused. How could he get his request across to this idiot?

Just then the inner door opened, and M. Huard came out. "Well well, look who's here!"

"Bonjour, M'sieur." Thomas doffed his hat.

"Ah, so, I thought it might be you, Thomas," which he pronounced in the French way: *Tomah.* "I have heard something about you and your Micmac friends."

"You did?" He wondered how that news could have reached him.

"News gets around on the coast, as you will discover. Now may I ask why you did not come work for me this spring?"

Thomas hung his head. "Forgive me, *M'sieur,* I have been unmannerly. But I have come now on a matter of some urgency. I shall be pleased to inform you of everything, but later on."

"And how can I help, young man?"

"By finding me your best surgeon here."

"Surgeon? We have only one, and he left last week on a schooner for Jersey. His replacement is due any day."

"No surgeon?" Thomas was stunned. An eventuality he'd not dreamed of.

"We have a woman; she claims to be nurse."

"No good, we need a surgeon, a real surgeon." Thomas walked back and forth in the office, like a man possessed. "We've got to do something. I have a Micmac man, the Chief in fact, out on the jetty and his life is in danger."

M. Huard shrugged. "I'm sorry, but what can I do?"

"I see." Now what next?

"Well, my boy, I do know where there would be a surgeon..."

"Yes?"

"On the *Bellerophon*."

Thomas turned pale. True. He'd forgotten. There would be one on the *Bellerophon*, and a very good one.

"Thank you, thank you very much." Thomas tipped his hat. He turned and hurried out of the office, trying to decide what to do now.

Little Birch saw him coming and ran up to him.

"No surgeon here," he said.

She looked crestfallen.

"But..."

"Yes?"

"There is one on the *Billy Ruffian* — on the man o'war out there."

"But that's..." Little Birch looked at him with pleading and frightened eyes. "You cannot go there, Thomas. You cannot."

He looked around helplessly. "No, for sure I cannot. But perhaps *you* could. You could bring the Chief out to the ship. You speak excellent English."

She looked at him as if he had gone crazy. "Me? A Micmac girl? They will catch me and take me away. They will not listen. You know that!"

"Bring Tongue with you."

"He's native too. They will capture both of us as prizes."

Also possible, he knew, with the attitude of those sailors to the "poor ignorant savages and their squaws." One so pretty as Little Birch, well, it didn't take much imagination to know what might happen.

But there was no time to lose.

He stood, undecided. All at once, he leapt into the canoe. "Take me to the ship!"

"No, Thomas!" Little Birch called from the jetty.

He waved back. "They might not recognize me. It's worth a chance. You stay here." As they paddled swiftly, he told himself, "Just don't think. You are doing the only right thing. Just go. And trust in God."

In four minutes they had arrived at the ship to be greeted by an astonished group of seaman, and one young Midshipman, new this year Thomas guessed. But no sign of Wickett.

Thomas called up, "Ahoy! May we see your surgeon, please? We have a sick man. Without immediate attention, he will die."

The Midshipman ran off. So now Wickett would be the next face he'd see — and Wickett would know him anywhere, no matter how different he looked. He waited apprehensively in the canoe floating beside the hull looming above. Fortunately, the sea was calm.

Soon the surgeon arrived and Captain Edward Hawker with him. They looked down.

"Surgeon, sir, we desire your help." As soon as Thomas began to speak, the surgeon, whom Thomas knew and had not overly liked, leaned close to his Captain and whispered. The Captain stared, as Thomas went on, "An Indian Chief must have an operation at once. Would you mind if we brought him on board to your surgery?"

Thomas caught the Captain's look of alarm. Yes, he did appear odd in his Indian garb, with long hair and a beard, but there was no doubting it: the Captain knew him as last year's deserter.

The surgeon turned to the Captain. "I believe a fee would be necessary for me to perform this outside the line of duty?"

The Captain nodded.

"So that's it, I'm afraid," the surgeon said gruffly. He turned away.

"A fee?" Thomas reached in his pocket. "Would this golden guinea suffice?"

The surgeon stared, then stepped back from the rail to speak with the Captain.

He reappeared moments later. "Very well. Bring him on board."

While a ladder was being let down, Thomas turned to see the marines' longboat rowing around the bow and coming right at them, pinning them against the hull. The marine Sargent stepped up and pointed to Thomas. "I arrest you in the name of His Majesty King George. Will you please step into the longboat, sir."

The four Micmac rose, unsheathing knives. One lifted his bow.

The marines raised their muskets.

Thomas calmed his friends. "No, I must go." He handed the coin to Tongue. "This is one guinea. When the surgeon is finished and the Chief is brought back and put in his canoe, give it to him. Not before."

Tongue nodded, staring at the gold glinting in the sun. The Chief had returned it to Thomas, and now it was going to save his life.

Thomas stepped into the longboat, knowing full well the punishment that lay ahead.

***

Thomas sat on a small stool in the dark brig, a bucket for slops at his side. Had he done the right thing? Where on earth was Wickett? Gloating in his quarters, probably. What about Little Birch now? What about his newly built cabin? She'd have need of it, or would she go back to her band? Of course. And his mother? And the good Marquis? He determined he would ask for a pen and paper, so that he might write to them, send them one last message.

He had been held here since noon, and now he sensed it must be night, for sounds on the ship had quietened. From experience, he knew punishments were administered at eleven o'clock before the noon meal. They mustered the whole ship and made the men watch.

He was glad, somehow, that he'd made it through the cauterization. There was every chance he would pass out before the worst of the pain. But he also knew they threw buckets of cold water over you to keep you awake. British Justice again. A devastating message to would-be deserters, he supposed. But still some did jump ship to seek new lives.

He wondered, when he died, if they would just throw him overboard? Or would they give his beaten remains a decent Christian burial? Well, he was in God's hands, and he devoutly offered himself up to his Maker as an all too human sacrifice.

Maybe if he got more paper, he might write Little Birch too. Someone might translate it, if not now, in a year or two. He wished he had also taught her to read. But perhaps a note would just make the wound of his death more painful. So he couldn't decide whether he should write to her or no. In the great despair that was settling on him, he could make no sense of any decision.

In a kind of torpor, he drifted off, only to be awakened by the brig door clanging open. No it can't be! Give me another hour, two or three hours, to have time to write, and... And then, he sighed and thought, perhaps the sooner the better.

It was the Captain.

Thomas struggled to his feet. "I'm sorry, sir," he began. "I have all my life wanted to live in the New World. To die if necessary, for a life of freedom."

The Captain nodded. "Well, my lad, the operation on that savage was a success. His life has been saved, and they've been sent off with proper instructions how to care for him." In the dim light of a low lantern that the Captain carried, Thomas watched his face take on a perplexed look. "You knew what would happen, and yet you still came." He shook his head wearily.

"Yes sir." Well, Thomas thought to himself, at least it's been worth it. "I did not doubt for a moment that our surgeon (whom Thomas knew as surly but an excellent practitioner) would save the Chief's life." He supposed that this made his punishment a bit more endurable, knowing Little Birch and her band would again have their finest hunter and leader. He went on, "I can only say I am heartily sorry for any disrepute I may have brought upon our vessel by leaving it."

The Captain nodded, and reached out to touch his arm. He coughed, and said, "Your Marquis, once he had received your letter, wrote me inquiring of the details of your misdeed. On my reply, he was kind enough to send by messenger a handsome recompense for all our difficulties. Very handsome, I must say. I did not know him

previously, but he is a man of distinction, with many con-
nections..." The captain paused and looked at Thomas,
seemingly trying to figure out how and why these strange
circumstances had come to pass. "He appeared thankful
for my having delivered you more or less safely into this
terrible wilderness, which apparently for years you have
yearned for, and which you now so obviously enjoy."

Thomas stood as one dead, at the same time surprised
at the largesse of his mentor, giving all that money.

"I did try to stop those marines coming to apprehend
you just now—" Thomas lifted his head. What was he
saying? "—but they fall, as you know, under another ju-
risdiction."

"Thank you very much, sir."

Captain Hawker heaved a sigh, and pondered. "Young
Thomas, I do believe you have reached the level of self-
sacrifice where His Majesty would largely approve, although he might not wholly approve of the object of your
largesse." Meaning the humble savage? Thomas thought.
Well, fie on him.

"I for one am pleased to have known a young man who
would willingly sacrifice his life for another. I am even
proud, yes, I do believe I am, that you have, for a time,
served under me. Though I'm not sure Wickett would
have agreed."

Thomas looked up, and frowned. Past tense?

"I managed to have him leave the ship in Portsmouth,
on our call there. I doubt he'll cause more damage to His
Majesty's Fleet." He gave Thomas a meaningful look. So
the Captain had known all along what was going on.
Well, of course, it was his business to know.

Thomas watched him carefully, hanging onto every word.

"So now my advice would be, you should move rather quickly."

"Move, sir? Quickly?" What was he saying?

"The reward that came my way, to be shared with my Admiral, has largely wiped out your misdeed. The Major of marines overstepped himself, as he does only too often. So now, lest I cause a mutiny, I am leaving you in the hands of two sturdy crew members. If they decide to row you ashore under the cover of night, what can I do about it? Your escape may be blamed on many things."

Escape? He's letting me escape? Thomas could hardly believe his luck.

"You see, I can divulge that your lord Marquis took the liberty of writing to the admiralty. On my next voyage, the rumour is that I might possibly be elevated to Commodore, due in no small part to my having helped you. So I now return the compliment. Go ashore a free man. But please, do take care to keep out of sight of His Majesty's Royal Marines." He reached out to shake the hand of his former Midshipman. "I am sure you will continue to lead a full and righteous life here in the New World. Good luck."

Chapter Twenty-Six

Paddling back to his brook in the canoe with the Chief, Thomas reflected on that unexpected outcome. The Good Lord had blessed him again. And happily, the Chief was improving. Little Birch had wasted no time after the operation in explaining to the Chief and his paddlers the nature of the punishment Thomas had faced. His reputation grew enormously, as a result.

Thomas, momentarily at peace with himself and with the world, tried to avoid looking ahead. Here and now, the Gaspé sun was glistening off the waves, and the cormorants and gulls were screaming their anguish at the intruders. His money could not have been put to better use, and although now there would be no safety net for the future, he thanked the Lord above that he had at least been instrumental in saving the life of one so important to his tribe.

But look ahead he must. He could winter in the cabin with Little Birch and try to live off fish in the frozen brook. Little Birch thought it was likely, though not sure, that the trout would continue to bite under the ice. Thomas had memories of One Arm fishing in the lake, so did not actually hold out too much hope for that. They could enlarge their own trapline, going farther back along the brook, snaring some of the small animals that must be around. But from what the Micmac had named his brook, Shegouac, empty, and from what he had seen, game was not as plentiful as around other rivers. And the Micmac always headed to the inner plateaus for winter food: he should take heed.

As the canoe thrust through the sea, he remembered the splendid offer that M. Huard had made, before he had left with the Micmac Chief. With the approbation of James Robin, he had offered Thomas a position in the woods. His going out to the man o'war to face certain death to save his friend had been noised about on the *barachois*, and Thomas found himself held an object of admiration.

"I see the way you work with oakum," M. Huard had said. "Why not you work in woods this winter? Four of my best men have leave. I pay you well."

"Well?" Thomas grinned. "I have heard what you pay lumberjacks, M. Huard, and I don't think—"

"Okay, okay, I make for you special price. Maybe I give for you heavy *vêtements* (clothing), too. Usually the men, they pay for dat."

"But I have no tools."

"I give you best tools, you only pay me half."

Thomas had to admit, it was an offer he should think about. Not now, later, when he had time.

And now he had time... Nothing but time. A decision had to be made. Here was a genuine alternative.

But what about Little Birch? Bring her to Paspébiac to live alone while he worked away in the woods? Wives did not go into the lumber camps with the men who themselves were packed into bunkhouses. Rent a room in town? Where, at one of the French settlers'? Would she enjoy being in one room, all winter long, with strangers — not for a second.

Discuss it all with Little Birch? Of course, but after they landed, after they were comfortable again in their routine.

Later as maple trees began to spread their flame across the hills, she resolved this problem neatly. She came up where he was working at the new site, cutting trees. She came over and said, almost shyly. "Thomas, I have some news."

"News? Where, from the band?" He frowned, how could that have happened?

She shook her head. "Just from you and me."

Thomas put down his axe, and mopped his brow. Though the days were definitely colder, his work cutting trees made him sweat. "I'm ready. What news?"

"I think I am making a baby."

"Little Birch!" Thomas was ecstatic. A new life? How much better could it get? He grabbed Little Birch and swung her round and round, laughing, with her joining in. Finally, they fell on the leaves in a tumbled heap.

But his next thought was, Oh Heavens! Winter! Now what?

That night after their chores were done, they sat eating round the fire in the cabin. She had fried tasty brook trout, about six inches long and golden brown, and boiled dandelions and tubers, with some Micmac bread. They washed it all down with wooden mugs of clear water from the icy brook — what more could a man want?

"That means you will have the baby in the spring?"

"Yes, eight more moons." She calculated on her fingers. "Just before the longest day of the year."

So what now? "Should we stay in our cabin for the winter, and risk having enough game?"

She shrugged. "You must decide."

"Oh no, we both decide, Little Birch, we both decide everything. Not the Micmac way, our way. We shall discuss it."

Thomas thought, more than ever, now she needed a good sturdy house, a fire with lots of wood stacked outside, and food for all winter in the larder. But how could he give that? He racked his brains. But try as he might, he could not see a way of making that wish a reality, this year. Soon perhaps. But not right now.

"I think you should be near the *Buowin* this winter. You might need him."

"Thomas, I need nothing." But she did look a bit doubtful. The *Buowin*, he would know what to do if anything happened while she was pregnant.

They discussed the matter until the fire died down, and agreed that perhaps, yes, he should work in the woods and Little Birch go back to her family for the winter. It would be an enormously painful separation, but he had to make money for the years ahead: they needed oxen and supplies; they could not stay locked in a cycle of need, summers at the cabin and winters in the interior, subject to starvation.

"I still don't like it, Little Birch," he said, "I mean, how will you survive? Who would help you and your family survive back in those desolate moose woods?"

"The Chief, he will arrange everything. You saved his life. He will take me and my family with him. Thomas, I am not the first woman to have a baby in our band. He will make sure it is well. He is a great hunter."

That did make a difference, Thomas thought. But he still wondered how he'd bear being separated from her for six long months.

But this was the only possible course of action. And so one day, when the first frost lay down a white sheen upon leaves and grass, the two of them began preparations. Finally, Thomas accompanied his wife back to her band for their winter's hunting.

Chapter Twenty-Seven

Nothing, Thomas swore to himself, could ever be as beautiful as a Gaspé woods in winter. The falling snow covered all the limbs, leaves, trails, and rotting refuse from a long summer. Across this virgin counterpane, the deft tracks of martin and lynx, hare and squirrel and bobcat, could be picked out among the lumberjack's spoon-shaped prints when they moved on snowshoes from the beaten trail into new areas for logging.

The air crackled with crisp light. The high clouds, bundling up as if in comforters against the freezing winds of the Gaspé winter, wandered across the deep blue sky, much deeper blue than summer. Chickadees chattered away with the nuthatches as they searched the icy trunks for bugs and sleeping caterpillars.

Never far from his thoughts was Little Birch, especially when the northern lights danced about the sky. He would lie at night on the straw thrown across the flattened logs of his bunk bed, and remember their first kiss. Although he was still worried about her, he forced himself to focus on the job at hand and prayed she would be all right back there in caribou country with the Chief's family.

The men worked in groups, each pair assigned a long strip where they would fell the trees, limb them, cut them into lengths for skidding by the oxen. The brush they tossed onto piles for later burning. Axe cuts rang through the muffled silence, echoing off the hills around; they worked always within a mile of their simple log bunkhouse. Give me some oakum and I can make this drafty place twice as warm, thought Thomas, or at least, half as cold. The floor was mud, save for a walkway down the centre between the bunks of flattened logs. Their fire sent its smoke up from the small stone circle into a hole in the roof directly above. No, the men were not taken care of quite as M. Huard promised. But Thomas's co-workers, used to this treatment, did not object, apart from cursing every morning as they awoke in subzero interiors to break the ice formed on their washing tubs.

Having to pair off, Thomas joined Marc Blanquart, an able young Frenchman who had been apprenticed to the company three years back, when only fourteen. He had arranged for his out-of-work father to come from France last year; he lived in a small cabin out by the woods in Paspébiac, whittling figurines and model boats that he sold to passing sailors during the summer. Marc's mother had died when he was young, and soon after that, his father had been injured in a mine accident near Lille. Marc's two sisters had been sold into domestic service in France, and Marc apprenticed to the adventuring Robin's clan. He could neither read nor write, as was the case with many of the indentured servants who worked for Robin's.

The bare trees, shorn of leaves, stood in a great silence that seemed to stretch almost back to the beginnings of the earth. Against a crisp icy landscape, pine and spruce added their dark green background to the stark skeletons of maple and spindly birches, all soughing in a wind that often rose to chill the bones and ice the fingers.

At dinner midday when they were far from the bunkhouse, one of the group would break off to coax life into a small fire on which they'd boil a container of tea. As the fire burned, it would sink deeper into the snow, so that after a few days it ended up two or three feet below. Not a lot of heat.

In the evenings, Thomas taught English to Marc and Marc taught him French. Hearing it all day long as well, Thomas was quick to pick it up again. Well, Thomas thought, I'm approaching the wisdom of Tongue, who knows four languages. How radical had been his change in attitude to the "simple savage" of his Navy years. That would be a battle against prejudice he'd fight the rest of his life, he figured.

One day the weekly messenger, who brought them supplies, handed Marc a letter received by Robin's on the last ship to arrive in the autumn. It had gotten mislaid by the administration, but in the end it reached Marc's father, who was now sending it on to Marc. Thomas watched his face as the letter was read to him by the Frenchman who had brought it. It really upset him. A girl? Thomas wondered. Yes, his little sister, in fact, who had been sold as a servant to one of the families in the middle of France. Much against her will, the master had forced himself on her, and now she had found herself pregnant. Once this was out in the open, she had been dismissed. She wanted his help, or that of the father.

What help could they give, he wondered. And what would happen to her, a young pregnant girl out of wedlock, wandering the streets? Marc was tremendously upset, but didn't seem able to share his feelings.

The next day, as the two of them worked at cutting their lot of trees, Thomas could see Marc's output was suffering. But he too, like Marc, felt stifled. Whatever could they do?

"I've got to go," Marc finally volunteered in French. "I cannot stay here longer. They must let me go back."

But as Thomas knew, no ships would ply the bay till spring, another month away. The shores were all iced in and the Gulf of Saint Lawrence was far too hazardous with many icebergs. No ships ever came or left the New World in winter.

And so the two friends, with Thomas comforting Marc as much as he could, struggled on through the long hard winter in this kind of captivity, with no respite from Marc's burning anger.

***

After what seemed to Thomas an everlasting age away from Little Birch, he woke to find that the low overcast clouds had brought forth rain. The snow began to melt. This meant hard slogging through the mush, but it did herald the end of logging. And with that, of course, Marc could make plans to get back to France and try to find his sister. Thomas would see his wife once again. He couldn't wait.

When finally the Robin's company brought the men back in a horse and sleigh to Paspébiac, Marc set about finding a way to leave on the first boat out. Luckily one appeared to be setting off momentarily, having been loaded during the spring breakup.

Marc brought Thomas to meet his father. A thin man whose frame seemed still too large for the wasted flesh that sat upon it, he embodied a life of deprivation born out in his pale, lined features. Most of all, Thomas would not soon forget the look in his eyes: a haunted stare without hope, without cause, a man who would surely himself succumb only too soon to the rigours of pioneer life, struck such a blow as the shame of his daughter.

Thomas forced himself to stay a couple of days with them. The old man was glad of the company, and talked a lot about his daughter. The father determined that he himself would stay, on the off-chance Marc might return with his sister and baby, so that they could all become a proper family. There would be opportunities for the sister to work here, Thomas knew, for many of the immigrants had pasts they did not want evaluated; here a man or woman would be judged only on the kind of work they turned out.

Thomas, with the old man, saw Marc off, a sad day for them both, but they wished him well.

Before Thomas left, M'sieur Blanquart made a point of giving his son's implements to Thomas: axe, saw, his peavy (pivot) and other items, including some clothes, so that now Thomas could dress like a Frenchman and was so much better equipped to clear his land. But he was aching to get back to see Little Birch and prepare for the birth of his new baby.

Marc's father had one friend, a fisherman, who agreed to take the two of them back to Thomas's brook. Having come to terms, in a sense, with His Majesty's Navy, and it being some two years after the actual desertion, Thomas felt secure enough to trust the two old men not to reveal his whereabouts.

After they beached the boat, Thomas led M. Banquart back to the brook to show him round his cabin, while the fisherman waited on the beach and smoked a pipeful. Walking up the now well-trodden trail, Thomas was apprehensive. How had the cabin weathered? Had it been discovered in the winter? Was it intact? He noticed that on the north slopes the snow still lay melting. The flat areas of the Hollow were running with a thousand rivulets from the heavy drifts along the sides. He was pleased that Little Birch had persuaded him to build their "real house" up on the flat land to the west.

As they reached the clearing, they stopped. On the worn face of M. Blanquart, the look of despair broke into pleasure as he saw the homestead. Thomas described his new life and promised that later, he and Little Birch would bring their new baby to see him in Paspébiac. It was almost as if the old man had found another family, and he later left with his fisherman friend greatly cheered.

Thomas was anxious to get down to Port Daniel, but he realized that he would have to do some preliminary cleaning of his cabin site after the long winter. He wanted it in good condition for the arrival of Little Birch.

Having said goodbye to the men, and put in a good afternoon of cleaning up, he fell into his makeshift bed in the cabin. Oddly enough, malevolent projections began to take over his dreams. The ghost of the cougar that had mauled him kept haunting his sleep. Finally one night, half-ghost but also very real, it snatched Thomas's newborn and carried it off in its jaws. In its lair, it began to feed the baby to its kittens, tearing it first into edible pieces. He watched the cubs chewing away on the baby's fingers. The little thumb, chewed, swallowed, now the next finger, while the cougar licked the cubs with a large — in fact, vast — tongue, slobbering over the remains of the baby, and nudging its armless torso toward the cubs. There, as a final gesture, she put one paw on its stomach, and ripped out the tiny guts. Thomas screamed and leapt off his mattress of cedar boughs and hides, panting. No more sleep that night. He stayed, swaying hands to head. Slowly his breathing returned to normal, and he dropped to his knees. He addressed his Maker earnestly, calling upon Him to chase away any returning chimeras. Then he dressed and went out to greet the thin, pale slip of dawn smudging the eastern sky.

* * *

Soon, May ended and he set off for the encampment, knowing his band would be back from the highlands. He longed to see Little Birch with the new life inside her.

He made the journey quickly, and tramped back, circling Port Daniel mountain, upriver into the encampment, heart in his mouth. Suppose something had gone wrong? He had not even let that cross his mind.

Two Micmac girls and a boy saw him and ran up gleefully, chattering excitedly. Would he play with them? He rubbed their little heads and eagerly headed for the wigwam of Full Moon.

He stood outside. "Little Birch?"

He waited, as he heard a rustle inside.

Through the entrance crawled his wife. She stood up awkwardly with her big tummy. And then they both fell into each other's arms, hugging as though there were no tomorrow.

"You're safe."

"Of course. And so are you!"

Several other children had gathered around to watch, and Elders on their conference log turned to smile at the happily wedded couple.

They just spent the rest of the day strolling and talking, while Little Birch happily recounted the many exploits back in caribou country and he the long days without her in the woods. He touched on the shame of Marc's sister, which seemed to make an undue impression on her. Too many omens.

Quite soon afterwards, Thomas was awakened by Little Birch. "I think the baby is coming."

But she had a look in her eyes that worried him. "Is everything all right, Little Birch?"

"Yes, my love, do not worry. All will be well."

Full Moon got up quickly and went to rouse the *Buowin*, the healer. She moved on to the next tent where Sleepy Cedar, the midwife, got up quickly and began to prepare the cloths and hides that she had ready, expecting this birth.

"Help me up, Thomas," Little Birch said.

"My love, you're fine where you are."

"No no, we go into woods."

"You what?" He frowned.

"It is our way: my mother and Sleepy Cedar, we go off to the birthing place of our band, and if we need him, the shaman, the *Buowin*, will come. We will return when the baby is born."

"I cannot go?"

"No, my love, that is not our way. You must stay here. I will be all right."

With some misgivings, Thomas helped Little Birch get up. By low moonlight they made their way to the edge of the clearing, where the little group had assembled.

"We have the place near the stream. All is prepared." Thomas heaved a sigh. He wished he'd known all this before, but yet, what could he have done? "Sleepy Cedar, the midwife, will look after me. If we need him, the *Buowin*, the shaman, will bless us and pray over us. We will be in a sacred place. All will be well."

"You're sure?"

She nodded, looking at him with her large eyes, wanting somehow to communicate something that she herself did not even know.

He forced a bright smile. "Whatever is your tradition, I am happy," he said. "You will have a fine baby. And I will love this baby as I love you."

He saw to his satisfaction that Little Birch smiled. And off she went with the three other women to give birth in their sacred birthing place.

Chapter Twenty-Eight

The sun climbed above and then passed its zenith. Thomas spoke to the Chief: perhaps he should go and see how they were doing? But the Chief gave him to understand he would not be welcome at the sacred birthing place. He must wait here, as was their custom.

He went for a walk, then returned quickly in case they were coming back. The sun began to drop, and finally settled low over the western trees. Thomas started turning in circles. He felt he was going crazy. Why wouldn't they let him see her? "Why is it taking so long? Why?" he kept asking everyone and no one.

He walked aimlessly among the wigwams. The tension building in his head was almost unbearable. "Something's wrong," he said to himself. "I know it, something's wrong."

At one point as the dusk began to settle, he thought he could hear Little Birch calling him. He heard her, he knew he did, and he grabbed One Arm. "I must go." But the Chief shook his head. "Every father like this. You no different," he said in surprising English. So he had been picking up words, thought Thomas, diverted for a moment. But he soon gave himself to his worries again.

Why was it taking so long?

Then suddenly he sensed a commotion. He put down the pipe they had given him to calm him. Two women were coming down the trail. He heard the distinct crying of a baby. His! Yes, his baby! He ran up to them and looked down at the bundle they carried. His child!

He chucked it under the chin, bent and kissed it. It looked perfect. So why were they all so solemn?

"All right? Baby all right?" he repeated in Micmac. Full Moon nodded, tears in her eyes. "Baby good. Healthy boy. Very good." The others nodded. "Baby good."

Then Full Moon gave the boy to the midwife, and turned to go to her wigwam, crying.

"But..." Thomas looked around. The midwife turned to the group that had gathered. She spoke to two young men who set off at a run.

"Where is Little Birch? Is she all right?"

No one would respond.

Before long the two men marched back. In their arms they carried the lifeless body of Little Birch.

Thomas stood like a statue, turned to cold stone. They brought her near. He stared down and then reached out and touched her pallid cheek. Her body was cold.

His beloved Little Birch was gone.

***

Thomas lay as one dead in the wigwam of Full Moon.

His brain teemed with nightmarish thoughts. Little Birch crying and naval floggings and Chiefs who lay dying, and moose killings and cougar attacks and all sorts of dread images. Then, he would be enveloped in a uniform greyness where no thoughts arose, no hope flowered. A dull grey throbbing pain suffused his brain and his whole body.

From time to time Full Moon would shake him and offer food. He would turn away; how could he face life? He didn't want his cabin, he didn't want his brook, he didn't want the New World. He just wanted to die.

Why had the Good Lord done this? What had He intended by this awful death of Little Birch? Thomas had heard from Tongue that she had not felt any pain. The bleeding, it just had not stopped, no matter what any of them did. She had drifted off, calling his name. Yes, he had heard that in the depths of his being.

He only vaguely remembered the ceremony as Little Birch was laid to rest. Through his tears, he had seen her mother place the implements she would need for her journey to the stars. He did remember going back into their tent and retrieving the saucepan which he had given her, and placing it on her bier. But as they walked away from the burial place, his heart was so torn in pieces that he felt he could not ever again bear such pain. It was worse indeed than when she had cauterized him. Worse than he could ever imagine. And again, he just wanted to die.

Once he awoke to find the gruel just beyond his nose on the bearhide mat. But he couldn't eat. Stomach and mind were both empty, and no nourishment for either could he ingest. Occasionally he gave himself up to a low moaning. No future, no reason to live, he wanted to end it all and join his wife among the stars. But these thoughts would evaporate too, and dull, grey gloom would envelope him again in its awful embrace.

He vaguely saw from time to time One Arm come in and go out. Even Tongue himself peered in under the lifted flap of the low entrance.

Time meant nothing, daylight flooded the wigwam and faded again as night and the sounds of night covered everything. How he longed to die! And be finished with all this struggle. He repeated over and over that the one purpose of his whole life had been Little Birch, and now that she was gone, he could see no reason to survive.

He found himself in a dark and immense cavern, where shadows were thrown on the walls as if on canvas sails, and these shadows moved, insubstantial, as though part of the wall of sail and yet each retaining its individuality — did that come from the shapes? Or from some curious blossoming of their souls?

As he was moving forward, he was stopped by a wide river, entirely black, as though running with ink. He let the water lap at his feet. Should he step forward into it? Should he try to swim across? Hearing a shout, he turned.

The *Buowin*!

They hailed each other in Micmac fashion. The *Buowin* waved for him to come back.

Thomas felt he did not want to leave the verge of this lake, or was it a river?

The *Buowin* came forward and stood beside him. They remained in silence, and then the *Buowin* took one of his hands. "I will show you wonders," he said, speaking oddly in faultless English in this visionary story. His voice was firm, but his grip even firmer.

He turned and, pulling Thomas, led him back over what seemed a rocky surface, but slippery, covered in slime. He managed to keep his footing, and after a long travail, they came upon a layered mountain. Ahead of him, the *Buowin* began to climb.

Thomas watched him, and then for some reason followed. Each layer was populated by figures in many different modes of costume.

Thomas found that the higher they climbed, the easier it got.

They arrived at a wall of burning flames.

The *Buowin* said, "We must walk through this."

"I cannot. I cannot ever."

"Hold my hand."

"No, we shall never make it." Thomas felt the heat. Any attempt to make a passage through would be doomed.

The *Buowin* tugged at him, as they faced the wall of flames. "You must have faith..." said the *Buowin* in tones oddly used by his clergyman at the castle, *"and I will bring you though the fire,"* quoting the Good Book.

In the centre of the flames, eyes shut tight against the heat, he felt a need to take in what was happening, and he opened them. All around in a purple glow, green streamers danced such as they had done that night he and Little Birch had seen the northen lights.

From out of the heart of the dancing colours, he heard, "I am here." The voice of Little Birch! "I will always be here for you in the dancing lights."

From the depths of his being he heaved a great sigh, as she echoed again: "I will always be here in the dancing lights."

He turned to the *Buowin* who had disappeared. "Where are you?" he called aloud. He felt a hand on his chest, and a voice answered: "We are here."

He lay back on the hides of the wigwam, and opened his eyes. The *Buowin* squatted next to him. Little by little, he began a Micmac chant. Oddly comforting. After a while, Thomas heard the shake of a rattle. Thomas found himself rocking to the gentle rhythm. The thrumming of some stringed instrument set up another rhythm. Was Tongue himself working that? Then Thomas smelt a sweet fragrance. He opened his eyes again. Herbs had been dropped into the coals, fanned alive by Tongue. Full Moon and One Arm had brought his baby near, with Brightstar; but inside, Thomas was alone with these two Elders.

After a time, Tongue began to translate the *Buowin*, "Thomas, the time has come for *Bilodua,* the Evil One, to leave you. Look. See. You can feel *Bilodua* is going. *Creator* is coming to help you. He will dissolve the darkness, Thomas. He will lift you up."

In the silence backed by the low humming of the *Buowin*, Thomas did indeed feel the blackness begin to dissolve.

"Thomas," went on the *Buowin* in Micmac, "you have a son, you must name him, you must give him the right name, you must give him life, you are his father, you must live and be strong to take care of him."

The words struck a loud chord in his soul. Why had he not been focussed on his son, that miraculous gift? How tight had been the embrace of that evil spirit.

"Thomas," Tongue went on, "your son is calling. Little Birch is speaking. She is begging you. Listen..." After a silence, Tongue continued to translate the crooning of the *Buowin*, in tones Thomas associated with Little Birch. "Please, Thomas, get up, take our son, love him, care for him. He needs you, you are all he has. Little Birch says, care for our son, our child we have made together."

Thomas felt himself respond, as though from a long distance away.

"Thomas, Thomas, live strong, be of good courage, lead our son. Make him strong and good as you are, Thomas," Tongue went on. "That is what Little Birch is saying."

The words entered Thomas and he could not help but feel their truth. He saw their light, he heard Little Birch in the windy trees and in the shaking leaves, in the words of courage, in the phrases of hope. He knew that Little Birch, with all her strength, would want him to do just that, just what she was begging through her medium of the *Buowin*. He sat up slowly.

Tongue watched him with his big serious eyes. The *Buowin* lifted his weathered hand and placed different herbs on the coals. The wisps flickered with an eerie green light. The smell began to intoxicate Thomas.

"Yes, Tongue," he said, "thank you. I will take the challenge, I will love my son."

He lifted his eyes to the heavens and said, "Thank you, Little Birch. I swear on the body of my son, I shall do as you wish. I shall be everything you ask."

And with that, he came out of the wigwam and took his baby in his arms, and stood looking around, as if he had been born again.

Author's Note

My great grandfather fought in 1805 under Admiral Nelson in the Battle of Trafalgar. When his man o'war, the Bellerophon, *came to the New World, he jumped ship and built his new home in the Gaspé. His youngest son, my grandfather James, was born in 1835, and my father, Eric, also a youngest son, was born in 1893.*

To commemorate these three ancestors, I write this series of largely fictional accounts of a family that helped found a real English community on the shores of the Gaspé Coast, and lived and farmed there for two centuries.

ACKNOWLEDGEMENTS

I could not have written this book without the encouragement and support of my wife, Joan, and the help of many friends and relatives. The input from them and those whom I name below, kept me on track; but, of course, any mistakes are my own.

Roger Pelletier, director of the Micmac Interpretation Centre near Gaspé Town, read my manuscript with great care and made very many helpful suggestions. At his museum I learned much of the Micmac ways of living and hunting, seeing actual wigwams, snares, and even deadfall bear traps. On one tour, I absorbed additional lore from a young interpreter, Peter Shaw, who still goes moose hunting every autumn with his Micmac grandfather. As Roger pointed out, my Port Daniel band is slightly less Europeanized than were many Micmac in the early 1800s, but we both preferred to show how they lived not so long before. I was very sad to hear that he took his life shortly afterwards.

Danielle E. Cyr, professor of linguistics at York University, lives in the Gaspé during the summers and produced, with Manny Metallic, the Micmac dictionary. She helped me with the native dialogue and other larger concepts. Finally, she read the completed manuscript and gave valuable suggestions.

Gilbert Sewell, who lives across Chaleur Bay in Pabineau, is one of the very few Micmac Elders who knows and understands the old ways, and indeed lives by them. He took Joan and me into his woods and shared many of his secrets. By observing him, we both became richer and we thank him.

Raymond Garrett, historian of the Gaspé and the foremost genealogist of the Garret and Almond families, provided me with a wealth of information. With James's first two children, I have presumed that for propriety's sake, he and Catherine might have chosen to adjust baby John's birth date to appear in records as younger than Mariah. But of course, this saga is fiction, relying only on facts to build a good story.

Elton Hayes, my cousin and a former breeder of race-horses, is wise in the ways of the Gaspé. Every week we got together with Gloria, his wife, to eat her dinners and swap ideas, which often found their way into the book. Elton has helped me with (and played in) three of my films.

Cynthia Dow, a distant cousin, was director of operations for the Gesgapegiag Band, one of the three Gaspésian communities on Chaleur Bay. She wrote her McGill University thesis on the Micmac, and gave help.

The Metallic Migmaq-English Reference Dictionary by Prof. Cyr and Manny Metallic (and Alexandre Sévigny) and the *Talking Micmac Dictionary*, a 6,000+ word Internet resource (http://www.mikmaqonline.org) for the Mi'gmaq/Mi'kmaq language, provided instant and helpful resources.

David Cordingly's exciting book, *The Billy Ruffian* (Bloomsbury, 2003) gives the complete history of the *Bellerophon*. From it I learned the captains' names and how the *Bellerophon* made its first trip to North American waters in the spring of 1813, and came back the next year. Cordingly writes such a readable and compelling narrative, replete with battles and twists and turns, that I urge everyone, whether interested in naval history or not, to acquire it.

I have been lucky with readers and editorial advice. First and foremost, Dr. Rex King and Pamela Ranger, both novelists of no little talent, followed the story step by step and gave many helpful suggestions throughout the long process of revision. Diana Roman, M.A. (Oxon), a striking young lawyer (at O'Melveny & Myers) with an intellect to match her looks, read this with an acute eye and wisdom. Nicholas Etheridge, retired diplomat and good friend now living in Victoria, has a splendid eye for the sweep of a book. He attended, and lives next to, St. Michael's University School where I filmed *Ups & Downs*. Also the New York playwright Oren Safdie, whom I am fortunate to call a friend (actually, ever since he was a little boy) was a great help as was my sweet cousin, Jennifer Hayes, who moved back to Shigawake after earning an MBA.

For help in Shigawake, I must credit Germaine Fitzgerald, who turned up each day to cheer me up, run errands, and mainly cook good meals. Our snowshoeing together through untamed wilderness "back behind" helped me understand more of how the Micmac walked and lived. Her father, Oswald, a lumberjack for fifty years, allowed me to use his personal recollections for background. For other revisions, I must thank profoundly the brilliant Cambridge-educated novelist and friend, David Stansfield, and Lynda Robinson who helped make the "Reading Guide" and corrected the French. And for those readers who are curious about the "Oh happiness bird," it's the white-throated sparrow (also called the "O Canada bird") heard all along the Gaspé Coast; the moose bird is a jay.

My cousin Ted Wright, the master researcher and fisherman-crab-trap maker, lives all year-round in the home built by my great grandfather and improved by successive Almonds. An absolute wizard of an intellectual, he knows so much about the history of the period, the British Navy, and so many other facts that were eluding me. He talked me through the chapter on oakum, and every morning would provide sage advice and imaginative speculation on what might have happened on this coast two hundred years ago.

I also wish to acknowledge now, rather than later, Doctors Noel Bailey Merz and Selvyn Bleifer, and others too numerous to name, for keeping me alive, and Edie Azaar, my Pilates teacher, and Emily Hinds and other trainers, for keeping me fit.

Here would be the place to thank my good friends Lynda and Harry Boyd, who continue to provide me with sanctuary in Toronto, and have made me feel at home in their Forest Hill home. Harry and I have been friends for six decades, from the time we played on opposing teams during the Oxford and Cambridge hockey game, and afterwards professionally together on Cortina d'Ampezzo's hockey team. His wildly busy wife, Lynda, associate director of all Advance Placement studies in Canada, still found time to make my visits painless — and full of cheer with her sharp, dark, and surprising sense of humour. Beverly Mitchell and Bernie Leebosh have graciously accepted Joan and me in their Westmount home through these many years since I sold my old mansion atop Mount Royal behind McGill University.

Apart from my wives and partners through the ages, I want to thank ongoing friends: Rick Klein and Mark Rosin, who have given me much friendship and sustenance over the past few decades. And also in Montreal, I want to mention my very dear Nina Safdie, and her partner Roch Carrier who continues to guide my career and inspire me with his prodigious output, no matter what august position he occupies.

The Bank of Montreal, which opened its doors less than a decade after this saga began, has accompanied me for almost eight decades with countless loans and lines of credit — even through those perilous years of film-making — and must also be acknowledged as a constant and reliable financial companion.

A NOTE ON THE SOURCES: In an old cardboard box in the basement of the New Carlisle Courthouse, I found documents to verify that Thomas Manning served on the *Bellerophon*, and other such details. For my belief that he came ashore in Port Daniel, and his subsequent relations with Micmacs, I have oral traditions dating from the 1930s.

Finally, any success this book might have is due to McArthur & Company, whose leader Kim McArthur I call Miss Whirlwind. She, with Devon Pool, director of publicity, Kendra Martin, head of production, and Ann Ledden, VP of sales, make up the most splendid team any author could wish for.

Shigawake, Gaspé Coast
June 2010

© Joan Almond

Paul Almond is one of Canada's pre-eminent film and television directors, and he has directed and produced over 130 television dramas for the CBC, BBC, ABC and Granada Television. Paul Almond lives on the Gaspé Peninsula in Quebec and Malibu, California. For a reading group guide, further historical background and more, visit him online at www.thealfordsaga.com